The Immortalists

The Immortalists

Andrew Hook

A version of this novel was originally published under the
same title by Telos Publishing in 2014. It has been heavily
amended for this edition.

Cover art by Edouard Noisette
(http://edouard-noisette.com)

ISBN number: 978-1-7398195-0-7

Printed and Bound by 4Edge

Published by:

Head Shot
85 Gertrude Road
Norwich
UK

editorheadshot@gmail.com
www.headshotpress.com

1
Eating Chicken

In sleep she was a flamenco dancer. One arm arced over her head, the curve bridging her hair that fanned cilia-like on the pillow, the other a mirror-opposite across her belly, as though she were cradling a child that might grow inside her womb. It could be prescient, Mordent thought, after that evening's lovemaking; but then no doubt she often slept that way. He wondered if he'd see her sleep like that again.

He stood in the shadows of his apartment, backlit by the glow from the refrigerator, scratching his balls with one hand and holding a piece of chicken in the other. It was 2am. They had retired early after some bourbon, some laughs, and a discreet understanding. It had been good, and then she had slept. For a while Mordent had listened to her breathing, and then he too had slept; but intermittently, the way you do when there's a stranger in your bed and you're the lamb that doesn't know if it's lying down with the lion.

Not that he was a lamb. More likely the other way around. But sometimes the lamb was also a wolf in woolly clothing.

The chicken drumstick was cold and slimy. He fumbled in the rear of the fridge and pulled out a half-opened tub of salsa. Dipping the chicken gave it a bloody head. The sauce was sharp on his tongue, but didn't improve the chicken's texture. He wasn't sure if he was hungry, but hunger empowered these night-time hours. Mordent had to be doing something instead of trying to sleep and thinking. Those thoughts weren't often what he wanted to think about.

The problem was all the dead. Those bodies that had been murdered, raped, mutilated, beaten, washed up on the shore bloated and white. The colours. Resonant purple bruises, yellow rope burns, blackened filigrees of blood striating the underside of skin that was stiffened like a hung pig. Expressions of fear, pain, a tightened rictus distorting features that once smiled and laughed; or worse, slack expressions and staring eyes of nothingness, as though the human had left. Just an empty sock puppet, devoid of the hand that gave it life.

Those were the victims. The innocent and sometimes not so. And then there were the faces of their killers, multitudinous characters often with no rhyme or reason. Bruisers and chasers, cruisers and wasters. Hired hands without grudges or family members that had shared photographs. A thin patina of respectability laminated some, but after a while you knew to see through it. Like wiping steam off a mirror. It came with the territory. It came with the job.

Then there were those killers who remained undiscovered. Who were waiting to fight and strike again, or who returned to loving families who were unaware of their crimes. Mordent had his own secrets but he couldn't imagine the horror of living with that knowledge. Not of having done the deed, but of allowing it to fester.

The girl on the bed moved. He watched her perform a silent dance, her fingers clicking invisible castanets, her legs criss-crossing under the bedclothes.

He should be there with her. Curled against her warm skin.

He took another bite of the chicken.

He wasn't in the force anymore. Had gone PI. Had a tiny office with his name stencilled on frosted glass that read in reverse from his side of the door. A stack of pencils rested within a used coffee mug, their rubber ends causing a chemical reaction with the dregs. A filing cabinet he hardly ever used took up one side of the room, screeching like a banshee whenever he opened it. He didn't do that often. A PC dominated his desk, the CRT screen indicative of his earnings. When he'd started the business he'd hired a secretary, a grim little woman in glasses. He'd fired her after she started bringing cakes into the office, mothering him with sinister intent. But at that stage he couldn't afford her anyway. Work had slowed to a trickle when it wasn't a flood to begin with. No reason he could think of, except he was no Sam Spade or Philip Marlowe. No craggy good looks, dames falling over him, or the attitude those black and white movies demanded. He was grubby, dishevelled, had been beaten round the block a few times. But he knew he was good, and that should have been all that mattered.

Yet still he saw the bodies. At the end of the paper-chase for missing husbands, wives, or children, offloaded in alleyways with rubbish bags as pillows, dredged out of the river bound with chains made of Mafia links, secreted in cabinets only occasionally brought out to play. Or the suicides. The lonely deaths. Slumped in cloudy cars, suspended from beams with toes inches from the ground, bullet holes in skulls seared with scorch marks, head-on collisions with stunned and stunted trees.

These bodies – murdered or otherwise – were reanimated in these early hours. Not literally, but they hauled themselves up from his memory and in some cases pointed accusing fingers as though he were the only one who could have helped them and it was entirely his fault that he had failed.

Mordent dropped the chicken in the bin. Reached out for the remaining bourbon on the bedside table. Thought of pouring a glass but necked the bottle instead. Fire burned away the demons. Yet still there were some that he couldn't forget.

2
Dawn of the Dead

When he awoke, sunlight backlit his eyelids. He opened and closed them slowly, adjusted his vision to a new day much like the previous. He was back in bed, his tongue retained the hum of the bourbon, the mattress retained the impression of the girl. He vaguely remembered movement, a whispered *Goodbye*. No doubt later he would catch up with her in some bar or another and attempt to recollect their brief interaction. However, for the moment reality blurred and he was immersed a dream, twisted within memory. Recollections of Simona, the retort of a fired gun, the burst of bubblewrap. She hadn't been the first dame to have pulled a gun on him, and no doubt she wouldn't be the last.

Dame.

So this wasn't the 1940s, but the word rolled off his tongue and sat pretty in the air in front of him. It was Mordent's way of dealing with things. Fictionalise it, noir-speak it, and maybe reality wouldn't press in on all sides like an untested electric blanket suffocating him with fear.

He pulled himself out of bed, glanced around for traces of the girl, but she had dressed and was gone. Under the fog of the previous evening's alcohol a name hung on a bent coat-hanger at the back of his mind: *Marina.*

She was a diamond. A few years younger, but also a few years wiser. Within the pale morning light Mordent couldn't quite believe she had been there. He stumbled into the kitchen where the smell of chicken caught in the back of his throat like a starched fart. He gagged. Coughed in the sink. When he ran the faucet it chugged like a steam train, spurting water like *it* was coughing. Creating a cave with his hands he caught the flow, splashed it over his face, woke up.

He booted up his PC over breakfast but there was nothing of interest. The piece of ham he slapped on his bread was overly pink. He folded the bread over to hide it and took a bite. Ate slowly. Then ran a hand through his thinning hair.

He was kidding himself about Marina.

Grabbing his phone, bag and keys he headed downtown to the office.

*

Traffic was light. Mordent tore through the streets like a Pamplona bull, dodging cars and pedestrians alike. He switched the radio to the news, but nothing was of interest, just the usual squeal about politicians and celebrities, both renowned for doing nothing that touched on his perimeter. As of habit, his eyes flickered constantly to the rear view mirror; being followed was an occupational hazard. Satisfied this was not the case he pulled a left into the underground car park that serviced his building, negotiated the barrier and parked in the concrete stillness.

Exiting the vehicle he caught his reflection in the car window. The glass coloured his face a darker hue, but his stubble was evident, his hair a wisp of nothingness. Heavy bags crowded his eyes. He slapped himself once across the right cheek, shook his head. Age had a habit of creeping up. He was becoming irascible within it, less tolerant; but less concerned about his physical appearance too. Again, thoughts of Marina flashed through his mind. He wondered if it might have been more than a casual pick up.

Morgan's Bar was his usual hang-out, but last night he had shouldered the door of an alternative establishment uptown. Ostensibly there to meet a client who never appeared, he had fixed his backside on a stool and watched himself sink several drinks in the mirror behind the bar. He had felt numb, displaced, and for a moment had been unable to feel the effect of the alcohol, as though it was his mirror-image drinking rather than himself. When the booze had hit it had been in one fell swoop, like a battering ram on a drugs raid. It was then that Marina had sidled up beside him, put her hand on her arm, and asked him what he wanted to drink.

A brunette, eyes as brown as the bourbon, slim but packing a little midriff weight, legs tapered into high heels, age around early thirties. At first glance Mordent had thought her a hooker. Second glance hadn't changed his mind. After three glances he'd decided it didn't matter.

According to her, they had a mutual friend.

Mordent didn't have any friends, but he hadn't been about to argue.

He hadn't been about to ask any questions either.

And so he hadn't. And so they'd ended up in bed.

He drew away from his car, took the stairs three flights to his office. Along the way he tapped his pants pocket for his wallet, removed it, counted the bills. Nothing appeared to have been taken.

At the top of the stairs, sitting on the metal chair with the worn seat that lived in the corridor servicing his office, was a client.

Mordent ran his hand over his hair. Straightened it. Reached for his neck to also straighten his tie and then realised he wasn't wearing one. He looked down at his shoes, brown, scuffed. The client looked at him and glanced away. Dismissed him. No doubt she was looking for someone cleaner. She was of mousy appearance, cardigan, tan tights, plaid skirt, shy eyes, unattractive in any sense of the word.

He pulled his key from his pocket and opened the office. Glanced at Miss Mouse who – as if she had been beckoned – rose and followed him inside.

He didn't like it. Mordent always needed a few minutes to settle before dealing with clients. Preferred to be sitting behind his desk waiting for the knock, letting them wait while he decided to answer, and – depending on the shape behind the frosted glass – playing the game of deciding beforehand whether he would take their business or not. More often than not, his silhouette hunches proved correct.

She had followed him in as though tied. A bag clutched between short fingers, head down as though examining the floor. She might have been a mother entering a headmaster's study, her son standing with his back to her in the corner, his ass raw under grey flannel pants. There was an apprehension of engagement. Mordent had the feeling this wasn't a new case, but one she had already tried with other PIs.

He busied himself, shuffled a few papers on his desk that were no more than bills, opened a window, glanced every which way but at her, and then – when he could avoid it no longer – beckoned for her to sit down.

'Early hours you're keeping, Miss ...'

'Davenport.' Her voice wavered, like a violin being tuned. 'And it's Mrs.'

Mrs Mouse after all, Mordent thought. *What a surprise.*

'So, Miss ... Mrs Davenport. How can I help you this morning?'

She had sat down with her legs straight, bag on her lap, as if she were sitting on a bus between two bums. Twice she attempted to clear her throat, but Mordent was sure it wasn't the vestiges of alcohol clogging her larynx. She didn't look the type. He thought of putting his feet on the desk. Thought again. There was a whiff of money. She wasn't rich, but would be a saver. Funds for a possible early retirement that could be heading his way if the price was right.

Again, that high forced-violin voice: 'I'd like you to look for someone.'

A husband? That would explain the nerves, the mousy appearance. There weren't many husbands who would stay around for that piece. Mordent was tempted to interject his presumption, but before his mouth opened everything flooded out of her.

'My son. I'd like you to look for my son. Patrick Davenport. He disappeared two years ago. Age 17. Last seen on the river ferry. Police assumed he fell overboard. Or jumped. There weren't many witnesses. He was on his way back from college. They couldn't find his bag. He wasn't into drugs or alcohol and he didn't have a girlfriend. Not that he didn't want one. He just disappeared. February 16th. Just disappeared. Disappeared.'

So that was it. A case colder than his morning ham. Mordent totted it up in his head. Expenses. Interviewing the ferry company. Checking with Missing Persons. What more could be done on a case two years old? Maybe he could interview college friends. Maybe he'd uncover a scandal. But what he wouldn't find was exactly what Mrs Mouse wanted. Any trace of her son.

Not that he said this.

He said: 'I'll need expenses. Fifty a day while I'm on the case. One week paid up front. Plus anything additional over and above that. I need details of which ferry, which college, names and addresses of friends and relatives. If you happen to remember who you spoke to at the police then I'll take that too.' He spread his arms in a welcoming, expansive, but also potentially ineffective gesture. 'Of course, I make no guarantees. But if I can find your boy, I'll do so.'

Mrs Mouse looked at him blankly. Mordent wondered if she'd heard. Then slowly, like watching dice roll onto snake eyes, something passed over her. Relief, he thought. There was an almost audible sigh, and a half-smile creased her mouth into something kissable.

'Thank you.'

She reached into her bag and pulled out a chequebook.

'I assume you don't take cards?'

Mordent shook his head.

She smiled again, as though they had shared a confidence. 'It's nice to find an establishment that's so...' she searched for the word, found it: 'old-fashioned.'

'It's the way I like it.' Truth was, he didn't want it any other way. Couldn't afford it any other way.

He watched as she wrote out the cheque. She had a little calculator on her cell phone to work out the cost. Not that old-fashioned. Not that bright.

After he'd folded the cheque once and placed it in his top pocket he listened quietly as she spent twenty minutes going through the information he'd asked for. He made notes on paper so that she'd approve, block capitalising the letters so he could read it later. When she left, his eyes grazed her rear. The frosty appearance had gone, she shook a little on her heels. But even from behind she oozed resigned desperation. What she'd bought was a little hope. After two years Mordent decided that was all she could afford.

As the door clicked shut and her silhouette receded, he put his feet up on his desk and closed his eyes.

Dead. Chances were the boy was dead. Mordent thought of the mythical ferry across the river Styx. From our world to the Underworld. A one-way trip. Wasn't it Achilles who was dipped in the river and became immortal as a result? Except for that troublesome heel. Mordent played with the idea of Patrick's immortality, then took his feet off the desk, booted up his PC and created a file for the boy.

In *My Documents*, adjacent to the new file, in a sub-file marked *Missing Persons*, were thirty-three similar folders.

Nancy Brooks.
Juliette Darnier.
Ruby Frost.
Annie Savage.
Dawn Thompson.

Those were just some of the names.

Mordent's filing system wasn't impeccable by any standards but he did do the basics. Added to the file name on five of the records was the word *Found*.

His filing system also contained the word *Solved*.

Found and *Solved* being two different things.

Dead bodies had the habit of staying so. They didn't move around. They just waited. Waited to be found by some two-bit PI or a dog walker. Or maybe by some kids digging in the dirt. Decayed as they waited, so identification would be obfuscated. As though they didn't want to be found, to be identified. And that was how most of them remained.

Mordent sometimes had nightmares about those thirty-three names. Of arriving at his office to find them all waiting in the corridor, exhibiting even less life than Mrs Mouse. Those accusing fingers once again.

The dawn of the dead.

Those bodies that didn't remain hidden tended to float. Those that were marked *Found* had been floaters. Mordent hadn't been the one who had found them.

As usual, when his tortured mind dwelt on such matters, memories of his father and of his reason for leaving the force pummelled his mind. Memories of digging in the dirt. He pushed them aside and got on with the day.

3
Buzz Cut

Mordent had exhausted all lines of enquiry within an hour after Mrs Mouse had left the building. The boy was in the river. Period. Lungs bloated. Body white. Eyeless. No doubt.

But the rent was due so he couldn't leave it there. Even if there was no body it didn't negate a crime. Sure it could have been an accident or suicide. But maybe Patrick had enemies. Mordent could work with that. Do a little digging. Even if digging was all he ever seemed to do.

Not that you could do much digging in the water.

He got up and walked to the window, the fabric of his chair regaining shape behind him. The glass wasn't often cleaned and the city's grime clung like bacteria to a Petri dish. The residue of dirty rain as permanent as a snail trail. The city was fundamentally dirty, Mordent thought. You didn't have to go all philosophical to believe it. The countryside was just as dirty when there were people in it. People were rarely anything other than dirty: overt or hidden.

Yet the window was clear enough to reflect the office door opening behind him. Mordent turned quickly, hand inside his jacket pocket. He had a habit of being nervous that was difficult to shake.

The guy was tall. Ducked his head to enter. Black-suited with the sleeves an inch too short. Clean-shaven. Blond. Hair buzz-cut to within a millimetre of his head. Young, perhaps; the tan deceiving. Certainly younger than Mordent, maybe the same age as Marina. Late twenties then. There was muscle between the material of his clothes. Mordent could almost see it turning like a well-oiled machine.

'And you are?' Mordent didn't stand on ceremony.

The guy smiled. 'A friend.' His smile indicated otherwise.

Mordent walked back to his desk, stood there. The heavy wooden structure a barrier, a shield.

'Last night you were due to meet someone.' His voice was monotone, factual. 'But he didn't show. We'd appreciate it if you didn't look for him.'

'I think that business is between me and my client.'

'You might find that you don't have any business.'

BuzzCut smiled again. One of his teeth was golden. It matched his hair.

'What is this? Some kind of joke?'

BuzzCut leant forward, his heavy hands with their big knuckles resting ape-like on the wood of the desk.

'Do I look like I'm joking, Mordent?'

He didn't. But Mordent couldn't help but smile at the corny dialogue.

'You take a course in intimidation?'

BuzzCut leant back, brow furrowed. 'A smart ass, eh?'

Mordent imagined a prompter, sitting in the space under the desk, whispering lines from a '50s pulp novel. It appealed to him.

'Smart enough to know you're just a monkey in a suit who's following orders. Who're you working for?'

BuzzCut stood back. 'You don't need to know.' He smiled again, composure regained. 'You don't *want* to know.'

'And if I continue on the case?'

'You don't continue on the case.'

'And if I continue on the case?'

'You *don't* continue on the case.'

Mordent thought of saying it a third and final time. Didn't.

'So I've been warned. Get out.'

BuzzCut turned, the top of his head grazing a loose ceiling tile. He ducked under the door again, looked back once at Mordent as though he were going to say something else, but didn't. Then closed the door behind him.

His silhouette stayed behind like a retina burn on the frosted glass before it moved away.

Mordent shook his head. It needed more than a boy scout to scare him.

He wandered over to the door. Opened it a gap, checked the corridor. It was quiet. He shared this office space with four other companies, although they barely acknowledged each other. There was a guy with white hair who researched family history; some kind of lawyer, although not the kind who he tended to meet; and a temp agency that ferried a veritable harem of girls up and down the corridor all day long. Not the agency where he had obtained his secretary, however. He had a feeling he wouldn't be able to afford even to look at them.

Back at his desk he opened the file on Constantin. It wasn't thick, even by electronic standards. He hadn't met the guy; it was an e-mail appointment only. Those business cards he had left in shopping malls were paying off. Constantin had some *information*. Mordent had no more than that. Other than the bar at which they had been supposed to meet. A couple of e-mails had been exchanged to set it up – and in the back of his mind, he had thought it might be a *set up* – but that was it. He fired a reply to the most recent e-mail, a polite enquiry indicating that he had been at the bar but no contact had been made. As he clicked *Send* he wondered if it would ever be read.

Someone knew about it though. BuzzCut was evidence enough of that. It bugged him that if he couldn't follow it up through lack of information *they* might think the warning had been successful. Perhaps he could switch his enquiry to BuzzCut himself. A 6ft plus goon should be easy to identify. He was moderately surprised he hadn't come across him before, but then allegiances changed so frequently in this city, people were brought in from outside, new faces arrived all the time. It was like a portal, a train station. But then everyone did that. A perpetual shuffle along the mortal coil.

He sighed. Having cases with little or no information seemed commonplace. Desultorily he clicked open a few other files, closed them. Got up, sat down. Pulled a cigar out of the box on his desk – the last cigar – and put it back. Nothing was doing.

Mordent's connections in the force were becoming few and far between. In the good old days there were people he could rely on, even in the few years following his *retirement*. But with Kovacs in charge of all the relevant departments, pulling strings and gaining information was akin to pulling teeth. An advocate of data protection – someone who saw it as a boon rather than a burden – Kovacs stuck straight down the line. Even the few drinking partners Mordent hung with would button their lips just in case. Even with the alcohol coursing through them.

But there was someone who might know about BuzzCut. A snitch Mordent hadn't called in any favours from for a while. He decided to go and tap him. There was little point in standing still.

*

Hubie Carpenter's lack of success was down to fast women and slow horses. Mordent had encountered him when he was a rookie cop and Hubie was on the straight and narrow. A chance meeting with a prostitute after a regrettable spur-of-the-moment decision had led to Hubie sitting in a cell for three hours. His head in his hands.

Mordent had watched him through the pinhole. He hadn't looked like a regular john. Smart shirt, tie loosened due to confinement, polished shoes. He hadn't oozed the desperation that a lot of the johns oozed, even before they were caught. Even so, as Mordent had peeped into that cell, he had known for a fact he was looking at a desperate man.

A desperate *married* man.

He had let him stew a little while longer. There had been enough stew for meat and potatoes, maybe even some turnip, by the time he'd opened the cell and had Hubie brought down to the interview room. By that time, Mordent had found out all about him. First offence. Either hadn't done it before or hadn't been caught before. A black mark against an otherwise impeccable business career. Married five years to Betty Harvard. One child. All this was something Hubie wouldn't want to lose. Mordent had known this. And he had exploited it.

Working in the City, Hubie had had his finger on the financial pulse. Not only had Mordent been interested in a few investments on the money markets – for his personal gain – but there had also been a rat by the name of Taylor that he had needed to keep an eye on. The usual: extortion, insider trading, possible embezzlement. Not the kind of stuff that usually interested Mordent, but a cousin of his had been singed in the stock market fire and had asked for his assistance. All trails had led back to Taylor. Hubie worked with Taylor. Hubie might have been innocent, but Mordent could see an arm twisted so far up Hubie's back that he'd be double-jointed by the time he left the station. And Mordent would have an eye on Taylor and Hubie would have his life back.

That was how it had been due to pan out. Like most things, it hadn't gone quite to plan. Mordent hadn't got Taylor, after assimilating the covert information Hubie had been able to provide. But Hubie hadn't got his life back either. His teeter on the edge of the abyss had driven him into gambling, and the self-destruction of his marriage had led him into women. Both sets of nags had bled him dry.

If Mordent had a conscience he would have considered himself partly responsible. Maybe he did. Anyways, he had kept track of Hubie's descent and swung by every so often. Feeding his gambling addiction also meant Hubie moved in the right circles. At least, right for Mordent. A word here, a nod there. The infinitesimal movements all added up. Prey was brought down by such means. Yet Hubie was discreet enough – insubstantial enough – not to get pulled into the aftermath. He was a good guy to stick with, so Mordent stuck with him. Until such time that Hubie's database of experience proved perilous, Mordent knew he'd be able to count on him for a solid source of information.

The drive to Hubie's office was sweet. The dirty city had opened up to blue sky, as though the clouds had been divinely pulled apart. Sunlight sparked. Traffic lights, the sidewalk, polystyrene food cartons, the wings of pigeons, the buttons on the coats of bums – all these reflected colour back to the sky. Mordent had the window down, the sunroof open. Jazz buffeted the car. Occasionally, with his arm hanging lackadaisical out of the window, he felt the urge to wave to pedestrians. Yet didn't.

Hubie lived several blocks away. Along the journey the traffic shed the expensive vehicles, as though they were weeded out, obliterated. By the time Mordent pulled up outside Hubie's office he'd passed two burnt out cars – still smouldering, twisted residues curling in the sun – and several others jacked up, tyreless.

It *was* tireless. The relentless effluvia of the city. Even under the blue sky. Which was why Mordent couldn't bring himself to wave. Give up a piece of yourself and something would take the whole. Even in jest, it was waiting.

Mordent parked up. Hopscotch grids tessellated the sidewalk: a secret city pathway unveiled like painting by numbers. Mordent knew the kids who made these chalked patterns weren't as innocent as the game suggested. There was a code hidden within the shapes, the integers. Step wrong and it was like stepping on a crack, falling through the pavement into another world. One to be avoided.

Not more than four paces from the car and he stood in some gum. Another four paces and he had to stop. The delay in his step, the *click*, the sheer filthiness of what was stuck to his shoe put him on hold. *Gumshoe.* The name had become synonymous with private detectives, but it wasn't because of chewing gum, romanticised by the downtrodden PI trampling equally downtrodden streets. Mordent had investigated it once, on the internet, between working on a case and watching porn. Gumshoe came from the late 1800s when shoes and boots were made of gum rubber, equivalent to modern-day sneakers. They didn't make much noise. As didn't the PI, sneaking up behind the low-life, quietly slipping between the flotsam and jetsam on the streets. Either way, either definition, his shoe stuck to the sidewalk all the same.

He swore and stood on one leg, regarded the glob of discoloured white and dirt on the sole of his right shoe. It was as he bent down, fingers poised to remove the gum, that his head lowered and avoided the bullet that cracked out of a nearby alleyway and embedded in his car.

The screech of his vehicle's alarm was barely louder than his pounding heart. Ducking into a doorway he grabbed for his gun, held it in a sweaty hand. Around him the streets were deserted, as though this were a high noon showdown. Litter blew along the sidewalk, a poor man's wedding confetti. Across the street a window banged somewhere, the bullet's echo. Mordent listened for footsteps, for anything. Yet nothing came. He beeped his alarm quiet. It was a full minute before reality reasserted itself. A car drove past, a teenager with his shorts hanging outside his pants rode by on a bicycle with his knees up to his chin, the air vibration of the bullet dissipated, ran to memory. Mordent stepped out of the doorway. He saw he'd taken cover in the entrance of a boarded-up pizza parlour. Nearby, where he thought the shot had come from, was an alleyway beside another pizza parlour. Looking about him one more time, he tried the door of the joint. It was locked.

Backing away to his car, he prised the slug from the driver's door. It was gripped like a young cunt grips a cock. Slipping it into his pocket, he looked around one more time. At the bottom of the road, barely visible, two heads were chatting. They weren't even looking his way. Feeling somehow cheated, he shoved a few coins into the parking meter and continued walking to Hubie's office adjacent to the closed pizza parlour. Still his foot stuck to the pavement, like a CD tripping a track, but now he blessed both it and the kid who'd spat the gum out.

Hubie lived and worked on the fourth floor. As usual, the elevator was out. The stairs ran around the outside of the shaft, like a snake coiling around a tube. He took each in turn, pacing himself. He wasn't the fittest PI around. Every so often he stopped and listened, started again. By the time he reached his destination his heart beat madly. Mostly adrenalin, little exertion.

Maybe he should have phoned ahead. But he liked to surprise Hubie. It gave him the advantage. And after he'd just been surprised it was only fair someone else had their turn. Cogs clicked in his mind, links between the bullet, his visit and Hubie. But he didn't really expect to find Hubie dead. And as it happened, he wasn't.

'Mordent.'

Hubie answered the door in a dressing gown and slippers. The faint tang of perfume hung in the air. The waste bin by the door was full of crumpled betting slips. Fast women, slow horses. Hubie lived adjacent to his office. The two rooms separated by no more than a door. The office was tidy. A desk. PC. Filing cabinet. All as in Mordent's office, but more for work and less for show. Hubie acted as a stockbroker to those who didn't know the market for themselves. Mordent was sure he creamed them; but then who didn't in this rat-filled city? The bedroom-cum-kitchen was a tip. As Mordent was led into the office, Hubie slipped into the next room to divest himself of the gown and slip on something uncomfortable. Mordent could hear voices. A girl's voice. Something that sounded like a kiss.

His stomach turned.

Hubie bustled back in. When they'd first met he'd worn contact lenses, but now he preferred glasses. He thought they added to his accountability. When clients were around he wore a thin brown cardigan with dark brown buttons. Sometimes, if he were feeling frivolous, a bow-tie. His hair was combed back, lightly greased. He had a good head of hair, even though he was now in his early fifties. On bad days, Mordent envied that look.

'Just let me tidy up.'

Hubie snatched what looked like women's underwear off the nearest chair. Filed it in the cabinet. No doubt under *W*, Mordent thought. Not for the first time did he run through the choices we make. The turns at which one life becomes another. The garden of forking paths.

Hubie proffered Mordent the denuded chair. Sat down on the other side of the desk, his back to the window. Mordent stood for a while. Tried to catch Hubie's gaze, which kept sliding as though on ice skates towards the bedroom door. Maybe it was an age thing. Maybe he preferred not to mix business with pleasure. Whatever, Mordent knew he shouldn't ask what was in the other room.

Instead he said: 'You hear a gunshot just now?'

Hubie stiffened. 'When? Right now?'

'About 15 minutes ago. Outside this building.' Mordent walked around to Hubie's side of the desk, pressed his face so close to the windowpane he could feel the cold millimetres from his cheek. Yet at that angle he couldn't even see his car, never mind Hubie's side of the street. 'Someone took a pop at me.'

'You're kidding.'

Mordent rested his hand on Hubie's shoulder. The thin material of his shirt couldn't stem the warmth within, and he found himself snatching his fingers away. Repulsed.

'Do I sound like I'm kidding?'

'We can all kid, Mordent.'

'Not all of the time.' He sighed. Sat down facing Hubie. Ran a hand through his thinning hair. 'Maybe I'm getting jumpy. Probably wasn't for me. Just a carjacker trying his luck.'

Hubie shrugged. 'Somewhere there's a bullet with everyone's name on it.'

Mordent thought of Simona. Thought of Alsiso. Another story, another time. Maybe there was.

Hubie cleared his throat. 'Look. I'm busy. Got some business to attend to. As I'm sure you know. Can we make this quick?'

'You and I,' Mordent began, 'are the same. Bottom line we're losers. Sure we might think we're big sometimes. Might think we're mighty big. But bottom line we're losers. What makes us different from the rest? We *know* we're losers. That's what. We know whatever we do won't make much of a difference, and we don't expect what we do to make us more than what we are. That gives us an advantage. You know what I mean?'

'I really haven't the faintest idea what you're talking about.'

'What I'm saying is that without aspiration we stay where we are. We're happy where we are. But there are others who assume that by making themselves appear big then everyone else will think they are. So they go up a level. And then they make themselves appear bigger again. So they rise again. And again. And again. But they haven't really risen at all. In fact, they've sunk to the lowest point. The elevator's gone down, not up. It's all been done with mirrors. But they have to kid themselves that they are up. That they're *up*. Right. Cos if they don't, then no-one is going to pull them from the floor.'

'I still don't know what you're talking about.' Hubie fingered his shirt collar. In his haste to get dressed he hadn't buttoned it properly. There was an extra hole at the top and a spare button at the bottom on opposing sides.

'You know a guy? Six foot plus. Blond hair. One gold tooth, bottom set on the right hand side. Hands as heavy as Rondo Hatton's, but face angelic with a twist of cruelty. Good dresser. You know someone like that?'

Hubie slowly shook his head.

'This guy, see, thinks he's going up. But he's not. He's going down. Sure he might have friends and associates who're telling him he's on a magic carpet if he plays his cards right, but sometime soon that rug is gonna be pulled out from underneath him and he'll fall. I want to know – now – the names of those he's gonna fall on.'

Mordent sat back. It was impossible to discern Hubie's mood. Over the years he'd honed his poker-face to a fine art. It was all he had, the appearance of knowing nothing. Just in case one day someone he didn't like assumed he knew something.

Hubie spoke. 'I gotta make the 2.15. There's a horse on it goes by the name of Derby Boy. I could make a little money on that one, enough to buy the girl next door a new pair of shoes. But I see its now 2pm and I don't suppose I'll get there in time. Shame. She could really have done with those shoes. And I could have done with her gratitude.'

Mordent pulled his wallet out of his pants pocket. Selected a few notes, glanced at Hubie, pushed some of them back. He put his feet up on the desk, the flattened-gum sole pointing Hubie's way. Then waved the remaining bills in the air.

'What do you say we bet on it?'

Hubie frowned. 'Bet on it? I thought I'd made myself clear.'

Mordent leant back in his chair. 'We go back a long way, Hubie. You got yourself into a jam and I got you out of the jam, but you ended up sticky anyway. Now along the way I've tapped you for information to keep you clean, but just like that gum on the bottom of my shoe, you've kept your head on the sidewalk. That horse ain't ever gonna come in, but we should bet on it anyway. We should place a bet as to whether or not the horse exists.'

'I don't get it. You've been reading too many cheap detective novels.'

'I've been reading your life story, Hubie. That's what I've been reading. And it's not an easy read. I'd place a bet that it doesn't get easier, neither.'

'Is that some kind of threat? Because if it is ...' Hubie rose from his chair, indignant; paused.

'Let's just cut the crap. Tell me this guy's name and the money is yours. You could get the broad some new stockings, as well as the shoes.'

Hubie grinned. 'Some detective you are. I've already given you his name: Derby Boy.'

'What the hell kind of a name is that?'

'I've heard it's the one he uses.'

'I call him BuzzCut.'

'Figures.'

They paused for a moment. Two boxers deciding if another punch was necessary.

'Who does Derby Boy work for?'

'Bataille.'

'*Bataille*?'

'You know him. Of course.'

Mordent held a breath. 'Of course.' He took his feet off the desk. Stood up. Pulled on the bottom of his jacket to ease the tension in the shoulders. 'How about Constantin? You know him?'

Hubie shook his head. Sincerely.

'Okay.' Mordent found he was mumbling. 'Thanks.'

He walked towards the door.

'Hey!' Hubie gesticulated at the money still clutched in Mordent's hand.

Mordent looked down. Seemed surprised to find the green stuff there. Then he yanked open the door to the bedroom and threw the bills inside. Closed it again. A shadow of a breast burred his vision.

'One more thing. You know anyone would care to take a pop at me?'

Hubie smiled again. A little more confident this time.

'Do I know someone who *wouldn't*?' he said.

4
Bar Story

Night found Mordent doing what he did best.

Hunched over a bar stool. Glass in hand. Staring at his reflection.

He called into Morgan's Bar for a couple of shots prior to heading uptown. The usual clientele sat huddled in shadows. Anonymity clouding them like a cloak of invisibility. Everything levelled. Once you were through the door you were safe as yourself, with all the glamouring layers of respectability, responsibility, pretence and substance stripped away. It was as though each soul in the dark was your own, a kindred spirit amongst alcoholic spirits. It was a haven, a sanctuary. A place where you came to be understood and where you didn't need to be understood. A bar where everyone *didn't* know your name.

It hadn't always been that way. Mordent had been a teetotaller prior to the force. The fog of alcohol never appealed. In those days he'd had nothing to hide behind. Straight cut, crew cut, uncut, never cut. He liked his mind clear, clean. He'd seen the others, hung-over, making decisions about people's lives when they couldn't make decisions about their own. Sometimes those were life or death. Or worse: decisions about their own lives. One or two hadn't ducked the bullet, hadn't seen it coming, hadn't realised someone was standing over them, that they were looking into the barrel of a gun.

He could remember his first drink. Unsurprisingly, there was death in it. A loose shot. A ricochet. A dead child. He was hustled out of the area, out of the station, out of the enquiry. Hustled into the bar. Repeatedly hustled into the bar.

A bottle, green, label peeling, cold to the touch, wet on the outside. *Take this.* He had necked it. Tilted his head as far as it would go. It had been okay.

The death had changed his stature at the office. Enhanced it. Like reverse psychology, he had become respected. One of the gang. He had no longer refused invites to drinks after work. His memories had been dulled. The boy's face had merged like a poor photo fit, a composite image sullied by the drink. He had used the alcohol as a tool, not a crutch. A blur. Rubbing away the edges, the sharp realities, the angles. Like walking through a haze without being hazy.

And Morgan's Bar was the extension of the alcohol. The cocoon.

The usual. It was never a question, always a statement. It was rare that Morgan said anything else.

When he did, it was more like: *Someone's been looking for you.*

'Someone's been looking for you.'

Mordent lifted his head from the glass he'd been turning in his hands, the liquid vortexing towards the centre. Its aroma rising off the swell, like sputum.

Morgan had one elbow on the bar, leaning towards him, his white apron speckled with something Mordent couldn't discern. His face held a ruddy complexion, as though palming a sunburn. Unshaven, his stubble grew through it like wheatgrass. Tufts of pepper hair protruded from his nostrils, his ears.

Mordent raised his eyebrows.

Morgan's voice was surprisingly sweet, not the gruffness Mordent always expected. 'Tall guy. Six foot plus. Blond. A bruiser. A clean guy but a bruiser all the same.'

'Thanks.' Mordent sighed. 'You get a name?'

'I don't think he's the kind of guy who gives a name.'

'I guess you're right.' Mordent paused. 'If he shows again, tell him something from me.'

Morgan shrugged.

'Tell him I don't want to buy anything.'

Down the other side of the bar someone shouted. Morgan grunted. Conversation over.

Mordent chucked the remaining liquid down his throat where it coursed like caustic soda. Stood. Steadied himself. The slight wavering due to stiffness, not alcohol. Onset of long-term health problems. Arthritis. A painful retirement. Unhappy death.

Possibly. He thought of Marina.

But there was another reason to go uptown. It wasn't just to see a girl.

Outside the cold air sobered him further, wind whipping into his face like the ice-queen's breath up close. He shook his head vigorously. Once. Twice. The first to clear it. The second to shake the Billy Joel song out of his head. He glanced left, right. No-one in the shadows. The bar's neon-coloured sidewalk puddles, where reflections of reality shook, wavered; beckoned as alternatives. But it had been a long time since Mordent was gutter-bound.

It was a short drive uptown. Just as the scenery had deadened that morning on the drive to Hubie's side of town, the opposite occurred in this direction. Streets took on illumination, people, gaiety – in the good old-fashioned sense of the word. From lone desperadoes on street corners to groups of friends hanging onto each other, couples walking side by side, couples holding hands, couples leaning into each other for warmth, security. From locked-tight disused bars to dingy drinking holes to wine bars to café-style restaurants with clientele eating and drinking under covered canvas on the sidewalk. It was like moving from night to day, from dark to light. Yet Mordent didn't like this side of the city. It was too open, too prone to cracking, to shedding that superficial happiness.

Or maybe it was just him. Gnarled. Susceptible to the underside. Having seen too much and understood too little. He couldn't plug a hole here. Wrong shape.

The bar had its own parking area round back. Not quite classy enough for a chauffeured service, still too classy for Mordent. He pulled up. Switched off the engine. Sat awhile with the same Billy Joel song running through his head as the engine cooled. Wondered how much he wanted a run in with BuzzCut. Wondered if he could avoid it.

Leaving the vehicle, he approached the bar from the rear. It was flanked by burly security in ill-fitting suits. He knew one of them. Ex-police. Couldn't recall his name but a good guy who'd stepped too close to the flame. He gave Mordent a nod as he entered the bar. Mordent nodded back. Code.

The interior was open-plan, a mix of tables and sofas. Bright reds, greens, oranges. The lighting bright. An open wound. No-one drank singly: all couples and groups. Dressed smart for an evening out. No-one drowning sorrows here, but celebrations, clan affirmations. He placed a hand casually in his pocket, wandered up to the bar.

It was served by three bartenders, two male, one female. Dressed in white and black, they moved like chess pieces, forwards, back, diagonally, sideways. The guys were clean shaven, the girl had her blonde hair tied back in a ponytail. They were fluid. One guy mixed a cocktail in a silver shaker, throwing it into the air for show. Two girls leant on the bar watching him, enthralled.

Mordent could feel himself folding in within his suit, closing down, retracting.

He recognised one of the male bartenders from the previous evening, beckoned him over. The guy slid between the girl and the descending shaker in one movement. He could have been a dancer. He probably was.

'Nice to see you again, sir.'

'Enough of that. Bourbon on the rocks.'

'Yessssir.'

The bartender wore a badge: *Mark*. Mordent watched as his drink was fixed. Wondered how to play it. He decided to pay over the odds. Slipped a bill across together with the exact change for the drink, so Mark could be in no doubt as to his intention.

'Anything else, sir?' Mordent watched as the bill was expertly, discretely, fingered away. A magician as well as a dancer.

'Last night I was in here waiting for a guy called Constantin. You know him?'

Mark shook his head. 'Do you have a description?'

It was Mordent's turn to shake his head. 'Just a name.'

'Not much to go on, sir.' Mark turned to go, another customer calling.

'Hey.'

Mark turned back.

'I didn't give you that bill to say *no*. That's for buying your time.'

'Sorry, sir.' Mark looked anxious. Mordent suspected every customer service move was watched in this joint. There would be plenty of bartenders waiting in line to pick up tips from sacked staff.

'Last night I left with a girl,' Mordent said, confidentially. 'What do you know about her?'

Mark smiled. 'She just came in.' He nodded towards the main entrance.

Mordent turned and saw her. She saw him. Smiled. Waved.

Maybe Mordent was wrong. Maybe booze did fog his memory. She couldn't have been that good-looking? Too attractive for him. He couldn't even recall what they had spoken about.

She slipped through the tables. She wore a silver blouse, dark skirt. The blouse rippled like water with two seals playing in it. The skirt was knee level. Legs slender, toned. Hair as black as the skirt. Shoes as silver as the top. She looked like she'd been expecting him, as if they'd made an appointment to meet.

Mordent couldn't remember making any appointment.

She sidled onto the adjacent bar stool, kissed him on the cheek. Her lipstick left a mark, which he touched with his hand, fingerprinted.

'How are you?' Her brown eyes sparkled, exuded a radiance he had trouble believing was directed towards him.

'I'm good. What are you drinking?'

She told him and he ordered. The pony-tailed girl brought over the drink. Smiled at him as she laid it in front of Marina.

'Sorry I rushed out this morning. Work beckoned.'

'Of course.'

'You look surprised to see me.'

'Did we have a date?'

She feigned shock. 'I should say so.'

'You should but you won't.'

She rummaged in her bag. 'No, you're right, I won't.' She pulled out a crumpled packet of cigarettes, crumpled it more when she realised it was empty.

'You can't smoke here.'

'I know this.' She looked up, smiled. 'So ... where do we go from here?'

'Where do you want to go?'

'It depends on who's taking me.'

'And if that person was me?'

'It would depend on who you are.'

Mordent smiled, his face an earthquake crack. 'That would depend on where we're going.'

Marina took an imaginary cigarette out of the crushed packet. Lit it. Placed it between her lips and blew smoke. A pretence.

'Shall we sit somewhere else?'

She slid off the barstool, hooked her left arm. Mordent took it. Led her into a corner. It was as though they were dancing, his legs clumsy. She glided, he stumbled. She eased between patrons, he knocked against them. Spatial awareness was natural to her. His car wasn't pristine. Hers probably was.

The table was tight, bolted to the floor. Mordent couldn't imagine it getting rowdy in this joint but everyone had to take precautions. He should have done, with Marina, the night before. He half-remembered whisperings of assurance that had pushed paternity suits out of his mind within the softness of her body. At that level, ground level, it hadn't mattered. And looking at her now he knew she could carry herself. Somehow, he trusted her.

'I know more about you than you think.'

Mordent jerked out of his reverie. He had been looking at Marina's knees, how hard they appeared.

He cleared his throat. 'Last night is a little fuzzy. What did I say?'

'Nothing to use against you in court.' She smiled. Then paused. There was a space. Mordent resisted the urge to fill it. 'I have psychic tendencies,' she said.

Mordent sighed, inwardly. There it was. Fruitcake. Why did every silver lining have a black cloud assigned?

That also explained the sex. Those New Age types were happy to jump into bed with anyone. Residual hippies.

The image of the baby that had flickered in the peripheries of his mind during the day changed to that of a disease. He swallowed.

'You're quiet.'

'Just thinking.'

'I take it you don't believe me.'

'I wouldn't say that. I'd say that *you* believe you.'

'So you're a sceptic?'

'I prefer my realities hard and fast.'

A thin sliver of memory passed between them. She smiled first.

'What if I were to say that you were surprised to see me but I wasn't surprised to see you?'

'I'd say it would be no surprise to see me in a bar.'

She folded her arms across her chest, inadvertently accentuating her breasts. 'But not this bar, Mordent. This isn't your regular hole. I wouldn't have seen you here. Other than yesterday, I mean. So is it just coincidence that I'm here again this evening?'

Again, Mordent found himself sighing. Second date and he was under interrogation. Why did women find it necessary to haggle? He could see the direction the conversation was heading, so finished his bourbon and came straight to the point.

'I take it you've got some information for me?'

Marina smiled again, wide, like a child confident it knew more than an adult. 'I have a body.'

Mordent laughed. Unusual for him. 'I've seen it.'

Marina blushed. 'Not mine, you idiot. Dead.'

'I suggest you contact the police. They're usually interested in that kind of thing.'

'I gravitated towards you yesterday, Mordent. I didn't know why, and I still don't. But then you mentioned you were a PI, and the visions I've been having started to make sense. I'm guessing it's a case you're working on.'

'Missing persons?'

'What else.'

He shrugged. 'Most missing persons end up dead. What are you seeing?'

Marina leant back in her seat, in her comfort zone. 'Imagine a fish-eye lens, a distortion. That's how I see things. Weird squiggles at the edges, occasional clarity in the centre. I'm seeing water. I'm seeing the underside of a bridge or a pier. I'm seeing a boy, maybe twenty years old. That number is coming to me. I'm not *seeing* it, if you know what I mean.'

'That could be anyone, anywhere.'

'I suppose it could.'

Mordent ran a hand through his thinning hair. He wanted another drink, but couldn't risk his licence.

Marina leant forward. 'What are you thinking?'

'I'm thinking that you should report this to the police. Have you dealt with them before?'

She shrugged. 'Not on this issue. I've spoken to a guy called Kovacs. He wasn't helpful.'

No surprise there, thought Mordent. Kovacs liked

things straight up and down, black and white. He paid no attention to this airy fairy stuff. No more than Mordent did himself, come to that.

'I don't really know what I can do.'

She crumpled, confidence gone.

'Here,' he reached out his hand, pulled her to her feet. 'Come home with me.'

'It's so fragile,' she said. 'You wouldn't believe it.'

With her warm hand in his, her body leaning against him, Mordent found that he didn't really care.

5
Get On The Mule

Dead.

Dead end.

Dead beat.

Dead broke.

Dead.

Mordent was at home. It was eight o'clock in the evening. Jazz bounced off the walls, vibrated the liquid in his glass. Outside, the night sky crowded against the window. It was never dark. The city didn't sleep deep. Like a cat, one eye open. Ready to pounce.

Dead end. None of his cases was going anywhere. Dead beat. Exhaustion permeated his body, his bones. Dead broke. No cases. No money. Dead. He might as well be.

Marina had stayed another night but it had been desultory. Passion was spontaneous, needed an impetus, no distractions. Yet she had popped an acorn into his head and it had started growing. Doubt about her, query about his cases. *Water*, she had said. Well, there was only one case he knew for certain where water might be involved. Patrick Davenport and the ferry to nowhere. Coincidence, surely? He hadn't even been on the case the night they had first met.

In bed her movements seemed calculated. He felt manipulated. Chosen. There was something unnatural about her. Otherworldly. Truth was, Mordent dealt in fact. Bodies. Fingerprints. The solidity of a gun or a fist. Sure, he had his intuition: but that was based on fact, which in turn was based on lengthily-acquired experience of the criminal mind and the way that people worked. Marina's visions were beyond that. Fanciful. Ethereal. He had come up against a few mystics in his time, and any shred of truth they offered could be easily derived from other sources. Usually subconsciously. An absorbed scrap of news, barely digested. The mannerisms of a suspect. A natural route upon which a body was likely to be found. Those were the psychics who predicted past events.

Then there were those who foresaw the future. 9/11. There were heaps of them. He didn't pay them any more regard than he did the prophecies of Nostradamus. He couldn't even predict the contents of his next sandwich. It was a blight, for sure. The belief that knowledge was held and yet couldn't be imparted to those in authority. It damaged those psychics' lives. An obsession. Then a conspiracy. A deliberate denial of the truth. Paranoia. The path was littered with broken glass. Everyone was against them. He'd seen it all before.

Marina, with her soft skin, doe eyes, hair black as squid ink, legs ready for wrapping; she was no different. He had no doubt she saw *something*, whether as a dream or as some form of reverie. Some kind of brain aberration. But it wasn't the future and it wasn't the past. And those people rarely saw the present.

He sighed. Stood. Pressed his face to the world outside the glass with its bright lights and steady dreams. Somewhere out there – alive or dead – were *all* the people he was looking for. The only thing he could be certain of was that they weren't in his apartment.

Ever increasing circles. That's what a missing persons search became. Start off local. In the home. Work. Regular haunts. Spread the net wider. District. Town. City. Spread the net wider. County. State. Spread the net wider. Country. Continent. Wider.

Then you pulled the net in, found it full of holes. The person was inside the holdall under the stair cupboard all along.

Otherwise it was like looking for a droplet of water in the glass. Position changed constantly. There were also those who didn't want to be found.

Once or twice a month Mordent regretted leaving the force. At least there his solved crime rate hadn't affected his salary.

Sometimes, though, you had to get on the mule.

A cinema. Classic. Laurel and Hardy. *Way Out West*. He could remember the scene. Night as dark as it could be in black and white. Hardy with a rope around his waist, the end looped around block and tackle. Laurel holding the other end like a child unsure of what it was. Unsure of *any* intention. *Tie that to the mule*. Then, insistent: *Tie it to the mule*. So Laurel ties the end of the rope to the mule. Blank expression. *Get on the mule*. Blank again. With a controlled frustrated emphasis: *Get on the mule*. Laurel gets on the mule, rides it, and up Hardy goes to the rooftop where they have to break into the saloon to steal back the gold-mining deed they've given to the wrong person.

Sometimes you just had to get on the mule.

However asinine it might appear to be.

Mordent had had several run-ins with Kovacs, right from his first day on the force. Steadily, Kovacs had risen above him. His standard, by-the-book approach winning favour with superiors. His face fitting like an ID shot of the perfect representative. Not that it had always been that way. Mordent recalled one scenario where he had got the upper hand. His mind lingered over the details. A remembrance of times past. When Kovacs had been green and Mordent had been a shade of something darker. But that was all water under the bridge, despite the grudge Kovacs held. Whether there was a body floating within that water was another matter.

Mordent sighed. It was time to pay Kovacs a visit. Time to get on the mule.

6
Old Scores

Mordent headed towards Police Headquarters. The car radio was silent. He needed a clear head. There were a few leads that he didn't have that required tidying all the same. Marina. Constantin. BuzzCut. He'd called in a few favours, made some enquiries, but nothing was going nowhere. He had to talk to Kovacs.

It bugged him. This need. This necessity to beg for information. But what bugged him more were unsolved cases. And more than that, unsolvable cases. He wasn't even sure if there were cases there at all.

Getting background on Marina would be useful. Business and pleasure. Constantin – with his request to see him and no clue as to why – was a loose end to dismiss. BuzzCut and his connections to Bataille didn't please him. Then there was that loose bullet. And Mrs Mouse too, should Marina be correct.

There was just nowhere else to go.

Outside the car the world rushed by. Rollerblades scoured the sidewalk, suits raced to meetings. Tourists looked up instead of down, bums looked down instead of up. Taxi drivers leant on their horns as though they were napping. Babies cried in perambulators. Women gossiped. Men looked at legs, breasts, bodies. Take a picture and the full schematic of life would be there. Take a picture anywhere, always the same. Snapshots of life. Life snapped and shot.

Each person carrying his or her own shadow, the prescient ghoul of death.

Unlike with Peter Pan's shadow, which had a mind of its own and became detached, Mordent knew there was no escaping the shroud that accompanied everyone within his view. It hugged them from behind. A tacky, sticky, almost palpable coating that held no menace, no personality. How did Woody Allen describe it in *Love and Death*? *Empty black nothingness*. It haunted him.

It didn't matter how many times you dulled it with alcohol or love or virulent dismissiveness. There it was all the same. Only those who had killed could really understand this. To take a life took something from your life. No matter the reason. There were no bad or good decisions. Just decisions. There were no bad or good people. Just people.

Killing someone was a great leveller. Much like Morgan's Bar.

And once you understood that. Once you understood that everyone was exactly the same on this road to nowhere. Once you got to that point. Then you could start to treat people differently.

Kovacs was a case in point.

However, Kovacs needled him. Knew where to turn the knife. He delighted in it. Could see through him. They were the same side of the same coin, only Mordent was sullied, Kovacs squeaky clean.

Mordent was waved through to the secure car park. Old habits died hard. He was respected here, still. Had despatched enough villains to gain notoriety, had remained irascible enough for those stories to continue without boredom. As he parked, in a reserved DI space, he smiled. His tyres squeaked in pleasure as he braked.

Sometimes it was good to come home.

He swung through the glass doors, up to the concave reception desk. Nodded at a few police along the way. Rookies regarded him curiously. He liked the power. Leaning across the front of the desk he caught the eye of Jamieson.

'Kovacs in today?'

'How's it going Mordent? Don't see you here much nowadays.' Jamieson beamed, his crooked teeth like badly-pulled shutters.

'You know how it is when I have to see the chief. He available?'

'Well, he's in. Don't know if he'll want to see you though.'

Mordent was already taking the stairs. 'I'll take that chance. Thanks Jamieson.'

First floor, second floor, third floor. Each mark in the stairwell familiar to him. The step with the missing plate still missing. The elastic band caught in the light fixture. The door on two with its number absent. The mould creeping like blistered ivy near the window. The smell of disinfectant, leather. The echo of his footsteps. Fourth floor. His destination.

Pushing the fire door open, he was assailed by his old floor. Kovacs hated him coming in like some kind of celebrity. As his hand was shaken, back was slapped, hair ruffled, he felt like a goal-scorer. He hated it himself. Camaraderie sat unnatural with him. But he tolerated it, because he could see Kovacs' face bisected and dissected repeatedly through the slatted blinds in his office, and even within that distortion he could tell that he was fuming.

Seconds later, he was standing in that very same office.

'Like a bad penny, eh Mordent, always turning up.'

'Nothing bad about me, Kovacs. I'm as clean as a whistle.'

'A penny whistle: a cheap, battered, aluminium penny whistle.'

'You've never liked me, have you?'

'I don't see how that's relevant.'

Mordent shrugged. 'I guess it doesn't matter.'

Kovacs remained by the blinds, watching the office.

'You know me, Mordent. I run a tight show. No room for mavericks here.'

'You know that's not the reason I left.'

Kovacs slipped his fingers from between the slats. They snapped together with the noise of a faulty firework. 'Maybe.'

He walked over to the fountain, pressed a button that released an arc of water into his mouth. Mordent remembered the time he and Jamieson had plugged the faucet with snot. It hadn't stopped the jet of water.

'I'm sure you can get the information you want from any of the goons out there.'

Kovacs wiped his mouth with a tissue from a box he kept by the side of the fountain. He folded it neatly. Placed it in the waste bin.

'You know me, Kovacs. I like to do things by the book, not behind your back.'

They exchanged glances.

'The thing is,' Mordent continued. 'You know everything. Those *goons* out there; well, they're good at what they do, but they don't retain information the same way you and I do. Especially you. And the information I'm after is both vague and specific, if you know what I mean. I'd like to discuss it with yourself, an expert.'

Kovacs took another drink of water. Another tissue. The same bin.

'Go for it.'

'What do you know about a psychic called Marina?'

Kovacs shrugged. 'I know she's not psychic.'

'We both know she's not psychic, Kovacs. What else?'

'She telephones occasionally. Bothers us. Claims she sees dead people but is never specific enough with the information to enable us to pinpoint who it might be or where they are. She often cries at the end of the call. Hooper speaks to her sometimes. You could ask him. He won't tell you anything I've not already told you. Why?'

'She's contacted me about a missing persons case.'

'Name?'

'Patrick Davenport.'

'No bells rung with me. But that's another department. I'm sure you've tried them.'

Mordent nodded.

'Is that it?'

'No. I'm looking for someone else. Guy by the name of Constantin.'

'Anything else?'

'Just that.'

Mordent was sure he could detect a smile, but maybe it was the movement of light behind Kovacs, a shift in the position of the sun creating a shadow like a scar.

'You come to me with a surname and nothing else?'

Mordent shrugged. 'You're the expert.'

'Leave it with me. I like a puzzle.'

Because you're a monkey, Mordent thought. 'There's something else,' he said.

Kovacs cocked his head.

'Bataille.'

'We all know about Bataille.'

'What's he up to?'

'More or less everything, but nothing we can pin down. He's a bit shaky. You know this. He wears a bulletproof vest and is greased like a pig. Nothing sticks.'

'One of his goons warned me about Constantin.'

'Then stay away.' Kovacs ruffled through papers on his desk like an old-style newsreader. 'Is that all?'

He didn't look up.

'His goon is six foot plus, blond hair, pretty boy, buzz cut. Might go by the name of Derby Boy.'

Kovacs shrugged, 'Goons are a dime a time.'

'There's something else,' Mordent sighed. 'Someone took a pop at me.'

Kovacs walked over to him. Patted Mordent's stomach. 'Couldn't have been a great shot.'

'I take it you don't take me seriously.'

'Mordent. I've listened to what you've got to say. I'll keep my ear open for anything about a Constantin. I don't see that there's anything else I can do. I don't think there's anything else that I need to do. You might have been big here once, but now you're just a guy on the street, and I've given you as much time as I would any guy on the street. Now there's nothing doing. Time to go.'

'Yeah, okay Kovacs. Time to go.'

Mordent headed out of the office. He hadn't expected much else. Hooper was hunched over his desk. The guy needed glasses; his nose was more or less touching the paper he was writing on. But a quick conversation revealed nothing further about Marina. She was a nut. Even in these politically correct times she was a nut.

A nut that was hard to crack.

He had her number stored in his cell phone.

So there was no case. He'd gone about as far with his enquiries as he could. Time to work on something else. Something that paid.

7
All That Water Under The Bridge

The river changed colour the further you went. Near the shoreline, despite the shallows, it was mucky brown. An oily tan tainted by silt and rust. Gaze-impenetrable. A few metres out the brown merged with grey. Rolling winter clouds against a sullen winter sky. If you looked hard enough you could make out twisted sculptures of bicycles, bedsteads: an underwater scrap yard. Where there were waves the water became clearer, its colour lost in reflections that dappled translucent shapes across its surface. In the centre of the river it was a writhing mass of speckled greens and greys, an undulating morass that battered and kicked. A bruise.

And then, in reverse, the colours retreated towards the opposite shore. It was in the browns that the bodies tended to be found. Swollen, white. Huddled just below the surface like milk in coffee. Folded over, as though in prayer, or spreadeagled as though sky diving. Either way, rocked by the slap of the waves. A final cradle.

Mordent shuddered. He leant against the rail of the ferry as it traversed North to South. A thin, reedy breeze tugged at his jacket like a child. He was at midpoint. Either side, the river stretched away. He was in the open maw, skyscrapers flanked the shore like teeth, the water a lolling tongue.

This was the journey Patrick Davenport had taken on his final day. CCTV had placed him entering the ferry, but CCTV hadn't placed him leaving the ferry. No-one had seen him jump or fall. No body recovered. No body would be recovered. Mordent was sure of that.

From the missing persons report it appeared Patrick had been alone when he boarded the ferry. Amongst other passengers, naturally; but not *with* someone. Mordent found it strange that a college student might be lonesome, especially if he thought of his own fraternity days. But then lonesome students were prone to lonesome endings. Lonesome town. How did the lyrics go? *Going down to lonesome town. Where the broken hearts stay. Going down to lonesome town. To cry my troubles away.*

Thinking of the song made Mordent remember Harry Town. One of his missing persons that had been found. Also in the water. Harry had been seen by a family friend leaving a salacious peep show establishment. Otherwise of good character, in his sixties, having married his childhood sweetheart. When Mordent met Harry a fish could swim from one eye socket into another.

The sides of the ferry were flanked with iron railings. A white-painted sheet-metal strip ran around the lower portion, preventing dogs or small children from slipping through. But the strip would be simple to vault. One, two, three steps and you would be over. Descending fast into the water less than twenty feet below. Mordent imagined the exhilaration of that jump. The point of no return. Sink or swim. It wasn't for him.

Death was pretty bad at the best of times. He wanted to go quietly. Preferably in his sleep. But if it had to be suicide, then he would use a method where he couldn't have second thoughts of turning back beyond the final opportunity to do so. The horror of changing your mind as the pavement rushed up to hit, as you roiled in the river, as your eyes struggled against the potency of the pills, as the chair wavered beneath your foot. Give him the certainty of a pressed trigger, the infinitesimal micro-second of a bullet leaving a gun. But even then, give him the courage to burrow it through his brain.

The ferry lurched: the swell from another boat causing a chain reaction. It looked cold down there. Mrs Mouse had indicated Patrick had everything to live for, as did the files. But it couldn't have been an accident. The ferry railings were testament to that. Even heaving someone overboard wasn't really a possibility. The CCTV had indicated the ferry was busy that late afternoon. It had been dusk, but not dark. Yet facts were facts. He had got on, hadn't got off. At the inquest, death by misadventure had been recorded. Without a body, there could have been no other conclusion.

Lifeboats were tethered along the side of the ferry. Could Patrick have descended? Hidden? For what purpose? Mordent scratched his head, miniscule slices of scalp embedding in his bitten fingernails. The slightly salty air stiffened his hair. Further along the channel, the river opened to the sea. Mordent had often wondered about the barrier between salt and freshwater, river and sea. Some fish were saltwater, some freshwater. How did they know? What was the physical boundary between the two? At what stage did the salinity prevent the freshwater fish from entering the sea, and whatever process worked *vice versa*? There was an analogy there – plenty, probably – if he wanted to dwell on it.

The crossing took twenty minutes. An additional five minutes each side to moor and discharge. It was a passenger ferry. There was a long, sweeping route for cars over a suspension bridge. That bridge was also a favourite for suicides. Why hadn't Patrick jumped there?

Kicking around ideas. Poking a chicken's entrails with a stick. Looking at tea leaves. It all amounted to the same thing. Speculation.

As the ferry disgorged its passengers, Mordent looked back at where they had come from. The opposite shore seemed far away. A gateway to a new land.

*

He walked through the college grounds. Tree-lined avenues arched overhead. Patchy grass – reasonably tended – mirrored green. He was out of place here. Average age nineteen. In the city, with its multitude of ages, he could blend in. Here he was a saltwater fish in a freshwater pool.

Tick. The first analogy.

Skirt walked by. He couldn't keep his head down. When it came to women there was no age limit. Apart from the legality. As he got older, there seemed to be more young girls around. He understood how frustrating it must be for the infirm*. Trapped in minds that were young, bodies that were old: the world flaunting itself before them.

At reception he was directed to the principal's office by a boy with a curious smile. Stairs turned in a helix. Legs went up, down. By the time he reached the office he was younger, regenerated. He'd been here before: disruptive behaviour, theft, suspected drug offences. Yet also: commendations, awards, achievements. His good outbalanced the bad; but despite dealing with hardened criminals, shooting an innocent man, and having writhed within the seething underbelly of society, he still found himself slightly nervous with trepidation as he knocked on the principal's door.

Old habits die hard. Even if a lot of water had passed under the bridge.

Dr Sternforth didn't succumb to the image his name suggested. Skinny with a skinny tie, thin moustache, mid-forties, corduroy pants, brown: he looked more a science teacher than an organiser. Mordent introduced himself and a reedy arm floated over the desk towards him. It had the texture of underwater flesh fallen away like a leper's. Yet his smile was warm, welcoming; and remained that way even after Mordent mentioned Patrick's name.

'Ah, one of our brighter boys, as I recall. Popular. Such a shame, such a shame.'

He beckoned Mordent to sit. Crossed his legs, sideways to his desk; the rub of his cords making a grasshopper sound.

'But this was some time ago. What brings you here now?'

'His mother, Dr Sternforth. You're probably aware a body has never been found. She wants some closure.'

'You won't find his body here,' Sternforth smiled; inappropriately. 'Although I understand her need.'

Mordent coughed. 'At the time, the police made a few brief enquiries with his classmates. I'd like to extend those enquiries, just to be sure.'

'Be sure? Of what?'

'Maybe that he was as well-liked and popular as everyone says he was.'

'I'm not sure I can entertain a private investigator running round the school disturbing students, bringing back harrowing memories that they've only just forgotten.'

'Harrowing?'

'You know what I'm saying.'

'Death isn't nice, is it, Dr Sternforth? What did you get your doctorate in? I'm assuming it wasn't humanities. What I've got is a grieving mother. A mother who – unlike your students – can't bury that grief beneath a cocktail of school friends and studies. A mother who's old enough to know that it doesn't get any better. A mother who could do with a little closure that I might be able to provide by asking a number of very discreet questions.'

'Of course,' Sternforth stood, 'you're doing this out of the goodness of your heart.'

'Nope. I'm getting paid. Just like you. This is how people live. I hope that's something you teach those students of yours.'

Sternforth blanked him. Glanced out of the window. 'Three years is a long time. Those students will be nearing the end of their education. These disruptions ...'

'... are a minor inconvenience. Give me some names.'

Sternforth hit a buzzer on his desk that sounded at the end of a corridor. He didn't speak. Mordent heard the scrape of a wooden chair leg on a stone floor, the clip of heels increasingly staccato, smelt a whiff of perfume, glimpsed a pair of beautiful eyes as the secretary entered. Again, if she were agency it wasn't any he subscribed to. Not that he imagined Sternforth appreciated it.

'Miss Burton, this is Mr Mordent, a PI. Can you ensure he gets the information he's asking for please?'

'Certainly.' Her voice was honey-smooth. She turned to face Mordent. She was older than he had thought; but she had clearly looked after herself. No doubt about that. 'Come this way.'

He followed the perfume trail and the wavering heels into her office.

In fifteen minutes he had details of two students who had been close to Patrick. One male, one female. It tallied with the information he already held. No surprises there. Yet following the official route was better than directly approaching the kids. Not only was it more professional, but it carried the weight of the school behind his investigation.

Miss Burton gave him a little wave as she closed her office door. Her red fingernails were like fireflies. He shuddered. Despite her looks, she was dangerous. Some women were too strong. Too self-assured. He needed the thrill of the chase, not easy meat.

8
All Your Friends Are Not Your Enemies

It was late afternoon by the time he caught up with the students. There was no point in disrupting lessons. Instead he hung around the quad, read pieces of work pinned to the walls like Blu-Tacked effigies.

The entire building was *No Smoking*. He wondered what the students did. Studied, perhaps. There had been a monsoon of gum judging by fat splats that speckled the pavements. He'd have had to dance like a loon to avoid it, but didn't bother. Stuff weighed on his mind. Being around academia reminded him of how well he could have done.

Being a police officer had had its benefits. As he'd worked his way up, the money had been good. Then he'd hit the ceiling. Following the Lazlo incident with Kovacs, that ceiling had become impenetrable. As the golden Kovacs boy had risen through the force, the ceiling had begun to descend. By the time Mordent had got out there had been but an inch crack above the ground to squeeze through. He had made it. Just.

Nowadays it was all specialisation, right from the start. He had a predilection for noir, but police work was all clean. No more the dark nights, long shadows, trilbies, cigarettes, heavies, trenchcoats, dames with guns, or the ability to throw a punch without a lawsuit. Occasionally those cases came. He cherished them. But they were few and far between. It was all DNA, forensics, fancy footwork. Getting out had regained him some semblance of his preferred role, yet watching these students with their lives before them ...

He shook his head. It wasn't jealousy. He didn't want their fractured lives, their virtual realities, the confusions that came with the onset of adulthood and the desperation of lost dreams. What he craved was the world that had already been and gone: the romanticised world of the PI that existed in movies and books. A world that had never existed, not in the way he imagined. But there was a tug towards it, a kinship, a love that he couldn't quantify.

Finally the building disgorged the students. He had waited outside the science faculty where both Greg Hammerton and Sue Sweeney had their afternoon classes. He had seen photos of them in the school yearbook, supplied by the secretary with the legs. Normal kids. Good stock, probably. They were looking for him as they came out, so the system worked and their tutor had been informed he was here.

Both were smartly dressed. Greg in a fitted shirt, tie, grey slacks. Looked older than his years. There was no dress code at this college, but there could have been. When you compared him to the other students, it was clear he had focus. Would probably enter the same profession as his father. Sue wore a long skirt. Had leather sandals on her feet. Her toenails painted green. A flowery top bunched out at the waist hid her figure, which looked like it might be okay. She was attractive and she knew it but she didn't want to flaunt it. No doubt she'd use it, as she got older, as she realised that you had to use everything in order to get where you wanted to be; but for the moment she was comfortable enough in herself not to need it. He admired that. There were far too many girls tarting themselves around. On the internet, on street corners, it all amounted to the same thing. And it was all too easy to succumb to temptation. Half his cases on the force revolved around young girls and misunderstandings.

First impressions. He wondered what they thought of him.

He waved them over. Was aware he was trying to look cool, to look like a detective they might want to talk to and share their secrets with.

'Greg, Sue.'

'That's us.'

'I just want a few words about Patrick Davenport.'

'That's a long while ago, man.'

Mordent glanced sideways at Greg. That *man* was affected; unnecessary.

'You try telling his mother that.'

Sue closed the gap between them. 'I'm sure Greg didn't mean to be flippant. It's just that it was hard for us. We've been trying to forget.'

Mordent thought about making a remark to the effect that Patrick's brain was being eaten by fishes, a sure-fire way to forget, but a slight tang in her perfume sobered him. 'Look. I'm not here to rake all that up. The boy goes missing. Isn't found. Probably fell or jumped to his death from the ferry. These are the facts. What I have is a mother who can't let go until she finds the body, so she employs me to make some enquiries. I'm gonna tell her the same thing but get the legwork in to prove I had an interest. This is how PIs work. So, to get back to where we started, I just want a few words about Patrick Davenport.'

Sue smiled. 'I'm sure that will be fine.' Mordent didn't look at Greg, but he suspected he wasn't smiling.

'The files I've seen suggest he was well-liked,

intelligent, had everything to live for. Did you see another side to him: drugs, drink, a girl, any periods of depression, suicidal thoughts that he might have expressed to his friends but not his family?'

'We can only repeat what we told the police,' Greg said. 'He was one of us. A regular guy.'

'Was it unusual for him to take the ferry alone after school?'

'Not at all. We live this side of the river, he lived the other.'

'Any enemies?'

'He was seventeen years old.'

Mordent shrugged. These kids came from stock where you wouldn't have enemies at seventeen years old, wouldn't have been involved in gang warfare, hustling, prostitution. Wouldn't have needed protection. But they still got killed or committed suicide all the same.

'How about something else? He specialised in science, right; just like yourselves? He mention anything about that?'

'Such as?'

'I dunno. Some secret project he was working on? World domination through genetic engineering? You tell me.'

'You're kidding, right?' There was an edge to Greg's voice. Mordent ignored it.

'You tell me,' he repeated.

Sue shrugged. 'He was like us. Just a student. You're looking for an answer that doesn't exist. It was a tragic accident that we've spent a couple of years getting used to. The loss of a special friend. What else do you expect us to say?'

Mordent didn't know. He no longer knew what he wanted from these guys. Something tangible, something he could go back to Mrs Mouse with. It wasn't just a body that was absent, but a reason. He felt she needed at least one of those for closure.

As usual, it was running to nought.

He delved into his inside jacket pocket, pulled out a couple of tatty cards.

'This is my number. Just give me a call if you think of anything useful. I know it's been a while. But anything. Please.'

Sue took both of the cards, slipped them into her bag. 'We will.'

He stood watching as they walked off. Just for a moment he thought Greg reached for Sue's hand. It was an automatic gesture, a familiar one. Their fingers nudged then moved away. Or was it just an inadvertent swinging motion from their walk? Either way, he suspected he wasn't supposed to see it. The detail was filed in the back of his mind.

There was nothing else to do. Go back. Phone Mrs Mouse. Tell her he had reached a dead end. Thank her for the money. Next time, maybe. No resolution. Nothing.

*

It was dark by the time he reached his office. He sometimes wondered if he should convert it, like Hubie. Sleep on the job, considering the amount of time he spent there. But he needed the distance. If nothing else, the journey to and from work with the jazz irrigated him. Put things into perspective.

It was with a sense of loss that he powered up his PC to obtain Mrs Mouse's contact details. It was never good to conclude an investigation with nothing, but to charge for it all the same. Like insurance payments: worthless without a claim. He imagined her sighing, flicking through the phone book, picking out another PI who would charge more and do none of the work. Just sit back for a few days instead of wild goose chasing it. The outcome would be the same.

People needed closure. Of this he was certain. Unknowing was worse.

Just like the certainty of death, and the unknowing of what came after it.

Life's eternal question.

After a moment, feeling the stillness of the building at night with the dark shrouding the windows, he got up and locked the door.

He decided to check his e-mails before obtaining Mrs Mouse's file details. And there it was: an e-mail from Constantin.

There was nothing in the subject line. He clicked it open.

If the e-mail could have spoken it would have been a mumbled apology. *Something came up.* There was little other detail. A suggestion he was being followed. Then an address. Another time and place to meet. That evening. Mordent knew that if this were a trashy detective novel he would arrive and find Constantin's body. A message from beyond the grave. He sighed, pulled open the wooden drawer of the desk to reveal a lolling, half-sunk bottle of bourbon, and poured himself a shot.

Should he stay or should he go?

The silhouette of BuzzCut burned on his retina. Bataille wasn't to be messed with. Yet he had nothing.

He couldn't be intimidated without knowing what he was being intimidated for.

The hands of his father's watch showed 9.20. Constantin had said 10.00. It would take him a half hour to get there. Time was of the essence. A decision had to be made.

So he made it.

The night was cool. The car heater was broken. He preferred to drive with the window open, but the temperature wouldn't allow it. His fingers hardened in the cold, evidencing the probable onset of arthritis. The thought itself chilled him.

Who would look after him in his old age?

Another unknown, uncertain question.

With the windows up, the car was a bubble. Life skittered past his view, the headlights illuminating a stage show of bums and whores, pirouetting on unsteady legs: either drunken or stilettoed. Or both. It was all greys and blacks, a monochrome night. The nearer the outskirts the grimmer it got. His clients were never in the salubrious parts of the city. He had Googled the address Constantin had given him. Flanking an industrial estate in an area that was marked for social regeneration, it wasn't the best place to meet someone at this time of night. As if to remind him, it started to hail.

Ice slapped the car, left beaten crystal imprints like striated windscreen chips. Within seconds the noise was deafening, like the knuckles of a thousand tiny demons rapping on the metal carcass. His wipers played ping-pong, battering hailstones left and right.

Mordent swore. Pulled over. Activated his hazard lights. It wasn't possible to see, yet several cars flew by while he was waiting for it to clear. Idiots. Some people couldn't wait for their deaths. Rushed into them headlong. White out.

The engine cooled. So did he. He waited.

After ten minutes he was back on the road. It was 9.45. He should make it in time. Should Constantin wait.

Whether or not it was his home address, of course, Mordent had no idea.

The road was slippy. His headlights illuminated a white-bobbled wetness, like the residue of an accident between a soda truck and a polystyrene truck. Fake snow. There was a lack of tension under his wheels, the hint of a slide. He *had* to open the window now, the screen fogged with condensation as the icy air met his warm breath.

The entrance to his destination was on the edge of the industrial estate. Standing alone, a six-storey building loomed like the remnants of Ozymandias, its previous neighbours demolished, a rubble-strewn landscape. Mordent wondered why it was still standing. No doubt some technical planning hitch. Lights beamed from various windows, making it resemble a confused lighthouse. Constantin lived on the third floor. A light or two showed there. It held promise.

He parked up. The building rose out of the ground like an extended arm in a graveyard from a B-movie horror film. Once the entrance had had a buzzer system, but this was long-defunct. The main door swung on loose hinges. The reception desk was empty.

He wasn't prepared to take the elevator. Inside his jacket his gun rubbed his ribs through the holster. He sneaked his fingers around the butt. It was quiet. Too quiet. Although better quiet than noisy. He could hear if anything was going on. Quiet beat noisy any day of the week.

As he reached the second floor he wondered why Constantin had been so cagey in his e-mails. Initially, he had thought security. Yet giving times and places of meetings was dodgier than supplying facts. He wouldn't have given it a thought if BuzzCut hadn't showed, but BuzzCut knew he'd been contacted. How had he known?

He took the final few steps.

Listened outside the door.

It remained quiet.

9
Step Away From The Girl

Mordent knocked.

There was a short wait before the door opened on a chain. A slice of face eyed him. Pale skin, blue eye, blond, about five foot two, male.

'Mordent?'

He nodded. The door closed a fraction to ease the removal of the chain, then opened.

Mordent was shown into a regular living area. Two sofas faced a CRT television set. A couple of aluminium foil trays lay on the floor. The wallpaper was 1970s. The place needed redecoration. A glass cabinet along one wall was filled with half-empty bottles of spirits and liqueurs. The curtains were closed: large orange spots complemented smaller green ones. It needed a makeover. A glance showed two doorways leading off into a kitchen and a corridor respectively. No doubt at the end of the corridor was a toilet and a bathroom with lime green furnishings. Mordent had been here before. It was every room in every flea-bitten dive that had once been loved and cared for but was now on the brink of disintegration. Too much to do and no-one to do it. This was a universal room in a universal building. Nothing unusual. Mordent wouldn't have paid it a second glance, if it wasn't for the girl on one of the sofas: her mouth stuffed with cloth and held by tape, her arms tied behind her back.

Constantin was sweating. Mordent looked for a gun. There was none. Constantin locked the door, and when he replaced the chain, Mordent noticed that his hands were shaking. He looked drained. As though he hadn't slept for a week. Not in the sense that the expression was normally bandied around, but literally *as though he hadn't slept for a week*. The room smelt of nachos and the dust burn of an electric fire.

'Sit down.'

It was almost an order, but it wasn't delivered as such. Constantin's voice was full of resignation.

Mordent pulled up a chair beside a table that was propped level by a fold of cardboard under one leg. Constantin sat on the empty sofa opposite the girl.

The girl looked from one to the other. Mordent couldn't calculate the expression in her eyes, but it wasn't fear, curiosity or helplessness. Her legs were tucked underneath her, as though she had been casually watching the television and hadn't changed her pose in the struggle. If there had been a struggle.

Perhaps she had nothing to do with it. Maybe he'd walked in on some sadomasochistic scenario. It wasn't for him to judge. The girl was old enough. And he had his own peccadilloes.

'I suppose you're wondering about the secrecy,' Constantin began, as though oblivious to sofa girl. 'Truth is, I have to be careful.'

'There was someone asking about you,' Mordent said. 'Big guy.' He paused. 'That girl over there, is she Bataille's?'

Constantin wavered. 'That isn't why I asked you here.'

'She's a little hard to ignore.'

Constantin stood, walked to the window and

parted the curtain. He waited a half minute. Sighed. 'Look,' he said. 'It's complicated.'

'I've got all night.'

He sat down opposite Mordent, the sofa springs sang. 'My brother is dead.'

'Go on.'

'Has been some time. I mean, like four, five years. I was there when he was killed. We were part of Bataille's gang. I had to keep quiet. That's why I'm living here, often drunk, spacing myself out, in this shithole.'

'What happened to him?'

'Thought he was clever, didn't he? Decided to cross Bataille on a drug deal, to cream off a little of the package he was due to collect. It was all done by weight. He didn't know. He gets the package, splices it, hides some, delivers it. Bataille weighs it. Like a feather against a heart. My brother's heart. So it doesn't balance. Bataille says he needs to make an example of him. He knows I'm there, watching like. It doesn't make any difference. Or maybe it *does* make a difference. Maybe he thought blood is thicker than water and thought like brother like brother. I dunno. What I do know is that they strangled him in front of me. That was that.'

Constantin swallowed. Mordent glanced over to the girl. Her eyes were wide.

'This was some time ago, you say.'

'Yeah.' Constantin leant back, as though his story were relaxing him, unwinding inside. 'You can understand why I haven't told anyone this until now.'

Mordent shrugged, 'He was your brother.'

'You know how things are. I had to demonstrate my loyalty. And if I didn't: the river beckoned.'

'So why now?'

'This is where it gets freaky.' Constantin licked his

lips, wiped his brow with the back of his hand, which came back shiny. 'A few weeks ago, they found his body.'

'The police?'

'Yeah.'

'So they pulled you in?'

'They needed me to identify him. So I did.'

'And? You're hiding out? You dobbed Bataille in?'

Constantin started to shake. He gripped his hands together as though they were one fist.

'Fuck.'

'Constantin?'

He stared ahead, at a blank space on the wall. Filling it in.

'He'd aged. He'd aged since his death.'

Mordent glanced over to the girl. Was there a trace of a smile under the gag? Constantin had slumped back. As though the effort of his last sentence had deflated him. There was no substance. The sofa absorbed him like a human throw.

Mordent chose his words carefully. 'It must have been traumatic. I mean, you must have buried this in the past, in the back of your mind, to deal with it. Seeing him again must have been a shock.'

'He'd aged.'

'There's no way to be tactful, Constantin. Bodies change after death.'

'He'd aged, Mordent. He was twenty-seven when he died. Had just had a birthday. Autopsy thought he was mid-thirties.'

'Autopsies get things wrong. You've been watching too much *CSI*.'

'Christ. I saw him killed. He'd aged.'

Silence fell in the room, as though the dark outside had managed to seep in the window, blanketed the three of them. Or as though a dimmer switch had been turned; shadowing their senses. Mordent turned things over in his mind. A petty crook, not in his right mind. A hostage. No visible weapon. BuzzCut. Bataille. There was something here, but the present situation needed fixing before he could get to the bottom of it.

'Where had the body been?'

'Warehouse. Down at the quayside. Bataille sealed him in a container and shipped it there. Warehouse belongs to Kirby Muxloe.'

Mordent breathed out. In doing so he realised he had been holding his breath, like in some cheap pulp novel. Kirby Muxloe was another gang leader. Although they didn't call themselves gangs: *businessmen* was the preferred term these days.

'Yeah,' Constantin went on. 'Thought it would be amusing to pin a murder on Muxloe's turf. Place has been crawling with cops.'

'So you've holed up here, kept quiet. Haven't told the police of Bataille's involvement for fear of retribution?'

'Something like that.'

'And the girl?'

'Lexi Leigh. One of Bataille's girls. As you guessed.'

'An insurance policy?'

'Right.'

Mordent stood up. Went over to the curtain. Looked out as Constantin had done. Rain fell like diamonds in the light from the window, disappearing into blackness. He could just make out his car, a lone beetle in a carpet of rubble. The way he saw it, Constantin needed police protection. Taking the girl meant there was no way back to Bataille. Constantin knew too much. But there were a couple of questions. If this was Constantin's regular pad, how come BuzzCut hadn't tracked him down? And placing the body at Muxloe's indicated Bataille had intended it to be found. Hadn't he foreseen what would happen with Constantin, even if it were to be five years after the event?

This was why he was a PI, he decided. To find answers to questions. It wasn't rocket science.

'There's a blond guy,' he said, 'six foot plus ...'

'Derby Boy.'

'That's it. Been asking after you.'

Constantin shrugged. 'Doesn't surprise me.'

'There's one other thing. He knew you'd tried to contact me. That night when we had the arrangement to meet at the bar and you didn't show.'

'No mystery there. I *did* show. So did he. So did you. You didn't see me. I saw you. I saw him. He saw me and you. Connections.'

'So you hightailed it out of there.'

'Wouldn't you?'

Mordent nodded. 'When did you pick up the girl?'

'After the bar scare, I needed collateral, something to bargain with.'

'Did you need that?' Mordent nodded towards the gag, the hand ties.

Constantin smiled, a crack in the cloud, 'You haven't heard her voice, felt her scratches.'

'You touched her?'

'No.'

'So ... why me? You know all I can do is go to the police.'

Constantin sighed. 'My number's up. The game's up. Either way it's up for me. Either the police or Bataille get me. I know this. But the police won't understand about my brother. He aged after he'd died.

I know what it looks like. But I'm not dumb. You'll understand.'

'I don't think you'll find anyone who'll understand, Constantin.'

'I tell you Mordent. You'll understand.'

There was a knock at the door. So quiet it could hardly be heard. The brief graze of a knuckle. Not a sound to get your attention, but one to scout, to determine a presence. Mordent held his finger to his lips. Constantin moved over to the opposite sofa, held the girl. From behind a cushion he pulled a knife.

'If that's them, she gets it.'

Mordent looked at her. Lexi Leigh. A two-bit porn star caught in the wrong business, or an aspiring starlet mixing with the wrong company. What was the difference nowadays? But she had nice eyes. He had to do something.

He pulled his gun from his pocket. Stood adjacent to the door, opposite the hinge. Listened again. There was a sound similar to a lock being picked. He glanced across to Constantin and the girl. They were directly in the line of fire should a bullet come through the door. That chain wouldn't hold anyone for long. Mordent decided to play a card. A card that knew someone was there.

'Who is it?'

There was a pause. The clicking sound stopped. 'Telegram. Telegram for Mr Constantin.'

Telegram? Mordent didn't know such things still existed. He slipped the chain link out of its slot and waited for the message.

The key fell backwards out of the keyhole.

Mordent flipped the latch, made things easier.

The door opened half a crack. Paused.

Mordent's card had worked. They didn't know

whether to go in all guns blazing or take the softly softly approach. But he still needed to be careful in case a bullet passed between them.

'Why don't you just come in? Constantin's not alone.'

The door edged open further.

'Smile,' Mordent said. 'You're on candid camera.'

Beyond the doorway, blackness resolved itself into the shape of two hoodlums. Mordent recognised one of them: it wasn't BuzzCut. These guys worked for Muxloe.

He kicked the door wider with his foot. Over on the sofa, Constantin held the knife close to Lexi Leigh's side. It wouldn't matter to these guys. She wasn't their dame.

As the inside of the apartment opened up to the men outside they seemed to relax. It was always the unknown that created fear, thought Mordent. The known was just a problem to solve.

'Come in,' Mordent said, his gun trained on both of them, held snug to his side. 'It's a bit cosy, but fine.'

'We're not here for you,' one of them said. He had a nose like Karl Malden and a scar that ran from the bottom of his left eye down to his cheek. His face was oblong, a patch of hair stuck up like newly-laid turf. His mouth a line, thin.

'I wasn't expecting you to be.'

'I know you,' said the other goon. 'You're a PI, used to be police. The name escapes me.'

'As yours does me,' Mordent said, keeping one eye on Constantin, who was twitching. 'Come out of the corridor, you're making it untidy.'

They shifted into the room. There was no bluster; they were like uninvited guests at the wrong party. Awkward.

'Seems like we've got a situation here,' said Mordent. 'I've established their position, so what are you here for?'

'Muxloe wants to see Constantin,' Malden-lookalike said. 'We're not here to hurt him, just have to take him in.'

'And if I don't allow that?'

'Then we need to review the situation.'

'I think you'll find you're outnumbered.'

They both laughed, uneasily.

Mordent knew if he could keep it sane they would have no place to go. Simmer. Don't boil. That was the only way to deal with these vegetables.

Then Constantin turned up the gas.

Even through the gag the three of them heard her squeal. Mordent swung around, gun remaining poised. Constantin had stood, hauling Lexi Leigh up with him, the knife pointed into her side, her white T-shirt bearing an increasing stain of blood.

'Get out,' Constantin shouted; it was almost a scream. 'Get out!'

The goons looked from one to the other. They didn't care.

'Constantin. Step away from the girl.'

'Get out!'

Lexi Leigh was trying desperately not to struggle. Her T-shirt rode up her body. Marks could be seen across her abdomen. Old scars. As Mordent watched, blood ran down one side. Only a surface wound, he was sure, but in any case he couldn't leave the goons unattended. A drop of blood caught the ridge of one of the scars, diverted and began a zig-zag along its length.

'Constantin, I've got this under control.' He kept his voice calm. 'Don't fuck it up.'

73

But Constantin was spooked, and backed away towards the kitchen. The goons didn't know what to do. They had no allegiance to the girl. Or to anyone, as it happened, other than Muxloe.

But Mordent had a feeling they wanted Constantin alive, not dead.

He turned to them. 'Wait outside, let me handle this.'

Again they were wrong-footed. They wanted to watch.

'Seriously. You can see how it is. There's nowhere for him to go. You're just making him nervous.'

The guy who recognised Mordent turned to the other. 'He's right. We can wait outside.'

'Wait up,' Malden said to Mordent. 'What are you doing here anyway?'

'Constantin called me. Wanted protection. The girl is Bataille's. He wanted security.'

The words were out before Mordent could stop them. Now the goons would want both Constantin *and* the girl. Their own kind of payback. He made an effort not to swear under his breath.

Constantin was in the kitchen doorway, had paused.

The goons weighed it up. No-one wanted a shoot-out.

'Okay. We'll wait outside.'

They backed out. Mordent closed the door, locked it, chained it, flicked up the latch. Turned to Constantin. 'Will you put that girl down?'

Constantin released her and she slumped to the floor.

Mordent went over, untied her hands from behind her back. She moved her arms stiffly to the front. Bruises a day or so old marked her wrists, although there were older bruises about her body that Constantin hadn't inflicted. Mordent started to care, then realised it wasn't his business.

He looked into her eyes. 'Are you going to stay quiet?'

She nodded.

'I'm on your side, remember this. Those goons work for Kirby Muxloe. You heard of him?'

She nodded again.

'Right. So you know it's best to keep quiet. Then we'll get you out of here and get that wound cleaned up. May I?' He pointed to her stained top and she nodded again. Lifting it up, he could see the wound wasn't deep. He felt like giving Constantin a slap, but he was still holding the knife, his eyes glazed over, knowing this was a situation he couldn't control.

Mordent slid off the gag. Lexi Leigh worked her tongue around her dry lips, reassembling her confidence. 'Thanks.' It came out as a breath.

'Get in the kitchen and wash that wound. Take a drink, while you're at it.'

He pulled Constantin into the living room, closed the door on Lexi. Constantin dropped the knife. Held his head in his hands. His earlier bravado shot to pieces. The crutch of the girl gone. When he removed his hands, bloody fingerprints populated the right side of his face.

'Easy,' Mordent said. 'I think the girl's more attractive to them than you are. From what you've said, I reckon Muxloe just wants a chat. He'll know it was your brother, will know you've spoken to the police. He'll have suspected Bataille dropped the body there. All he'll want is confirmation. He drops you, police are rammed against him. But if his goons return with the girl, then that's a trade off. You owe her to keep her safe. If she gets killed, that's your responsibility.'

Constantin started to shake. He was weak. In way over his head.

'They're not going to wait outside that door forever. Get a grip on yourself.'

'What are we gonna do?'

'You're gonna go outside and hand yourself over. As *my* trade off, I'll take a look at your brother's body. And I'll keep the girl here.'

'You think they'll let her stay?'

'They've got me to deal with.'

'So why can't I stay here with you?'

'They're not going to leave with nothing. Trust me, you'll be safe. And if I return Bataille's girl, maybe even he will look kindly on you.'

Constantin shuddered. 'I didn't touch her.'

'Didn't say you did.'

'And you'll look into my brother? He aged, Mordent. He aged after his death.'

'I'll look into your brother.'

For a moment, Constantin's eyes flickered with gratitude. Then they hardened. Mordent knew he was steeling himself for a meeting with Muxloe.

'Okay, I'm ready.'

Mordent went back to the door. Stood adjacent again, flicked the latch.

Outside, he could almost hear the anticipation as the lock clunked.

'Constantin is coming out,' Mordent said. 'That's who you came for. The girl stays with me.'

The voices were too low for him to hear.

After a pause: 'That's fine.'

Mordent turned the key, hooked off the chain, kept his gun – once again – snug to his side.

When the gap was wide enough for a body to pass through, Mordent bundled Constantin outside.

'And remember,' he said. 'Me and the girl are witnesses. Anything happens to him, Muxloe's in deep.'

'Yeah, sure. We'll pass it on.' They were laconic, now they had their man.

Mordent closed the door. Bolted it. Chained it. Locked it. Went over to the window and waited and watched. After two minutes the group moved from the projected light at the front of the building into shadow. There was a car parked under a tree. One of them went in the front, two in the back. After another short while, the car lights sparked to life and they drove away.

Satisfied the situation was resolved, Mordent headed to the kitchen. His gun remained in his hand.

10
In The Heat Of The Moment

Lexi Leigh was sitting at the kitchen table, making a peanut butter sandwich. She looked up, her smile bright: 'You want some?'

Mordent shook his head.

'I haven't eaten all day.'

She folded the bread in half, overbit it. Mordent imagined the peanut butter sticking to the sides of her mouth. Imagined tasting it.

He saw the bruises on her arms and wrists, the scars across her stomach.

'You wondering how I got those?' She pulled her T-shirt down, so only her belly button was on show. 'Just what happens.'

'You need someone who should treat you right.'

'Maybe I like being treated this way.'

Her eyes showed otherwise.

'Wait here.'

Mordent returned to the living room, began moving stuff around, searching for anything that might be evidence. In these situations, it was never clear what might be useful and what might be trash. Sure as hell he didn't expect to find anything, and it didn't take him long to realise that was the case. When he returned to the kitchen, the girl was nowhere to be seen.

He listened. There was a hissing noise from the end of the corridor. She was taking a shower.

He walked quietly. The carpet thin under his feet, the wallpaper a dirty blue. He didn't want to touch it. There was a smell permeating the air, thick like chocolate but not as sweet. The bathroom led off to the right, the bedroom straight ahead. He flicked a switch and bugs ran off the bed and onto the floor. The curtains were closed. Underpants plastered the floor. The thick smell of dope. Mordent reached into his pocket, pulled out a handkerchief and put it over his nose. Then he returned it to his pocket, the 'chief not much cleaner than the room.

He pulled open a couple of drawers: a gun, a Bible, a book. He flipped the book over: Dan Brown's *The Da Vinci Code*. No surprises. There seemed to be just as many of those in the world as there were Bibles. And just as useful.

There was nothing else to see. Mordent hadn't expected anything. The hiss of the shower was white noise in his ear. It was running longer than was necessary.

He backtracked out of the bedroom, opened the door to the bathroom. Lexi Leigh's pale silhouette could be seen through the steamed glass of the cubicle. Mordent glanced at the bath. A ridge of scum delineated the watermark. The shower seemed the best option. On the floor lay a stained T-shirt, shoes, jeans. In the midst, a pair of off-white panties bearing a trace of skid.

The steamed mirror bore lettering: *Get in with me*.

Mordent paused. Against the panel he watched as Lexi Leigh's body occasionally touched the glass: a moment of clarity.

He unbuckled his belt.

11
The Cold Light of Day

Mordent was awakened by the trill of his cell phone. Eyes closed, he reached out an arm, found it on his beside cabinet, determined his location. The inside of his mouth felt like the residue of an afternoon nap.

Maybe it *was* afternoon. Light filtered through his curtains. He squinted at the phone, couldn't see the display, answered it.

'Mordent.'

'It's Kovacs.'

'Courtesy call or something special?'

'I'm doing you a favour, giving you the heads up.'

'Oh yeah. On who?'

'On the Davenport boy.'

Mordent tried to sit, his elbow depressing the pillow so he rolled instead, banged his head on the cabinet and dropped the phone.

A tinny voice, as though from afar: *Mordent, Mordent!*

He reached for the phone. 'Sorry, I slipped.'

'Well, there's a body. No surprises there. Guess where we found it?'

'In the river?'

'No. In a box. More like a container. It had been shipped.'

'Shipped?'

'Yep. Special delivery.'

'Where?'

'Well, that's the thing. We don't know.'

'You're not making things easy.'

'If there was a label on the container then it isn't there now. The truck was found abandoned on the highway. We're trying to trace the plates. If you ask me, this is a body that was intended to be found.'

'Cause of death?'

'Unknown, at present.'

There was a pause. Mordent wished he would hurry and wake up.

Kovacs spoke: 'Don't you think it's a bit of a coincidence that this body turns up just after you've started looking for it?'

'Someone's doing me a favour.'

'Perhaps.'

'I guess you want me to come and have a look.'

Kovacs sighed. 'Maybe it's me that's doing you the favour. God knows why. But I'm interested in why you name-dropped him the other day, so get yourself over here and we'll go down together.'

'It'll be like the old days.'

'Not quite. You've got thirty minutes.'

The line went dead.

Mordent heaved himself out of bed. He was naked, and this surprised him. He glanced over at the other side of the bed but there were no telltale clothes that indicated a female occupation. He'd dropped Lexi Leigh off at her apartment around three o'clock in the morning. She'd given him a conciliatory kiss. *Thanks for saving my life.* Although he wasn't sure he'd done so. Delayed the inevitable perhaps.

As he'd driven back to his apartment he'd thought of Marina. It was hardly normal for him to have slept with two women in one week. Both had been satisfactory, neither did he want to see again. Marina had been exciting, yet her psychic nonsense indicated that all the best things turn to rust. Lexi Leigh had been impulsive. He regretted it as much as a bird might regret alighting on an unearthed electricity wire. A quick shock, then it's all over. Although he didn't regret it *that* much.

Slipping on his clothes he wondered about Patrick Davenport. Wondered if Mrs Mouse had been informed. Like the other women, he didn't want to see her again either. He could bank her cheque, refund anything he wasn't entitled to. Close down the file on his computer. Another dead body. Sometimes he wondered what he'd do if he found someone alive.

Out of the apartment. Into the car. His life.

The streets were busy. His dashboard clock showed 10.30. Lack of sleep fogged his motions. He stalled the car before he left the garage. Something heavy hung at the back of his eyes. He remembered a cartoon where a drugged cat tried to prop its eyelids open with matchsticks while a cartoon mouse attempted to pull them shut. *Tom and Jerry*, no doubt. His eyes felt the same. Dragged right down.

Life was becoming harder as he got older. Somehow, somewhere, he had done something wrong. Surely it was supposed to be the other way around.

The streets were wet, slick. Even in the daylight everything was dark. The underbelly remained, just below the surface. If you looked close enough you could see the grime on the freshly-cleaned sidewalks, between the cracks. Nudged into the mortar edging the bricks in the buildings. On the bottoms of people's shoes, scuff marks on clothing, bags. It was all there. You just had to see it.

Constantin was the dirt hidden at the back of the sofa, Lexi Leigh the tidemark round the bath, the hair in the plughole. Bataille and Muxloe were acid rain.

Mordent supposed he would have to follow up Constantin's allegations about his brother. However weird they might seem. He tried to keep his word on the basis that what goes around comes around. Not that he was into karma, but a lubrication of the wheels in this business tended to yield results. If he did as Constantin had asked, maybe one day Constantin wouldn't put a bullet in the back of his head – even if he was told to.

He pulled into the police car park. Kovacs was standing by his vehicle. Looking at his watch.

When he shook it, Mordent knew he was on time.

He parked up.

'Get in.'

They headed off. Kovacs had a driver. It was cosy in the back, just the two of them. Mordent could tell Kovacs was uncomfortable by the way his body seemed to hug the door, putting as much space between them as was physically possible, trying not to show it.

'We're heading upstate,' Kovacs said.

Mordent nodded.

'Truck was stopped by the side of the road. Routine traffic patrol. Been there a couple of days. Inside, one container. Inside, one body. Patrick Davenport.'

'Identification?'

'Simple. Had his student card with him. Photo was old and the body decomposed, but recognisably him.'

Mordent wondered if Kovacs knew about Constantin's brother. For him, the word *container* rang as loud as someone banging a wrench against the side, trying to wake up the dead within. What he wasn't sure of was whether or not to reveal his card.

Holding an imaginary rod and line, he went fishing instead.

'Seems a weird place to dump a body. You say you think someone wanted it found.'

If Kovacs had any cards he kept them close to his chest. If he were a fish, he'd be cunning.

'I think it was placed there. Deliberately in a container. To implicate someone who may or may not be involved.'

Mordent shrugged. 'No doubt I'll find out when the time comes. Fished out of the river?'

'Pardon?'

'You say the cause of death hadn't been determined, but I thought it might be evident if the body had been in the river.'

Kovacs sighed. 'We'll see when we get there. I know how he was supposed to have died. Give me time on this; we've only just found him.'

'Still not sure why I'm tagging along.'

'You know well enough.'

They stayed silent, each contemplating the other's thoughts in an uneasy truce.

Finally, Mordent chanced it.

'You don't know, do you? You've got no idea what's going on. That's why I'm here.'

Kovacs looked out of the window. They had left the city behind. Verdant scenery rushed past, a flicker-book display of pointillism. Autumnal colours. Above the landscape, a pure slice of blue. It was beautiful, Mordent admitted, once you got out. Yet stretching behind the car was a thick piece of elastic, ready to pull them back into the city. Just as it was taut.

Kovacs spoke: 'You're here because – despite our personal differences – I find you useful. You're here because you're acting in an official capacity as employed by Mrs Davenport. You've made recent enquiries, while our trail was long cold. Is that enough for you?'

Mordent let it lie. Squeezing info from Kovacs was never easy. He gave as much as he wanted. That was all.

After thirty minutes – Mordent's head nodding against the window frame, pulling himself from sleep as a drowning man might occasionally surface – they parked up behind a truck surrounded by police vehicles. Kovacs got out first, Mordent reassembling himself within his suit like a pile of laundry brought to life.

'Here we are.'

Mordent followed Kovacs like a lap dog, knowing that under different circumstances it might have been the other way around. He growled under his breath. If Kovacs heard it, he didn't turn.

The air was fresh outside the car. As well as the regular vehicles, an ambulance was parked near the truck. There was a gurney beside it. The ambulance staff were smoking, taking their time, waiting for Kovacs to give the scene a once over, rubberstamp it before they could get going. One of them recognised Mordent, raised an eyebrow. Mordent raised one back, gave a half-smile.

A white sheet covered the body, which was strapped to the gurney. Features were delineated beneath. Mordent realised how nondescript those sheets were until, like unveiling a ghost, you pulled them back and saw what no-one wanted to see. Your future.

A gloved hand revealed the body.

Three years can do a lot of damage but, for a corpse, Davenport didn't look too bad. His face was pockmarked, skin blackened, like a survivor of a black and white minstrel show. But the features were clear. Death had aged him, naturally; he looked much older than his seventeen years. But he was recognisable from the photos Mordent had seen on the police files, on the news streams. Mrs Mouse wasn't going to be a happy mother.

They both nodded and the blanket was replaced. The gurney was hitched into the back of the ambulance and it drove away slowly.

Then they pulled themselves up into the back of the truck.

Kovacs spoke to an officer inside.

'Just had confirmation that this truck was reported stolen last night, sir. It belongs to Bataille. Normally does the cake run. For his chain of baker's stores, as you know.'

Kovacs nodded. Leant over the side of the container where the body had been found. It was relatively clean. 'I don't think he's been in there long. Certainly not dumped there when he was killed.'

Mordent raised both eyebrows. 'I guess it can't be anything other than a suspicious death.'

'I guess not.' Kovacs paused. 'Seen anything you want to comment on?'

'Only what you've seen. That the body was meant to be found. But why, after three years. And where has it been?'

'Did Mrs Davenport make any suggestions as to why she'd contacted you?'

'I got the feeling she was a desperate woman. That she'd tried all other avenues of enquiry. Certainly all the official avenues. That I was her last resort.'

Kovacs stroked his chin. 'And then there was a body,' he said.

'And then there was a body,' Mordent repeated.

Kovacs sighed. 'There's something else. We had a call. From the psychic woman. She tipped us off.'

'Specifically?'

'Almost.'

Mordent ran a hand through his hair. A few strands came back with it.

'I know something else,' he said. 'I know about Constantin's brother.'

Kovacs looked him clean in the eye. 'Thought you might, when you casually name-dropped him yesterday. So, what have we got? Tit for tat? If so, what's Davenport's connection to Bataille?'

Mordent shrugged. 'Sounds like police work to me. I had a body to find. I didn't find it. You did. End of my story.'

'You're a hard man.'

'So are you, when you need to be.'

If it was a compliment Kovacs didn't take it. The line of his mouth hardened. 'Best be getting you back to the city, unless you want to walk.'

'I'll take the ride, thanks.'

It was a cheerless journey.

12
Office Work

Mordent wasn't a gambler but there was a stack of cards in his desk drawer. When he wasn't busy – which was often – he played solitaire.

His PC could run the electronic version, but the appeal was different. With a pack in front of him he knew the order of the cards was predetermined. With a virtual pack – despite the certainty of the number-crunching computer – he didn't trust it as a fair game. And if nothing else, he always wanted a fair game.

It was like watching an old black and white monster movie. A guy being chased by another guy in a rubber suit. You always knew – in theory – that the 'monster' could catch the guy. Yet with CGI, despite the detail of the monster, subconsciously you knew the guy could never be caught. It was all running against a green screen. And if nothing else, Mordent needed the possibility of being caught.

By a monster, or otherwise.

He bit the bullet. Gave Mrs Mouse a call.

She already knew. He detailed what he'd done. Said he'd return some of her cash. She told him not to bother. He half-heartedly insisted. At the end of the call he felt a ham, but took her money anyway on the proviso that should he be able to help the police with their enquiries then he would.

He flickered his mouse over Mrs Mouse's file. Wondered if he should mark it closed.

But he couldn't. Because there was one word: *container*. There was Constantin's brother and there was Patrick Davenport. Nothing in common apart from the inside of a metal box, with Bataille at one end of the spectrum and Kirby Muxloe at the other. A tainted, rusted rainbow with a stolen pot of gold.

He couldn't let it lie.

Finally there was Marina. His hand rested on his telephone receiver but he didn't make the call.

She hadn't called him, after all.

He ran through their lovemaking. Bodies and memories commingled. Marina. Lexi Leigh. His own, degenerated effort. Where did one stop and the other begin? Age was a leveller when it came to recollections. You filtered and discerned, applied your own parameters, kept a lot of stuff buried. One hell of a lot of stuff.

He turned over a card. The Queen of Spades. Wasn't that significant? He didn't know, but the dark queen always appealed. Probably Marina could tell him more. If he wanted her to.

Sighing, he picked up all the cards, gave them a quick shuffle and replaced them in the pack. It was then, at 2.30 in the afternoon with the sun making a white square of his window, that Sue Sweeney knocked on his door.

He beckoned her in. She was wearing a long denim skirt that ran to her ankles, and another flowery-hippy top. She still wore sandals, although Mordent questioned her wisdom in this weather. She was nervous; that was evident from the way she fumbled the door handle. Once within the intimacy of the room it was all too personal. Too confined. Too *contained*.

'Sit down.'

She pressed the fold of her skirt between her knees as she sat. He imagined she would have the same nerves entering principal Sternforth's office; have the same trepidation. He didn't imagine that she entered his office that often.

Again, he contemplated her features. Pretty but not flaunted. Good cheekbones, good breeding. Demure: but he guessed she would come alive in bed, like a delicate flower that bloomed only once every couple of years. Then it would spread.

'How can I help?'

Her voice shook. Not a death rattle.

'You gave me your card.'

'I gave you two cards. You kept both of them. What was it with Greg Hammerton?'

'You spooked him. I don't think he liked your tone of questioning.'

'Questions have a way of getting answers, whether they're answered or not.'

'You're very direct.'

'I try to be.'

She blushed. Mordent wondered how direct she wanted to be. He wouldn't push it. She was an open clam with a pearl inside, but he had to be careful that she wouldn't close up. His aggressiveness was flirtation with the right kind of woman. And Sue Sweeney was certainly the right kind of girl. Although he probably wasn't her right kind of guy. She was a fish out of water.

'So,' he said, softening his voice, 'back to the question. How can I help?'

'There's something I thought I should tell you that I didn't want to tell you in front of Greg or over the phone. Something about Patrick.'

'Go on.'

'Well, you see, Patrick and I, we ... well, it was just once really ... but we ...' The words stopped in her mouth, like a train hitting the buffers. There was nowhere further for them to run.

'You were lovers.'

She nodded.

'While you and Greg were going out together?'

'Kind of.'

'Did he know?'

'No! That's why I wanted to tell you privately.'

'Are you sure he didn't know? Isn't that why you're here? In case he knew?'

'How do you mean?'

'Jealous people do strange things.'

She stuttered, fell over her words: 'Greg wouldn't do such a thing.'

'So why tell me?'

Sue Sweeney remained quiet, looking at her hands in her lap as they made a motion like she was washing them with soap. A Lady Macbeth movement. An admission of culpability, of guilt.

'How long was it after this affair that Patrick disappeared?'

'It was the following day. We'd met up occasionally, done some heavy petting; nothing too serious. I liked him. Greg can be a bit dominant. We were young. We *are* young. I didn't want that kind of commitment. Patrick was different, shy. Maybe I preferred him, maybe things went a bit too far. Anyway, we made out. It was all good. The following day, he disappeared.'

'And you've been wondering if it was because of that?'

'I didn't know what to think. I couldn't confide in anyone. So I closed up. Hid it all away.'

Mordent sighed. The problem was, it was too little too late. Greg and Sue were out of the equation. Whatever had happened to Patrick had nothing to do with either of them.

She didn't know, either. She couldn't know.

He would have to tell her Patrick was dead.

'I don't think you have anything to worry about,' he said. Then he stood, walked to the window, looked out at the dirty city and the streets below. Cars, people, movement. 'What do you think happened?'

'I think he got on the ferry and didn't get off.'

'That's what you know. What do you think?'

Behind him, he could hear her sobbing. All the pent-up tension, all the months, years, of fretting, were released. He still stood with his back to her. She had to deal with this alone.

After a short while, she sniffed back the residue. He wondered where she kept her handkerchief.

'I think he felt so guilty about what we'd done – he was best friends with Greg – that he heaved himself over the side of the ferry and into the water.'

'Have you been on that ferry?'

He turned, she nodded.

'That's one hell of a heave.'

She sniffed. 'There's no other explanation, is there?'

Mordent shrugged. 'There's no record of Greg getting on or off that ferry.'

'So there *is* no other explanation?'

'Possibly not.'

She sighed. He wasn't sure if it was in relief or release.

'I suppose I've made a bit of a fool of myself.'

Words stuck in his throat. He walked over to the chair. Watched himself place his hand on her shoulder.

She didn't flinch.

'There's something else.'

She turned her head, looked up. Tiny trails etched her meagre make-up, a cleared pathway after rain.

'Patrick's body was found. This morning.'

The slight solace she had held momentarily was gone.

*

After Sue left the office Mordent opened his desk drawer and poured himself a neat twist of bourbon. Sank it.

He imagined a puddle of tears under his visitor's chair. Rising. Sue swimming as Alice had in Wonderland when she was shrunk tiny-size. He didn't need to deal with this. Emotions were beyond his capabilities. Taking another shot, he closed his eyes, slept.

In his dream a monkey rode an ocelot offering cigarettes to Marina. She pointed and he entered her head, searched through a pile of bodies, all naked and dead, until he found the container holding Patrick Davenport. Inside was Sue Sweeney, performing a sex act on his corpse. He lifted her away, weeping. Under Davenport was a body that he knew to be Constantin's brother. Under that, another body. Under that, another. He realised the container was bottomless just as he was falling into it. He awoke with a bump.

He'd fallen off the chair. Dark had come early. The lights were off in his office, the glow through his glass door from the corridor being the only illumination. His screensaver was black. He rose to his feet, his legs were stiff. Another hint of things to come. Jiggling his mouse he brought a blue screen to life. His hand looked cold, dead in that light. Walking around the side of his desk, touching the surface to determine the way, he flicked on the switch, dispelled the shadows.

His mouth was dry, his tongue carpeted like the hallway of some posh residence. Somewhere even *he* wouldn't have a client. He glanced at the time. Already 8.00 pm. Those late nights were catching up with him. It suited his noirish sensibilities to hug the dark, but it played havoc with his sleeping patterns.

Returning to his desk, he opened and closed files. Played solitaire in a desultory fashion. Watched an episode of *The Simpsons* online. Nothing satisfied. If he went home, there was nothing for him. He toyed with phoning Marina, giving her the placebo of the Davenport body as an apology. Yet all along he knew he was just putting off the inevitable. He had to take a trip to the morgue.

He'd made a promise to Constantin and he was going to keep it.

*

Martens started the morgue nightshift at ten o'clock. Mordent didn't want to clear this one with Kovacs. He suspected he'd been given too much information as it was. But Martens owed him one. He'd saved his life, once; not in the same way he'd saved Hubie's, but just as effectively. Martens would always owe him. Big time.

The reason: he'd once caught Martens fingering a corpse.

Plain and simple. Fingers tucked where they shouldn't have been.

But what was it to him? The stiff was dead. No good in reporting it. What it was to him was information. A card he kept calling on long after he'd left the force.

He decided he might even take a look at the Davenport boy once he was down there.

He sank another bourbon, watching the clock tick around to ten. Slowly.

Night suited him. A convenient overcoat. Shadows gave him a good profile. Dames were easier and drink tasted better. The sky wasn't as open above you. It all hunkered down after dark. It was two days since he'd been to Morgan's Bar. Morgan would be hiring out his stool.

As the second hand ticked over he dialled Martens. Told him what he wanted to see. Left the office to do some work.

13
The Dead Lay Still

Another journey through the darkness. Mordent's motor ticked over. A soft hum vibrating the pattern of the night. He clicked his recent cases over in his mind. They all slotted into place as dead ends. BuzzCut linked to Constantin linked to his brother linked to Muxloe. Mrs Mouse linked to Davenport linked to Bataille. Bataille linked to Muxloe. All dead ends all right and none to do with him.

Except something.

The pot shot outside Hubie's.

He'd tried not to dwell on it, but it bothered him. Hung in the back of his mind as the bullet might have done, had it found a home.

Was it random, or more? If it was linked to Constantin, what was the fuss? According to Constantin the police would have been well aware of the death of his brother, so what would be the reason for taking him out of the investigation? Especially since all he had at the time was a name.

Something didn't add up. But what was it the film director Godard had said? We understand that one plus one equals two, but we don't know the meaning of plus.

Lights streaked his vision, searing beacons against the darkness. Vehicles almost nudged, seemed compacted in the dark. The highway was a pack of shuffled cars, slots created then filled. Motorbikes weaved in and out, a disorganised convoy. Snug inside, couples sat apart, staring ahead, barely mobile even while travelling at speed; or otherwise held hands, chatted, safely cocooned in a bubble of unreality, yet hurtling towards their inevitable deaths.

One way or another they would all arrive at Mordent's current destination: the morgue.

Some in a better condition than others. But dead all the same.

A bottle of bourbon rattled in Mordent's glove box, but it was rare that he drank while driving. It served as a reminder that solace was at hand, should he need it. A persistent tapping, like that of a narcolepsy sufferer awaking in a coffin, tentatively wondering whereabouts they were. He shook his head: images of death crowded in and he didn't like it. Soon enough, the accusing fingers of those he failed to find would start prodding the spongy corner of his brain. A persistent nagging he wouldn't be able to shake away.

He'd seen plenty of corpses in his time and they all looked the same: devoid of life.

Not such an obvious statement as it might seem. Some relatives clung to the physical status of their loved ones, were desperate to retain something of the person they had been. But Mordent knew they were empty shells, nothing more. He had no belief in the soul, but everyone died the same way: lack of oxygen to the brain. And brain dead equals dead. Ultimately.

He took a right off the main highway. There was a cacophony of horns as the car behind him changed lanes and did the same. His eyes flickered to the rear view mirror. A black car, normal plates, two guys in the front. He went a couple of blocks and took a left. The car followed. After another block he took another left, and then again, until he had made a square. The car was still behind him. No doubts. He was being followed.

Yet they were being cack-handed about it. Too close. Too obvious. Amateurs? Or maybe they wanted him to know he was tailed. A warning rather than a threat. He gunned the engine and sped up a couple of blocks, took a right, then a left, then a right. The city's backstreets unfolded in his memory like an ancient scroll. This had been his beat. He knew every nook and cranny, every crevice. While the city was a grid, this older section was a maze. The roads were short, with not a great deal of space between one turning and another. After a few minutes he pulled back onto the main drag, a street parallel to the one he'd been on before. The other car was no longer in sight.

He slowed, pulled over, parked up by the side of the road. The street was deserted; then, like treacle being poured down a blackboard, the road began to glow. Three or four cars passed in quick succession, their lights picking up every pit and bobble in the tarmac. Time was regained, the traffic steadier, but still no sight of his tail.

Either Muxloe or Bataille. Both knew of his meeting with Constantin. He wondered what Constantin had said.

He pulled away from the kerb, re-entered the traffic stream. After five minutes he was parked at the hospital. Flashing his PI badge at the front desk, he made his way to the elevator. Hit *Basement* and descended to the morgue.

There might be a reason why it wasn't on the top floor. Maybe the same reason that you didn't put raw meat above cooked meat in the refrigerator. But he had the feeling it was more deliberate. A hiding away of death in a building of which the intention was to prolong life. A metaphor for heaven and hell? Or did the bottom floor hasten a quick getaway. The vehicles that left that part of the building were unmarked.

Martens didn't look like a corpse fiddler. Smart in his long white coat, no glasses, hair neatly coiffured and not greasy, he wouldn't have looked out of place in *ER* or one of those other high-budget hospital shows. But whenever he saw Mordent that tanned façade would slip, the mask revealed. He couldn't hide it, no matter how hard he tried. And Mordent knew that so long as he couldn't hide it, then Martens was his for the taking.

A body was on the slab as he entered. Martens leant against a worktop, cup of coffee in a nitrile-gloved hand.

'Taking a break,' Mordent growled. The subtext hung in the air like the smell.

Martens gulped his coffee. When he placed the cup on the side it rattled a nervous beat.

'Always good to see you,' he said.

'I imagine so. Wish I could say the pleasure was all mine, but you know how things are.'

Martens nodded. Despite the coffee, his mouth was dry.

'It's been a while.'

'It has,' Mordent said, 'but then I'm like an elephant, I never forget.'

Martens mumbled something under his breath. Mordent had the feeling he wished he could forget. He wondered if Martens had ever risked it since. Not that it mattered. Once was enough to tar him. Thickly.

'You got the bodies ready?'

'Not out, no. Don't want to attract attention. Come over here.'

Mordent passed the corpse on the slab, a girl, her nipples pale and hard, breasts firm in death. A sheet covered the lower part of her body. Bruising discoloured her neck and arms. Three out of five fingernails on her right hand were missing, lined up neatly alongside her. Martens had been looking for something under those nails. A DNA-trace to her killer. Picking her apart as though she were a child's doll. Did it really matter, once they were dead?

By the time she was buried those nails would be restored. Her family's final memories of her would be angelic. The funeral parlour's work as restorative as plastic surgery. All traces of infiltration and dismemberment repaired.

The body, of course, would still be dead.

Mordent stopped by Martens at a row of metal doors that always reminded him of a bank's security deposit boxes. Thin card inset into the front of each box determined the occupant. Martens reached towards one box at floor level. Tugging the handle he pulled it open, the container wheeling out swiftly on well-oiled runners.

'This is Robbie Constantin. Unlike most of the other bodies here, he's not fresh, as you know. Dead four, five years in my estimation. Strangled, as you can see by the marks here and here. Open and shut case. No DNA matches to any known criminals. Body won't be released for a while yet, due to ongoing police investigations. What else do you want to know?'

'How old would you say he is?'

'Mid-thirties. Skin samples indicate as much.'

'But you know how old he is.'

'Twenty-seven. People age differently. Some people your age have a full head of hair.'

Mordent ignored him. 'There should be some decomposition, surely.'

'He was found in an airtight container. My professional opinion is that he was put there shortly after he died. Bone tests would assist in confirming an age, but that's just not necessary. We know who he is. We know how he died. We know exactly how old he is. Why do you want to know?'

'Someone said something.'

'That crazy brother of his has been talking to you?'

'You got that right.'

'Mordent, he's not going to age after death. It might appear that way, but it can't happen.'

'I know this. What I want to know is why Constantin thinks it's happened. Don't nails and hair continue to grow?'

Martens smiled. 'That's a common misconception and an optical illusion. After death the body loses moisture, dehydrates. That causes the skin to shrink around the skull and skeleton, exposing more of the hair follicles, more nail. That's what makes it look like it's still growing. Of course, down at the parlour they'll moisturise the body to compensate for that, but it's certainly not growing, Mordent. And if brother Constantin hasn't seen a dead body – or certainly, not one of anyone close to him; or even more importantly, not one several years dead – then he's going to be perfectly susceptible to that illusion.'

'I guess so. Although growing and ageing are two different things.'

'Then believe what Constantin tells you. I'm sure he's trustworthy.'

Martens pushed the corpse back into its slot with his foot.

'I've done what I said I'd do: check out the corpse. Just fulfilling an obligation.'

'Whatever.'

Mordent shot Martens a look, 'Gone all teenage on me have you?'

Martens shrugged. 'It happens.'

'Nothing to do with that girl on the slab, I hope. Thought you'd given that up. Or are you keeping your hand in.'

Martens muttered something under his breath that Mordent couldn't hear. Didn't need to. He turned his back and moved towards another metal door, swung it open and pulled out the body.

'This is the Davenport boy.'

Mordent took a look, although he'd seen it all that morning. He didn't let Martens know that.

'And this one, how old would you say he is?'

'Looks early twenties, although he went missing at seventeen. I'd say he's been dead three years. Difference with this one is that the cause of death is still unknown. There's been some internal bruising, but it'll take more time to establish.'

'You not working on it now?'

'Didn't come in on my shift. Clements is dealing with that one.'

'And he won't tell me anything, so I'll have to rely on you.'

'I'll tell you what I know.'

'Good.'

Mordent fished a handkerchief out of his pocket, blew his nose. It made no difference. The smell of death and disinfectant would remain in his follicles for a few hours yet. 'Just one more thing. He didn't drown, did he?'

Martens shook his head. 'He certainly didn't drown.'

'I didn't think so. And the container?'

'I'd say he hasn't been airtight the whole of his death. But he's been there at least two years.'

'So there's a link?'

'You're the detective.'

'We're all armchair detectives, Martens. Just answer the question as straight as it came.'

Martens closed the door on Davenport. 'I'd say there was a link, wouldn't you?'

'I would. And I don't like it.'

Mordent headed towards the door. His steps felt heavy. He didn't like the way things were falling into place. Falling out of place.

He stopped.

'There's one more thing.'

'You're getting more Columbo-like every day. Failing memory?'

'Are there any other container deaths?'

Martens shook his head. 'Not yet.'

'Let me know, will you, if any more come in. I doubt Kovacs will bother to update me.' He waggled the fingers of his right hand.

Martens turned his back, muttering. The shadow of a memory hovering over him like a cloud.

14
Where Did The Girl Go?

By the time Mordent returned to his apartment it was well after midnight. The streets weren't deserted – the city came alive at night with new people, new possibilities – but even in the throng of the midnight express it was clear no-one was following him. That possibility increased rather than decreased the closer he got to home, but he was satisfied when he arrived that there was no danger. Maybe they just wanted to keep an eye on his movements, not restrict them. Or him.

Yet confrontation excited him. Sometimes it was an indicator of how life was, how it should be. It helped him to confirm he was still alive.

At first when he unlocked the door to his apartment he didn't notice the difference. He turned on the lights, dropped his clothes on the sofa, walked in his underpants through to the kitchen, slugged some milk from a rim-encrusted bottle and spat it in the sink. He swilled his mouth with water, put the bottle back in the fridge, walked through to the bathroom and performed his ablutions. Looked, for a short while, at his grizzled face in the mirror. Gurned. Cleaned his teeth, head down, watching the sink froth. Spat again.

He turned off the bathroom light, walked through the living room and into the bedroom. Pulled down his underpants, scratched. A sound like sandpaper on wood. He stood naked at the window awhile, watching the remaining lights of cars wink their way across the streets like slow fireworks. In the apartment across the way a light was on. He saw an old man watching a flickering box in the corner of the room; half-dressed, standing, as though caught like a rabbit in headlights. Striped-pyjama bottoms, bare chest. Then the television flipped to black and Mordent watched as the man pulled on the pyjama top, turned to look out of the window, turned off the light.

Mordent wondered how many silent figures stood in darkness looking out at the world. Did all the windows in the apartment opposite – at least eighty of them – contain men looking back at him. Passive observers.

When he turned back to his own darkness, he saw the red light blinking on his landline.

Sometimes the difference between knowing and not knowing was subtle.

He picked up the phone, dialled the messenger service number. Pressed through the menu options to access the call. He pressed the phone to his ear as though expecting a whisper.

Soft, female, recognisable.

'Hey Mordent. It's me, Marina. I lost your cell phone number so dialled your office number. Remember the body? I told you I saw something, but even though we made love I guess you didn't believe me. There's something else I know, but the phone isn't the best way to communicate, is it? Too impersonal for me. Give me a call or come over: 373 Acacia Lane West, Apt 16. Big brownstone building, you can't miss it. If nothing else, we can entwine again. Ciao.'

The voice gave him goosebumps. He wasn't immune after all.

But it was late. He returned to the bedroom, slipped under the sheets. Sank his head on the pillow. Slept.

There was a dream of violets, canapés. A large office, open-plan, partitioned cubicles. Someone told him to collect leaves to put on grass to make it grow faster. He pulled them off a low-lying plant, their texture waxy under his fingertips, droplets of rain running off them like glass balls. Stuffed them in his pocket, made his handkerchief wet.

Although it was a bright day, a shadow approached from the rear. A menace. When he turned to look, the shadow was behind him. He turned again. Again, behind him; as though it were tethered like a kite to his back. Whichever way he span he couldn't get rid of it. He slipped. Fell into the violets and canapés, broke a table laid with a white cloth, twisted his ankle. When he looked down at his shoes they were clogs. He looked harder, and the wood of the clog was the wood of the table. They melded together. He struggled, but couldn't get them off.

The shadow darkened, pitch black. He realised his eyes were closed. Woke.

It was daylight, or thereabouts. Pale morning pressed softly against the windowpane like a ghost. Condensation pooled on the sill, where a sluggish autumnal insect had drowned. He noticed a fresco of mould rising on the inner wall, patchwork black. Paint puckered around a crack, open petals. Details bored into him, patterned his mind. He saw all this in one moment as he woke, as though he had been staring eyes open instead of sleeping.

It had the lucidity of a dream.

He eased himself out from under the covers. It was cold but he kept going: dressed, cleaned his teeth, ate the knob-end of yesterday's baguette with a smear of butter and paté, drank black coffee with no sugar. Paused.

There was little for him to do.

He powered up his PC and deleted spam from his e-mail account. There was nothing of any importance. He e-mailed Constantin. Informed him that he had seen the corpse of his brother. That nothing untoward was obvious. He mentioned his fee but didn't expect one. Wondered, even, if Constantin would ever get the e-mail. Although he didn't think Muxloe or Bataille would sail too close to the wind.

All that was left was Marina. He gave her a call.

Her phone rang without answer.

From an inauspicious start it was a day of non-events.

He tried her number again. The urge to see her was returning, whether from boredom or curiosity. Hang the eccentricity. Anyway, he wondered what she had told Kovacs. The hint of something new she had 'seen' was only mildly intriguing. It was matching the unknown to the known that grabbed him.

He accessed the previous day's voice message again, made a note of the address. Picking up his gabardine coat he slung it over one arm, checked the gun in his inner jacket pocket and headed down to the car.

The day had continued its pale blue start. Just cold enough for scarves and coats, but warm enough for them to be unbuttoned, flying. The breeze was light. Perfect weather. He drove and regarded the human existence of flotsam and jetsam, mostly smiling, mostly cheerful. He wound down the car window, allowed the jazz to break through to the outside world, provide a soundtrack for the day.

Marina's building was on the corner of Jasmine Avenue and Acacia Avenue West. Quiet area, no trouble. He parked nearby a fire hydrant. They always reminded him of the movies – he'd never seen one where a car chase didn't result in a jet of water. From his experience, this was a fiction. Packing dimes into the meter he headed up the twelve steps to the entrance of the brownstone. It was an unattended building with no reception. The left side of the doorway held thin white cards adjacent to well-worn metal buttons. He flicked his finger down the list, found Marina, and continued. It always paid to know who was in a given building. Finding no other name familiar to him he pressed his finger on the bell.

Just as the telephone, no answer.

He waited. Tried again. Rang her cell phone from where he stood, listening above the mild traffic noise for the chance of hearing it ring. Not that it was likely, but best not to rule anything out. After more non-replies, he pushed three buttons simultaneously. One occupant let him in.

The inside of the building was dark, a concrete stairwell ascending in a rising square, like a twisting Christmas decoration. It was clean, though; no unpleasant smells. Not the kind of building Constantin would have lived in. The elevators were to one side. He glanced at them but decided to walk. Marina was two floors up. He didn't expect her to be there. He was going to look inside.

It wasn't a hunch, just curiosity.

Mordent found that curiosity normally equated to the best hunches.

Outside her door he placed an eye and then an ear to the keyhole. Blackness. Quiet. He knocked: softly, then loudly. No response. He rang her cell phone and could hear nothing, rang the house phone and heard the echo.

No-one picked up. No-one came to the door.

He wished he had a skeleton key but knew they were really useless. At least, they were for exterior doors. Cabinets, handcuffs, vending machines, there were certainly skeleton keys for those; but the idea of a key that could open all locks was pure myth. Instead, there were other ways he knew to open locked doors. It was just that they didn't conform to his noirish sensibilities. With certainty, he tried one of them now.

The door clicked open as easy as placing a hand in a bowl of water.

He entered and closed the door behind him.

The pad was tastefully furnished. Clean modern lines with a few antique pieces of furniture spotting the room with pockets of golden brown. Tall plant stands commingled with lamp stands, like storks with one leg broken off. The floor was tiled, a rug in the main living area a potential death-trap. Mordent nudged it with his foot and it held; sticky backing. A large flatscreen television dominated one wall. He couldn't imagine Marina using it. Maybe it came with the apartment. Like his, this place was rented; most of them were. A brown leather sofa came with scratch marks down one side. He wrinkled his nose. Cat. Found one in the kitchen asleep on a worktop. A negligent guard. He scratched its belly while glancing at the empty food bowl. No indication of whether the cat had been fed the previous night or that morning; although its water was also low.

He looked in the waste bin for signs of breakfast and found nothing. A plate and a clutch of cutlery lay in the sink. The curtains were open. The cat stretched, looked around, nestled down again. It was a tortoiseshell; multi-browns carpeted its fur. Short-haired. Less mess. Mordent wasn't keen on cats, but he wasn't averse to this one.

He checked in the bathroom. Standing room only. No bath, a shower, one toilet. Clean. He followed through to the bedroom. Again, empty. A canvas print of *A Mermaid* by John William Waterhouse hung above the bedstead. The bed sheets were clumsily made, but that meant nothing. No-one made a bed properly anymore. Not like his mother did when he was a boy.

The mirror by the dressing table reflected his image back at him. He pulled open the drawers, found a few interesting sex toys, some condoms. He ran a hand absentmindedly through her knickers. Nothing hidden at the backs of drawers or under the bed.

Clean.

He wondered how long she had been gone, where she had gone.

He knew she might be at work. He had never asked about a job. It hadn't arisen during their conversations. He was breaking and entering, committing a felony.

Still, it bugged him.

Maybe the intuition 'psychic' Marina obtained came from this apartment, because there was a tingle in the hair at the base of his skull.

No signs of a struggle.

He stopped in the kitchen. Fed the cat. She didn't go for it. Had been fed that morning. Everything was all right, then.

But it wasn't.

He looked again. This time, not for the things that were there, but for those that weren't. Her cell phone, handbag containing everyday items, the coat she had worn on their first meeting, the shoes that matched. All indications were that she had gone out unhurried. He found her passport, a photo four years old, an indifferent look on her face. He glanced in the fridge, saw a lipstick smear around a bottle of water that didn't rub off when he ran his thumb over it. Half a bottle of red. A third of a New York cheesecake.

Something still wasn't right.

He cut himself a piece of cheesecake and sat at the kitchen table. The knife was sticky. The cat unwound, jumped onto his lap, pawed at the cake. When he threw a bit to the floor the animal looked at it without comprehension, pawed his hand. Something was missing.

The cheesecake was thick in his mouth, glutinous. The biscuit base was dry.

He realised what he was looking for.

Standing up, jettisoning the cat with the movement, he walked back into the bedroom. Saw the pen on the bedside table. No notepad.

Marina had mentioned that she usually received her 'visions' at night, sometimes within dreams. He knew of a writer who always kept a pen and pad by his bedside. The guy had said that if he awoke in the night with a great idea and didn't write it down then all he had in the morning was the memory that he had a great idea. The realisation, not the idea itself. It wasn't that the written idea turned out to be great in the morning light, but it was a safety net, just in case, a confirmation.

Marina would have had a pad by her bed. He searched for it.

After fifteen minutes he stopped searching. It wasn't anywhere in the apartment and there wasn't a rectangular piece of cardboard in any of the bins to indicate she'd simply reached the last page.

The pad had been taken.

She had been taken.

A subtle link, but he saw it and knew it.

He finished off the cheesecake.

15
A Mouthful Of Nose

Before Mordent left Marina's apartment he hit the redial button on her phone and reached his answer machine.

He declined to leave a message.

Then he dialled Kovacs from his cell phone but got no response other than a police operator confirming he was out. He hung up when they asked for his name.

There was no address book by the phone. Nowadays most numbers were saved on cells. He didn't know if Marina had any friends or family; knew nothing much about her. What he knew wasn't enough.

He'd have to come back to feed the cat until she turned up.

He said his goodbyes in the kitchen. The cat's teats could be felt through its fur as he stroked its underbelly. It stretched, claws unsheathed. Curled up again. He wanted to curl up with it, but instead he left the apartment and travelled down to the street.

BuzzCut was leaning against his car. Hands in his pockets. He wore a smart suit, looked like a city worker rather than a hood. His shoes were black, polished, reflecting the sunlight back to the sky. The two top buttons of his white shirt exposed some pale hairs at the base of his throat. He wasn't wearing a tie. Hoods rarely did. One fight too many and you could be strangled. Bow ties never caught on.

Mordent couldn't make up his mind whether to ignore him or engage him. So he stood at the bottom of the steps to Marina's apartment, weighed up what BuzzCut might know.

'Social visit?' BuzzCut's voice was a low purr. It gave nothing away.

'That would be my business.'

'I guess it would.'

'I could ask the same of you.' Mordent walked towards his car. The street wasn't quiet but it wasn't busy either. On the opposite kerb there was a car parked with its engine running. BuzzCut saw him look over.

'Someone wants to see you.'

'Bataille?'

'Good guess. He wants to thank you for getting that girl away from Constantin.'

'Tell him to send me a telegram.'

BuzzCut made a short movement in his right hand pocket. A directional movement, indicating Mordent should walk over to the waiting vehicle. A hand movement that suggested there was more than a hand in his pocket.

'Come on.'

'I've got things to be doing.'

'You ain't got nothing doing.'

Mordent smiled. 'If I ain't got nothing doing then I must have something doing. Double negative.'

'Smart guy.'

'Smarter than you.'

Mordent walked around to the driver's side of his own vehicle. BuzzCut followed. Walked close.

He snarled in Mordent's ear: 'I could make you.'

Mordent made a sudden ducking movement, turned his head inwards and around and barrelled BuzzCut in the chest. He put his arms around his waist, pinned BuzzCut's pocketed hands to his side. Despite the difference in stature he lifted him an inch off the floor, unbalanced him, swung a foot to catch his heel. BuzzCut went down hard onto the tarmac, almost pulling Mordent down with him. As he rolled on the ground, his size making it a laborious business for him to regain his feet, Mordent walked over to the car with the engine running.

The driver looked nervous and amused.

'Where'd they get him from?' Mordent asked. 'Out in the boondocks?'

The driver said nothing.

'I understand Bataille wants to see me. I imagine it's in my interests to come along.'

The driver nodded. 'I wouldn't mess with Bataille.'

Mordent watched the driver's eyes flicker to a shadow behind him. He turned around sharp, caught BuzzCut with a glancing blow to the chin, which simply bruised his knuckles. BuzzCut backed him hard against the car. One, two blows to Mordent's stomach. He bucked backwards, jerked his head upwards in a head-butt, but got just a mouthful of nose. Another blow to his solar plexus winded him. BuzzCut stood back. A small crowd had gathered on the pavement. They moved cautiously away as BuzzCut swung his gaze.

'Get in the car,' he whispered. 'You were gonna do that all along.'

Pain seared along Mordent's left side. He closed his eyes, focused on the glow illuminating the back of his lids, decided he'd made his point. When he opened his eyes he was glad to see that the back of BuzzCut's suit was torn and wet from his roll on the ground.

'The gene pool you crawled out of was stagnant,' he growled.

'Get in the car.'

BuzzCut stood back, manoeuvred Mordent towards the rear door, opened it, half-pushed him inside. The seats were leather, cold, snug. Mordent shifted over to the right as BuzzCut got in beside him.

'Now shut up and keep quiet,' BuzzCut said. He reached into Mordent's jacket pocket, pulled out his gun. 'I'm keeping this for a while. You'll get it back. I told you, Bataille just wants to see you to thank you for bringing the girl back. The violence was all yours.'

Mordent nodded. 'I had a hunch you'd be here.'

'You've got more hunches than the hunchback of Notre Dame,' BuzzCut menaced.

Mordent laughed. It hurt his side. 'That's just the one hunch.'

'You calling me ignorant?'

'Derby Boy, if ignorance is bliss then you're approaching nirvana.'

BuzzCut grunted. Called through to the driver to get them going.

Mordent nursed his ribs as they entered the traffic. It had been foolish to engage in the fight, but he hadn't been prepared to go quietly. Even so, he needed some answers to questions that he wasn't sure existed.

There wasn't much history between him and Bataille. When he was in the force, Bataille hadn't been in the area. He'd moved up from the East to fill a gap created through the redeployment of another gang. A little internal ballet with bullets. Some of his businesses were legit, others less so. He had 'more front than Blackpool', although Mordent was aware of the saying more than the English town itself. His own tiny slice of ignorance.

Ignorance abounded in this world.

He glanced down at the knuckles of his right

hand. Not too badly damaged. Bataille would notice them if they shook.

Outside the car, pedestrians struggled to keep up; yellow cabs with their temporary occupants weaved in and out of increasing traffic. Mordent wondered how he would be getting back to his vehicle, but he didn't wonder *if* he would be getting back. They were heading towards one of Bataille's business concerns. The bakery, no doubt. Mordent would have felt happier if he wasn't already full of cheesecake.

They pulled up kerbside beside a glass-fronted building. The letters *Big Cake* were stencilled on the pane in pale, off-white lettering. Through the glass Mordent could see the open shop. Girls in starched white clothing and black tights worked the tills. Beyond the counter there was a door leading into a kitchen. A heavy black man was kneading dough. Mordent wondered if he was for show.

BuzzCut nudged him in the ribs. 'Get out.'

Mordent exited roadside, walked around the back of the cab to the sidewalk. He grabbed the passenger door handle and opened it, held it for BuzzCut before he could get out. 'After you,' he said.

BuzzCut muttered 'Smart guy', before edging him into the store.

They slid through the customers as though they weren't there. They were walking on a different plane, the bread roll and cream cake clientele inhabiting an alternate reality to the rest of Bataille's business associates. The two worlds were parallel, running together but not connecting. There was almost a physical difference between them.

BuzzCut punched some buttons on a door adjacent to the kitchen. It opened to the bottom of a stairwell. They went up.

At the top was a corridor linking the stairwell they had come from to a door at the opposite end. No side doors, no pictures on the walls. Maybe it was Mordent's imagination but the tunnel seemed a funnel, like one from *Alice in Wonderland* or the original *Willy Wonka* movie. The realisation that cake also featured in both of those almost made him smile. Although he was sure that would be where any similarities ended.

BuzzCut knocked on the door. A shadow passed across the back of the fisheye. The door swung open and they entered. BuzzCut stood to one side, ushering Mordent through.

He hadn't been sure what to expect, but the room was entirely normal. A desk, a PC, a flipchart off to one side with some figures written on it in red marker pen. Some charts on the wall, their staccato lines ascending. Carpet thick in cream. Walls also cream. The smell of a rich cigar permeating the atmosphere but not overpowering it. On the side of the desk – heavy, mahogany – nearest to him sat a young blonde with legs and lipstick. Again, not from the agency he had once subscribed to. On the other side of the desk, lounging, sat Bataille.

The door closed behind him. BuzzCut stood handle-side. Hinge-side stood a man with a weasel face and whiskers. Neither of them was smiling.

Bataille was.

He said something to the secretary that Mordent didn't catch and she rose, glanced his way, and exited via a side door Mordent hadn't noticed before. He took one last look at her legs and heels as she closed the door. A bubblewrap fantasy.

Bataille stood. Extended an arm, a hand. He was of average build, average looks, average height. He looked like he should be fronting an insurance office rather than a barrelful of hoods. He certainly didn't look like a baker.

Mordent advanced, took the hand and shook it. The grip was firm, held onto his for a little longer than necessary. Then the palm opened, the fingers splayed, directed him to the chair the secretary had vacated, which Mordent found still warm as his buttocks pressed into the leather.

'Mr Mordent, we meet at last.'

The voice was sly, powerful.

Mordent crossed one leg over another. 'I didn't know you wanted that pleasure.'

Bataille smiled. 'I hope my goons didn't rough you up too much.'

Mordent shook his head. 'Not at all. I started it.'

'Then I hope you got as good as you gave.'

There was a pause. Neither of them seemed willing to fill it.

Bataille said: 'A couple of nights ago you freed a little bird for me. I just wanted to thank you.'

'She got caught in a net that she didn't know how to get out of,' Mordent said. 'I trust she's now safe in her nest.'

Bataille sat motionless. 'She extends her thanks also.'

'She already thanked me after I freed her.'

'Maybe she did.'

There was another pause.

Mordent stood. 'If that's all ...'

'I can be a patient man,' Bataille spoke, each word a careful enunciation, 'and I can be more of a help than a hindrance. But to do so I need to know the full facts. Have you seen Constantin since that evening?'

'I think that's between me and my client.'

'There's an exit from this building,' Bataille said,

'which doesn't go through the baker's shop. A quiet exit. You can leave from that exit or you can leave through the store.'

'Do I have a choice?'

Bataille spread his hands wide. 'You know you do.'

'I haven't seen Constantin since that evening. I guess Muxloe's still got him, or he's hunkered down somewhere like the dog that he is.'

'How much did he tell you?'

Mordent sat back down. 'He told me about his brother.'

'All circumstantial evidence.'

'Tell me about Davenport.'

'Who?'

'Patrick Davenport. The kid found in your bakery container yesterday morning. Don't tell me you haven't heard about him.'

Bataille smiled. 'Oh, the boy. A plant, of course.'

'Tit for tat?'

Bataille shrugged.

'Why am I here? You think I know where Constantin is? Maybe you're getting nervous about who he's gonna tell.'

Bataille made a triangle from his fingers. 'We told you to stay away from Constantin. The fact that you're here isn't my problem.'

'I got a client named Mrs Davenport who'd be very interested in what happened to her son.'

'You can't hang that on me.'

'Not yet, maybe.' Mordent stood again.

Bataille stood too, extended his hand as before. 'I'll arrange for someone to take you back to your vehicle.'

'Don't bother. I need the exercise. And I'll make my own way out. Thanks.'

Mordent turned and headed for the door, between BuzzCut and Weasel-Face. They let him pass. BuzzCut handed him his gun, barrel first. As he returned along the corridor he waited for footsteps behind him, an arm around his neck, a rabbit punch. Nothing happened.

He let himself back into the baker's, thought of buying a cake just for the hell of it, but changed his mind and hit the street. It had started to rain. He pulled up his collar and droplets trickled inside it. Their coolness against his neck indicated how hot he'd become. The brief meeting with Bataille had told him nothing, except that they wanted him to know he was in their peripheral vision. Yet even after three or so days on the job he didn't know if there was a job to be on.

He had to mix it up. He decided to visit Muxloe.

Raising his hand he hailed a yellow cab. He was sure he caught a glimpse of BuzzCut in the rear view as they pulled away from the kerb.

16
Hubie Doobie Doo

Once he'd collected his vehicle – four wheels still intact – he drove to his office. In the corridor of his building he passed one of the girls heading to enrol at the temp agency. She gave him a smile as she walked towards him that evaporated when she saw he wasn't part of the company she was trying to impress. He would have been impressed by her company, but would never have that opportunity.

He powered up his PC, flipped the switch on the kettle that stood by the small sink in the tiny bathroom behind his desk. The coffee tasted better than the cheap brand that it was. It was only after the first mouthful that he realised his mouth was dry. He ran his tongue over his lips, moistened them. When he swallowed, his stomach hurt. He unbuttoned his shirt, looked at the bruises that were starting to form. Mild discolouration under his skin. It had been worth it to get BuzzCut on the ground.

Sitting down, he checked his e-mails. None from Constantin. The rest were the usual spam of Cialis and offers from Russian ladies. He sent another e-mail to Constantin, using the *Request read receipt* through Outlook. Just to check if he might be there and hiding.

He pulled the cards from his desk. Shuffled them. Ran through a quick game of solitaire. The joker appeared midway through the game and he discarded it. Face down.

He ran a hand through his hair. Wondered what he wanted. In the corner of his eye he imagined Patrick Davenport standing beside him. Mrs Mouse remained his client. Occasionally he found it useful to put himself in their position. Find out what they wanted, and then work out what he could do about it.

If it sounded obvious, then it wasn't. What people wanted, what they said they wanted, what they really wanted even if they didn't know what they wanted, could often be different things.

Mrs Mouse wanted her son found. But more than that, she wanted to know if he'd died. And now she knew he had died she would want to know how he was killed. And then she would want to know who the killer was. Once that was determined, she'd want the killer brought to justice. Mordent couldn't do all of those things, but the police could determine how he had died, and he could determine who was the killer. Or, on the slim chance that he wasn't killed, how his body came to be in that container.

So he had to visit Muxloe. Of that there was no doubt.

But there was another client. A shadow client. And that was Patrick Davenport himself. And he would want more than his mother. The dead always would.

And technically another client: Constantin. But he had resolved that. Hadn't he. There was a reasonable explanation for why his brother appeared to have aged.

Then another shadow client: Robbie Constantin. It was clear from his brother's account that he had been murdered by the Bataille gang. But it wasn't his responsibility to notify the police. Constantin could do that himself. But he hadn't and probably wouldn't.

A moral dilemma.

If he squinted really hard, the body of Robbie Constantin could be seen standing next to that of Patrick Davenport.

There was another body. One that he didn't want to see.

He tried Marina's cell phone and then her home number. Still no answer from either. Maybe she'd simply left town for a few days, although that answerphone message hadn't intimated anything of the kind. If he still hadn't heard from her by the morning he would pay the cat a visit. The status of its food bowl would indicate if she had been home, or if arrangements had been made. He wasn't hopeful.

The phone clattered. It was Bakelite old-style with a traditional ring. Mordent thought it gave his office some gravitas, but mostly it made him jump with the dependability of an alarm clock.

'Mordent?'

'Speaking.'

'It's Hubie. Can you come over? I've got some information for you.'

'Isn't like you to offer your services, Hubie.'

'Well, that's as maybe. But you'd want to know this, Mordent. I'd rather not tell it over the phone.'

Mordent made a mental note of the number of people who preferred not to say things over the phone in the delusion that it wasn't secure, could be tapped. From his experience, that was rare: the stuff of movies and pulp novels.

Nevertheless he made arrangements to see Hubie that afternoon.

There was nothing left to do. He wanted to know how Davenport had died but Clements wouldn't give him that information. He'd have to wait to speak to

Martens on the nightshift.

Everything seemed to happen at night. All wet gunmetal streets and long shadows. Hoods with hats pulled down over their eyes. Soft punches breaking the silence. Booze and dames and chains and boots. The crack of a pistol, shattering the night sky. Clouds scudding across a black background, like theatrical silhouettes. The moon breaking through, illuminating the killer.

He craved it. It fed his soul.

He had an hour or so to kill. Headed to Morgan's Bar.

*

Although the sun was still shining it was dull within the bar. The only lights were those that glittered from the insides of the bottles. The overheads were muted. There were no gambling machines with their incessant, persistent displays and random noises. No spotlit pool tables. No cosy corners with individual wall-lights. No square glows from cell phone displays. Morgan's was a cave, a throwback to spit and sawdust times. Even the sunlight on the immediate sidewalk seemed to acknowledge this. There was shadow beneath the awning.

Mordent's glass fitted within the palm of his hand. A magic trick.

He called Morgan over. 'That tall blond guy you said was looking for me, a few days ago. He been in again?'

Morgan shook his head.

Mordent shrugged. 'He found me, anyway.'

Morgan nodded.

Someone else entered the bar, and Morgan moved across to serve them. Conversation closed, in any event.

Mordent sat, watching his reflection in the mirror behind the bar.

Sometimes he wondered why it was there. The mirror, not his reflection. He supposed it created imaginary space, widened the room, so that even those sitting right at the bar weren't on the edge.

It also prevented anyone sneaking up on you.

Not that there was trouble here. Morgan's record was immaculate.

The liquid coursed down his throat. Hot yet cold.

His reflection looked older than him, but he knew it was just perception. It was like going to the barber's. More grey hair fell into his lap than he assumed was on his head. Death didn't sit easy with him, nor did the aging process that led to it. A constant reminder that death was looking over his shoulder, tapping him. His fingers couldn't clench the glass indefinitely.

He glanced at his watch. Left the bar before he got too maudlin and before the seat refused to let him go.

Halfway to Hubie's he realised he was being tailed.

It was unlikely to be BuzzCut. It was more than a possibility it was one of Muxloe's goons. He didn't fancy another scrap, another fist in the ribs or a gun in his shoulder blades. He took a left and then another; repeated the motion, made a square of it. Back on the main drag the car had gone. He couldn't quite believe they were so stupid. Maybe it had been his imagination after all.

He parked outside the empty pizza parlour as before. Remembered the shot. Followed the trajectory to the alleyway beside the parlour and walked down it about fifty yards. It opened onto a small walled garden, the rubbish bins of the pizza place groaning black plastic bags. He kicked over a few cardboard containers, stood on his toes but couldn't see over the wall. The closed pizza parlour was boarded up at the back as well as the front. No-one had tried to force it.

If the shot *had* come from that alleyway the other day then he could have trapped the culprit there. Maybe it was a pity he hadn't. Although knowing how a rat behaves when it's cornered, maybe it was a bonus.

He took the steps to Hubie's office. Knocked on the door. This time when Hubie answered he was appropriately dressed. The door to the bedroom was closed. It was quiet.

'Mordent.'

'Hubie.'

'You better come in.'

Outside the window, twilight was starting to fall. Long shadows elongated Hubie's furniture, spread like an ink stain along one wall. Mordent wondered what Hubie would see in a Rorschach test. A horse, neck extended, meeting the camera of a photo-finish line. A leg, also extended, leading from the slit in a chemise up to the thigh in a V. Maybe a girl on a horse. Maybe a horse on a girl. Whatever he saw, it wouldn't be an inkblot.

'You've got some information?'

Hubie nodded.

'I'm guessing the reason you won't give it over the phone is that you want paying for it.'

'You're a cynical man, Mordent.'

'How much is it worth?'

'Enough to make a 14/1 bet worth betting on if the horse comes in.'

'Not enough to pay for the horse itself?'

Hubie shook his head. 'Certainly not.'

'Go on then, spin me a tale.'

Hubie leant back in his chair like it was junior

story time. A smile played around his lips. It was predatory and a little disconcerting. Mordent wondered how he managed to attract his fast women. He gave the show of having money, even when he didn't. So that would be it. Hubie's lips curled further back from his teeth. A grin.

'I heard something about Derby Boy and Bataille,' he began. 'Thought it might interest you from your little visit the other day.'

Mordent nodded his head. Didn't pander Hubie by actually saying, *Go on*.

'Word on the street is that Bataille has an interest in life expectancy. Derby Boy used to work in cryonics. Not scientifically, of course, but in security. I did a little digging and it appears he left his previous employment in an unceremonious fashion. Suggestions of stealing: information and ideas. Nothing unexpected, of course, for a man of his character; but enough for them to give him the chop.

'He went to Bataille specifically. Direct from that previous employ. Has risen fast in the ranks. Suggests he has given Bataille something that he wants. He's not liked amongst some of Bataille's other men. They find him cocky, a golden boy. Which is how come I got this information. Does that help?'

Mordent sighed. Shifted his weight in the chair. Delayed his answer to negate any eagerness. Lowered the price of the information through his non-verbal reaction.

'Well?'

Hubie's quick insistence indicated he needed the money faster than Mordent needed to lose it.

'Backtrack a bit. How do you mean Bataille has an interest in life expectancy?'

Hubie leant forward, conspiratorially. 'Bataille's

father died four years ago. Heart attack or cancer, the details are sketchy, but one of the *big* ones. You know what I mean? Word has it that his mother is in the same way. What goes around comes around. Runs in the family. Bataille has been making some enquiries, some investments in the cryonic market. Probably been examining other methods and means. Word has it he's twitchy. Has seen the writing on the wall.

'You mentioned a guy called Constantin the other day. I've made enquiries about him too. I know the allegations he's made about his brother.'

'You know how hokey this sounds, Hubie? Sounds like you're giving me the runaround.'

'You asked for information,' Hubie said, petulant. 'You got it.'

'Remind me about cryonics.'

'They freeze you when you die, with the aim of resuscitating you when science has advanced sufficiently to bring you back to life.'

'So it's a scam.'

'Potentially it's a scam, potentially it's the future.'

'You and me, Hubie, think it's a scam. Right?'

'That's as maybe.'

'Just like you're an atheist until you can prove the existence of God.'

'Mordent. For some people it's an insurance policy. One that's just as good as the existence of God. We all need a security blanket from time to time.'

Mordent reached for one of the cigars that were on Hubie's desk. Clipped the end off. Lit it. Sucked on it and took in enough smoke to blow out again. He was no longer keen on cigars. But he needed something to focus his mind.

'I don't quite see as how this is information I should pay for.'

Hubie stood. Leant forward with both hands on the desk. 'Constantin said his brother aged after his death.'

'Yeah, but the whole point of cryonics is to freeze the body, halt the process of ageing and decomposition. How do you explain the body ageing after its death? The reason is, you can't.'

'Of course I can't. It's irrelevant. What's relevant is that Bataille has an interest in it. Bataille makes money out of things he's interested in, or alternatively he pours money into things until they start to make money themselves. Derby Boy is part of that racket. I ain't supposing Bataille's cornered the market in immortality Mordent, what I'm flagging is that he's interested in it.'

Mordent puffed on the cigar. 'I'm still not sure that's information worth paying for.'

Hubie reached over the desk, snatched the cigar from Mordent's mouth. 'I'll take this back then.'

Mordent watched as the tip was crushed in the desk ashtray. Miniature sparks blew, like a meteor hitting the earth.

They watched each other as the clock ticked. Hubie sat down.

'Constantin says his brother aged after death,' he finally said. 'What if Bataille is working on stuff that could give that appearance. Just imagine how much money could be up for grabs. If someone else thought it was genuine.'

'Enough for Kirby Muxloe to have an interest in it.'

'Maybe.'

'Yet these are businessmen. Grounded.'

'So? They'd conduct experiments, do tests. Whatever. Who said it was a dead cert?'

Mordent stood. Reached into his jacket pocket and pulled a few notes from their resting place. Tried to hand them over to Hubie, who just looked at them. Mordent placed them on the desk, fanned them.

'If you win,' he said, 'give me this cut back.'

Hubie nodded.

'Another thing,' Mordent said. 'Your body or your soul, what would you choose?'

'Someone else's body,' Hubie said. 'One with curves and breasts and a big ass. Get some of that and my soul would take care of itself.'

Mordent grinned. 'Your asshole, maybe. Be seeing you Hubie. Over the next hundred years, if you're right.'

He closed the door behind him.

Descending the stairs, he mulled it over. Hokum, pure and simple. But it didn't matter what he believed. What mattered were all the others. Bataille and Muxloe, Constantin and BuzzCut. Hubie was right: there was money to be made. Scam or no scam. But, more importantly, was there crime?

Somehow, he just couldn't see it.

He sat in his car awhile. The question of actual crime was a sticky one. He remembered an incident that had occurred shortly after he'd left the force. A puzzle. Something that needed unravelling, but where the element of *crime* hadn't been obvious. It had also been around the time he'd met Maria. Marina minus the N. He wondered where she was right now.

As he drove, the wheels turned like his memories, flicked up detritus, covered ground that had never been forgotten. The tarmac progressed from smooth to bumpy until it was impossible to drive down that road at all.

17
To All The Girls I've Loved Before

Mordent pulled over sharp and parked at the side of the road.

His eyes were too wet to focus properly. Not with tears, as such, but their rheumy equivalent. He had split from Maria within a year of their marriage. What had seemed perfect on the surface had been crème brûlée. Easily cracked. They had parted amicably, but what had been intense was now disparate. Eighteen months had passed. They were still married, on paper. But it was tissue paper. Wet. Thin.

His life was littered with the lipsticks and heels of discarded girls. Goofy girls with braces on their teeth from high school days, confident girls with marital intentions in his late twenties, dumpy girls whom no-one else would look at in his thirties, whores and sundry undesirables in his forties. Leaving the force had left him with less access to company. He wasn't into picking up women; they generally found him, gravitated to him, then, like comets, span away from his magnetic field. They were greased pigs. Some, literally. All that passed in his memory were a succession of bums, boobs, legs and open smiles. Yet settling down had only exacerbated those frustrations.

It was the old saying: you only want what you can't get and you don't want what you can get. It was his saying, in any event, regardless.

He decided to drive to Marina's apartment. Knew he was putting off seeing Muxloe, but hadn't quite decided what he was going to do about it. Anyway, he was worried about the cat.

It was late evening by the time he arrived. Darkness pushing twilight into night. He parked up as before. Rang the same three buzzers after there was no answer from her apartment. As he ascended the stairs, a prescient feeling of dread prickled the hairs on the back of his neck. Her door was closed but there were scratch marks around the lock. They seemed to be recent. Taking his gun from his pocket he stood for a moment. Wondered if anyone was inside.

It was the old light bulb question: the one where you're standing outside a hermetically sealed room containing a light bulb hanging from the ceiling. One of three switches outside the room turns on the light bulb, but you can't tell which one from outside, as they're not labelled and you can't see into the room. You can flick any or all of the switches as many times as you like, but only once can you open the door and see the bulb. So how can you tell which switch operates the light?

It was all down to heat. Turn on one switch and leave it for a while without entering the room. Then turn it off and turn on the second switch. Enter the room. If the light is on then it was the second switch, if the bulb is warm it was the first switch, and if the bulb isn't on or hot at all then it's the third switch.

Mordent needed to increase the heat.

He knocked on the closed door.

Waited.

Listened.

He could hear nothing within the room, but knew that if someone was there they would have moved close to the door.

He knocked a second time. Louder. Then suddenly he put all his weight against the door and charged it open.

There was a crunch and a yelp as the door smashed into the face of the person stood behind it.

An amateur. Obviously.

He hoped it wasn't Marina.

He closed the door swiftly and grabbed hold of the dirty lapel of a guy with a bloody nose. There was a gun on the floor. He kicked it to one side. Twisted the guy's arm behind his back and turned him to face the wall. Kicked his legs wide and stood between them. Leant against him. The guy seemed wired, his eyes white, breathing ragged.

'Fuck,' he said.

'Ain't it,' Mordent replied.

He continued to hold him, pressed his gun against the guy's ribs on the side where his arm was twisted.

'Suppose you tell me what you're doing here.'

The guy's breath hung in the air with a trace of salami.

Mordent twisted his arm further.

The guy gasped. 'Watch out, you'll break it.' Blood had trickled into his mouth. His teeth were red.

'Give me a reason why I shouldn't. Breaking and entering was an offence the last time I looked.'

'You're not a cop.'

'Doesn't matter. So, back to the question, what are you doing here?'

The guy relaxed. Stopped struggling. It was the old Houdini trick. Tense when being tied up and the ropes would be loose when you relaxed. Then you could struggle free. But Mordent knew the trick and had one of his own. He was a python. When the guy relaxed, he tightened, and he would continue to tighten every time the guy relaxed. For as long as necessary.

'I'm choking here.'

'Back to the question. What are you doing here?'

'I can't answer if I can't breathe.' The words rasped out, as though blown through a tapering tube.

'You're answering fine now.'

The guy coughed. Blood speckled the wall, tuberculosis in a handkerchief.

'I was sent to look for something.'

'Find it?'

'No.'

'I can check.'

'I didn't find it.'

'What were you sent to find?'

'Anything.'

'I need more than that.'

'You're really hurting me.'

Mordent tightened his grip. His own arm was beginning to go numb. He jiggled his gun in the guy's ribs.

'Look, I don't know a lot, okay. Was supposed to find something that showed she might know certain stuff.'

'Stuff?'

'She's psychic, right? Maybe there's stuff written down. I dunno. Let me go.'

'Who you working for?'

'I tell you that, I'm a dead man.'

'I'll keep it quiet, let you go. Just tell me.'

There was no answer. The guy was mulling it over.

Still no answer.

'We can do it my way or I can turn you over to the police. Where's the girl?'

'We don't know.'

'Who are you working for?'

'Muxloe.'

Mordent released his grip, stepped back quickly and bent to collect the guy's gun from the floor. He wasn't under threat. The guy slumped down the wall to a seated position, fished a piece of tissue paper from his pocket and held it to his nose. Red spread through the paper like the opening titles of a cheap horror movie. He must have been in his late-thirties. Old enough to know better. Mordent wasn't sure of his story but knew that he wouldn't get any more. Muxloe must be worse off than Bataille if his employees were as useless as this one.

Mordent pulled up a chair. Sat on it legs astride like Christine Keeler and leant on the back. Couldn't be pushed over that way. He watched as the guy regained his composure if not his confidence.

'I think you've broken my nose.'

'Count yourself lucky.' Mordent glanced quickly around the room. It hadn't been turned over. Just a few items ruffled. Maybe the guy hadn't been here long. The cat was watching them both. Curious. Then it started licking itself. 'What does this girl have to do with Muxloe?'

'I tell you, I dunno. I was given a job to do and I'm doing it. I don't work for Muxloe.'

'He's contracted the job out?'

'You could say that.'

Mordent sighed. Organised crime was in a funny state of affairs.

'You don't know where the girl is?'

'She's not here.'

'Don't get smart. Has Muxloe got her?'

'I dunno. I just know she's not here.'

'One final question, laughing boy. Have you been tailing me?'

The guy coughed up a smile. It was pained, looked like it hurt. 'Not me. I don't have a car.'

'Get up.'

Mordent watched as the guy pushed himself to his feet. He stood by the door, expectant.

'Well?'

'I'd like my gun back.'

'I bet you would. Treat its loss as a lesson.'

The guy swore. Took a couple of steps toward the chair before Mordent's right hand gestured with his own gun. The guy thought better of it.

'You watch your back,' he coughed. Blood ran down his hand.

'Out,' Mordent said. He watched the guy's back as he opened the door and closed it behind him.

Mordent waited a good couple of minutes. Then went slowly to the door and locked it from the inside. The wood had splintered but it still closed. He put the chain on. Put his eye to the fisheye. Nothing.

He returned to the chair.

Detective work was like a jigsaw puzzle without the box. Everyone held a piece, no-one knew the full picture. You had to gain a piece with every encounter and most of them were sky. Once you had all the pieces, you had to put them together. There would always be missing pieces. Even once you completed the puzzle there would be missing pieces. If it got to trial, the jury would be presented with the same pieces in a slightly different order from that in which they were found. Together, they would have to imagine the missing pieces. It was on those imaginary pieces that cases were often decided. Not the facts, but the imagination of the jurors.

Mordent imagined where Marina might be.

He imagined what the implications were should Constantin be right.

He imagined what the implications were should Hubie be right.

He imagined what life would be like if he hadn't left the force and had Kovacs' job right now. Things would be easier, most likely.

He imagined himself with a conscience or responsibility.

That one wasn't too hard.

He got up. Looked over at the cat. It had been fed. Maybe the guy with the broken nose had more conscience and responsibility than he credited him with. Maybe more than himself.

He made a quick check of the room. Other than a few disturbed drawers there was no great indication of a search. What concerned him more was that Muxloe was interested. Did that add credence to Constantin's claims? Was it suggestive that Muxloe wasn't holding Marina? Did that mean Bataille had her? Or was she actually away, visiting unknown relatives, her phone signal in the boondocks and unable to receive calls?

If only the latter were correct.

He stood by the window, his reflection imprinted on him by the darkness of the night. Lights from buildings shone through that reflection like sunlight shafts bursting through the bodies of exposed vampires. The twin glows of parallel traffic signals populated his eyes. He was marked out like a constellation. *Cop with gun*. Star sign: changed daily.

He wandered into her bedroom. Was tempted to spend the night.

Did.

18
Kirby Muxloe

He awoke suddenly, unaware of his location. A filigree of dream slipped away from him, as though he were caressing a woman in a negligee. He fought to regain it, failed. A half-sense of loss flittered like REM over his awakening eyelids. He sat up, naked. Regarded the room. On one corner of the bed was Marina's cat, and its presence placed him, fixed his whereabouts like a pin through a butterfly.

He rubbed his eyes, picked out grit. While everything screamed *Marina* he felt it was Maria he had dreamt about. Longing pulsed through him, as though he had been injected with empty desire. Love was the drug.

He could smell Marina's perfume on the pillow. No doubt that would have sparked the dream.

Mordent wondered if he wrote down all the clues he had gained so far in a notebook on the bedside table, whether he would wake with the answers in his head.

There was never that easy option.

He got up. Wandered to the bathroom. Shut himself in the vertical glass coffin of the shower and turned on the water. The heat was wrongly calibrated and he jerked backwards as the cold hit him. Gradually the water warmed. He placed his head under the shower hose. Water streamed off him as he kept his eyes clenched tightly shut. He remembered almost drowning. Attempted to brush the water away from the top of his head, but it was constantly replenished. He hung there for a while, between dream and reality, fantasy and truth. When he turned off the water, the cold speckled his body with bumps. He stumbled out, reached for a towel that hadn't properly dried. Rubbed the steam away from his gaze in the bathroom mirror.

If Muxloe was looking for a bedside notebook then that meant either he didn't have Marina or she hadn't had it with her when she was taken.

There had been no signs of forced entry.

If she hadn't called him then he wouldn't be there. Wouldn't be aware of the possibility of her disappearance.

Everything screamed *set up*.

Why was he getting the feeling that he was being played off between Muxloe and Bataille? He had nothing to give either of them, knew nothing. Were they somehow using him, or was he just another pinball in their machine – being battered from one station to another, completely randomly, scoring points along the way.

He genuinely didn't know what he thought anymore. Or what he wanted to think. Or what he was expected to think.

So he had to visit Muxloe. Couldn't put it off any longer. He was reminded of the scene in *Annie Hall* where Alvy Singer – Woody Allen's character – discusses Kennedy assassination conspiracy theories in order to avoid sex. His own avoidance mirrored it. But then you couldn't put off permanently what needed to be done.

He had history with Muxloe, unlike that with Bataille. They had crossed swords, almost rubbed noses, on at least three occasions while Mordent was on the force. There was no respect between them. Muxloe regarded Mordent as an interferer, someone whose allegiance couldn't be bought. Not that Mordent didn't take the odd backhander; just not from Muxloe. The reason was simple. Muxloe couldn't be trusted. As well as the usual concerns about dodgy dealings, there were rumours that Muxloe was peddling child pornography. Regardless of the truth of the matter, Mordent wouldn't touch him.

Unlike Bataille, Muxloe lived way out of the city. Had large premises within a forested area. An old colonial property. Wooden façade, pillars either side of the porch. But it was just a front, literally; the back of the building had been extended in concrete, spread long and to the sides, as though the original building was but the mouth of a long beast, the new one the elongated body. It had given Mordent the creeps both times he had gone there. Once with a warrant, the second time covertly – undercover – through a window. Neither time had he met with any success.

He couldn't even remember what he had been looking for.

Mordent fed Marina's cat. Wondered what it was named. Wondered if he should rename it. Temporarily. Just so he could call it something. But the thought of doing so shook him inside. Like walking over Marina's grave.

He wondered if he'd find her at Muxloe's. Like Lexi Leigh. Trussed and gagged and needing a peanut butter sandwich.

He needed a peanut butter sandwich. He took a look through Marina's cupboards, bathed in the light from her refrigerator, flicked through the slices of bread and discarded those blue with mould. The two

ANDREW HOOK

remaining browned in the toaster while he returned to the refrigerator and opened the ice box. Stuffed right at the back, behind cubed water, was a notepad.

He gave it a tug but it didn't budge. Paper cracked in his fingertips. He ran his thumb over the twisted wire of the spine. If he defrosted the fridge, any lettering would be ruined by melted ice. Even if he hacked it out, the surrounding ice would turn to water. Marina hadn't thought this through. Truth was, she hadn't expected to be away so long. It had been an impulse hide, and not a bad one, but ultimately the notebook's secrets might be permanently erased.

He buttered the toast. Chewed slowly, the hot butter activating his saliva glands as he masticated. Warmth, home, remembrance. Golden summer light. Snug winter nights. He thought of the notebook.

What could it contain other than the imaginings of a slightly scatty, possibly crazy female? But weren't they all scatty, crazy dames when it came down to it? That was why men loved them.

He switched off the refrigerator and then rummaged in the bedroom until he found the hairdryer he was looking for. It was pink, with an elongated snout. It reminded him of an aardvark he'd once seen at the city zoo. Directing the blast of hot air at the notebook he dried it as it melted. Halfway through, the pages fanned as the base of the notebook stuck, reminding him of the tendrils of an anemone, clinging to a rock. He wondered about the glut of animal imagery entering his mind. Maybe the cat had done something to him, something bestial, while he slept.

It took ten minutes, but the notebook came free.

It was in no state to be read. Ink blurred the pages like bedsheet residues. The centre pages stuck together like dirty magazine stains. He turned the hairdryer on

144

low and fanned warm air across it, tried several angles. It was a hopeless task. Like making love to a beautiful woman, it had to be done slowly to get a result. Hard and fast just wasn't going to work.

He turned the heat on low in the apartment, and laid the notebook carefully against a radiator. He felt safe in assuming that Marina's apartment wouldn't be searched again. Hopefully, by the time he returned, there would be something salvageable to poke through. Even better, Marina would be back and they could go out for dinner.

Mordent realised he hadn't had a proper meal for a long while. His trash can was littered with the aluminium containers of TV dinners. Their blandness had coated his tongue and desensitised his taste buds. His own fridge contained little but chicken drumsticks.

He finished up the last bit of toast, gave the cat another stroke. Then he left the apartment as quietly as if Marina were asleep there, making his way down the concrete steps and onto the sidewalk where he had left his car.

On the journey to Muxloe's, it didn't appear that he was followed.

The day was crystal blue, a sky seen from underwater in a Caribbean sea. Clouds were brilliant white, newly washed. The air as crisp as notebook pages, the breeze as cool as minted breath. He hung his elbow out of the car window, his fingers tapping along the hulk of the vehicle as jazz sweetened its way out of the radio. If it wasn't for his destination the day would be perfect. As he approached the highway leading out of the city he almost contemplated taking an extended holiday in the mountains, but Muxloe beckoned as surely as roadside semaphore.

He skirted trees, gravel side roads, lost lanes, the

highway tapering to a point the further he went. Traffic stopped consisting of commuters, became long haul. Increasingly he passed trucks, decreasingly roadworks. It was a good fifty kilometres from the city before he reached the turn-off to Muxloe's pad. There was a metal sign by the side of the road, displaying the name of his haulage firm. Another front for Muxloe to hide behind.

Stones flipped a halo as he exited the highway. Two hundred metres later he was at the electric gate, pressing a switch and announcing his presence.

'Who?' The feminine voice was crackly, almost electronic.

'Mordent. M. O. R. D. E. N. T. Here to see Kirby Muxloe.'

'There's no appointment showing.'

'I don't need an appointment. He knows who I am.'

'I know who you are, Mr Mordent. I'm just saying there's no appointment.'

'Muxloe will want to see me.'

'Perhaps if you had phoned ahead ...'

'Listen. *Miss*. I'm not going to drive all the way back to the city and wait for you to wipe your nose. Go and tell Muxloe I'm here and have him tell me to go if necessary. Until then, I'm staying put.'

The system crackled. Died. Mordent sat still. Watched a squirrel chase a nut. The metaphor wasn't lost on him. It raced up the tree, bark affording a natural foothold. When it disappeared the system crackled again. 'Mr Mordent? Mr Muxloe says he will see you. Please drive on up.'

The gates were slowly swung open by unseen hands.

The drive was long and curving. Well-tended lawns scattered with brown and red leaves proved there was life outside the city. Established trees and bushes pushed out of the ground, a tacit reminder of nature's growth. Dotted about the estate, a couple of black-suited security types meandered with nothing to do and too much time on their hands. Good work if you could get it, Mordent mused. Not that he wanted it. Their black suits were soiled, blots on the landscape. Life's detritus, no good and vile.

He pulled up front. A shadow emerged from the doorway, took on flesh and colour as it came into the light. He opened his door before it could be opened for him. Got out, carefully. The shadow smiled, a row of yellowing, cigarette-scummed teeth making a poor greeting.

'I'm here for Muxloe.'

'Of course, Mr Mordent.' The man's voice was soft, girlish. Mordent wondered if it had been the voice on the intercom. 'You may leave your vehicle there. Come with me.'

He followed into the building. The darkness swallowed him up.

Down a corridor with the curtains all closed.

Rooms led off the hallway. Mordent's gun hung heavy within his jacket. He glanced from side to side. Most of the doors were closed. Occasionally there were scenes of decadence. Large, glittering chandeliers, polished oak flooring, antique furniture. He couldn't abide luxury. Wasn't jealous of it, just found it unnecessary. An ostentatious display of wealth that smacked of the reasons how that wealth had been obtained. Even legitimacy didn't legitimise it for him.

The man's footsteps echoed in the corridor.

They took a left at the end, then a right. No-one else was in sight. Finally, after what seemed several hundred yards, they approached a set of large wooden double doors. There was a chair outside, and Mordent was beckoned to it as if he were a patient in a doctor's waiting room.

'Wait here, Mr Mordent,' Girl-Voice said. He rapped on the door swiftly and without waiting for an answer opened it and stepped inside.

Mordent stood up. He backtracked a short way down the corridor. Tried a door to the left, which was locked. One to the right led to a small office with plush carpet, similar antique furniture. The only sign they were in the 21st Century was the obligatory desktop computer. Mordent couldn't tell from this angle whether it was on or off.

Gumshoe.

His life seemed to be a series of corridors and doors.

Walking from one to the other, from one person to another. Not just professional, personal too. Always something in another room. He closed the door softly, returned to the chair.

Before he could sit down, the double doors opened and he was beckoned inside.

Muxloe and Bataille were at once different and the same. Same low life, same high standards. They dripped with sleaze so nothing would stick. Same professional business fronts, same illicit dealings. They were two sides of the same double-headed coin. Yet they were still opposite. Each one clawing at the other to get more of the business share. Greed drove the both of them. Greed and hunger. Two sides of another coin.

Mordent entered the room. To his surprise it was tiny, like an anteroom. One side was all glass window, looking out at the lawn. Two of the other walls were flanked with bookcases. Muxloe sat on the edge of his desk. He was a tall, well-built individual. Clean shaven, smart suited. Rings circled most of his fingers. His shoes shone, but Mordent would bet the notebook on the radiator that he didn't polish them himself. Muxloe would employ someone to take a shit for him.

He remained seated on the desk as the double doors closed softly behind Mordent's back.

Smiled.

'Mr Mordent. What an unexpected surprise.'

'Lay off the screenplay, Muxloe. This ain't scripted.'

Muxloe's smile didn't flicker for a moment. He reached for a hardwood cigar box that sat beside him on the desk. 'Cigar? I don't smoke myself.'

'I do, but I'm choosy who I smoke with.'

Muxloe closed the box shut with a click.

'You love the dialogue, don't you Mordent. Every time we meet it's the '50s all over again. Shadows and fog. Wet streets and dames. I'm sure even now you're noiring up my responses. Changing the word dames to dames. Making a big deal out of nothing. We all have our hang ups, but yours are worn on your sleeve.'

Mordent grunted.

'So, what are you here for? I'm a busy man.'

Mordent walked over to the desk and parked himself in his second leather chair in two days. Muxloe watched him, sat also.

'I've been hired by a certain Mrs Davenport to find out what happened to her son.'

Muxloe reached into his desk, pulled out a sweet, unwrapped it, popped it into his mouth.

'Am I supposed to know who this Davenport boy is?'

'You tell me.'

'How about you tell me if I don't.'

'There's more. I was with Constantin when he was picked up by your hoods.'

Muxloe smiled. 'There you go again. *Hoods*. Rather dramatic, isn't it?'

'It doesn't matter what you call them, it amounts to the same thing. There's more. I ejected an intruder from the apartment of Marina Gonzales yesterday evening, says he was working for you. Gonzales' whereabouts are unknown.'

Muxloe ran the sweet around the inside of his mouth, like a boy with a race car on a toy track. 'So just like a war veteran gets medals pinned on his shirt you want to pin these problems on me.'

'I just want simple answers to simple questions.'

'You're not on the force now, Mordent. I have no obligation to answer any of these questions.'

Mordent nodded. Crossed one leg over the other. Leant back. 'No, I'm not. But the latter two pieces of information have yet to be imparted to the police. And should that be done it won't be me you'll be talking to, but someone who'll expect you to provide the answers.'

'You think you're the lesser of two evils?'

Mordent shrugged. 'Are you going to tell me the answers or not?'

Muxloe crumpled the sweet wrapper between long fingers. There was a sound like a squirrel rustling leaves. 'You know about Constantin,' he said. 'You know his brother was found dead on our property. We just wanted a chat with him. To find out the story.'

'I haven't heard from Constantin since that night.'

'Maybe he's lying low. He was fine when he left here. Of that there is no doubt.'

'You know what he said about his brother?'

'Tell me.'

'That he had aged after his death.'

Muxloe laughed. 'Again the dramatist.'

Mordent leant forwards. 'What can you tell me about immortality?'

Muxloe's face became stone. 'Everyone believes they're immortal until they die, Mordent. Then they don't believe anything anymore.'

'And that's what you believe?'

'What is this, a philosophical discussion or police ... I mean ... detective work?'

Mordent sat back again. 'Just trying to fill in the pieces.'

'You gotta be careful you don't dig a hole that's filled in with you inside it.'

'Is that a threat?'

'Did you hear what I said? Didn't sound like a threat to me. Or are you still switched on to noir-mode. Everyone knows why you left the force, Mordent. You couldn't hack it. There's no reason to suggest you can hack what you're doing now.'

Mordent grunted. 'You've answered one question.'

Muxloe took another sweet from his desk drawer. Hard-boiled. He offered it to Mordent, who shook his head. Muxloe shrugged then unwrapped it. Popped it into his mouth. The previous sweet hadn't dissolved. They clicked together like pool balls.

'You come to me with answers rather than questions and expect me to match the answers. You know about the Davenport boy already.'

'I know it was a tit for tat body swap. I don't know who killed him or how he was killed.'

Muxloe shrugged. 'So, you know the answers. What do you expect me to say?'

'How about Gonzales?'

'Never heard of her. I'm a busy man, Mordent. I employ thousands of people in purely legitimate businesses. If you thump someone and he uses me as his get-out clause then I can't be held responsible for it.'

'Word on the street is that you can't be held responsible for anything.'

'*Word on the street*.' Muxloe snorted, derisively. 'Here we go again. You've been watching too much *Police Squad*. Shall I be a caricature villain to your caricature cop? Oh wait, not a cop. A PI. I could probably think of a few words to match those initials.'

Mordent reached into his pocket. Pulled out his gun. Turned it around in his hands.

'What is this? A show of strength? You're not about to kill me. I'm not quite sure what you're doing here, Mordent. *Are you?*'

'Tell me about Bataille.'

'There you go again. Asking me questions to which you already know the answers. Bataille and I are not drinking buddies. You know this. We've had our spats. I don't need to say anything else.'

Muxloe reached for a buzzer on top of his desk. Mordent didn't stop him.

'Now, if you'll excuse me. As I said, I'm a busy man.'

Mordent stood. Put away his gun. 'You think you're smart but I'm smarter. You think you're quick but I'm quicker. But there's also smarter and quicker men than me. You should watch your back Muxloe. You're not a popular guy.'

Muxloe gestured to the room, his manner suggesting he was referring to the whole building rather than the library into which they were squeezed. 'Do I look like I need to be popular?'

The door opened behind Mordent. He turned and Girl-Voice stood waiting.

'If you would come this way, Mr Mordent.'

Mordent got halfway to the door before Muxloe said, 'And if there's anything else you need, e-mail me. You don't need another wasted journey.'

'I got all the information I needed,' Mordent grunted. He turned and followed Girl-Voice out of the room.

They made their way down the corridor in silence.

In a small room just before the main hallway Mordent glimpsed someone he recognised.

They hadn't seen him.

His car was parked outside. It didn't look like it had been moved. He got in behind the wheel. Had to manoeuvre around a car that previously hadn't been there, and made a mental note of its plate. Then he drove back down the long drive. The squirrel was in hiding. As he approached the large metal gates they opened automatically to ease his egress.

He drove a hundred yards down the road then pulled off onto a dirt track, turned around in a clearing almost suited for the purpose, and waited.

He clocked his watch. Early afternoon. Shade from overhead trees darkened the vehicle's interior and patterned it with henna-like tattoos. As he watched and waited, leaves fell from the branches, curling colours of browns and autumnal reds, glorious in their death throes. The warmth of the engine soon left the vehicle. The sun's distance sufficient to have changed summer to fall. Mordent preferred the temperate seasons: fall and spring. People were malleable during those months. In summer and winter they became as extreme as the weather.

Time ticked on. Mordent thought over his meeting with Muxloe. He was no closer to finding Marina, and he was sure Davenport's manner of death would be gleaned from Martens that evening. Why had it seemed imperative to contact Muxloe? Was his brain sparking connections that only tenuously existed, his synapses muddled. Muxloe had seemed to greet him with some amusement. While it hadn't unnerved him, it did make him query his intent. Was he really some two-bit PI moving from one dialogue to another? Like a plot device? He shook the thought out of his head; blurred it. Life was complicated enough without adding complication.

After an hour he got out of the car. Found a sizeable tree and urinated against the trunk. Steam rose from his piss, the smell pungent. He took a walk afterwards, stretched his legs. Wondered what piece of immortality he might want for himself.

What was it Woody Allen had famously said? *I don't want to achieve immortality through my work, I want to achieve it by not dying.* How did *he* want *his* slice of immortality? Warhol had said that in the future everyone would be famous for fifteen minutes. Was that all it took, fifteen minutes to gain that immortality? Not in Mordent's mind.

Traffic on the road was light, so when he heard a vehicle he returned to his car. It was approaching three o'clock. He turned the engine over. Waited.

Within a few minutes he pulled out behind the vehicle that he had seen at Muxloe's. There was one occupant. The driver was also the person he had seen at Muxloe's. He sighed and hung back, just within distance but not so close as to cause suspicion. As the afternoon wore on, he began tailing Greg Hammerton.

19
Soft Shoe Shuffle

If there was one thing Mordent was certain about it was uncertainty. The way the puzzle pieces fit together wasn't always the way it seemed they might fit. In the mind's eye, the finished result was oblong. In reality, it could be a snowflake pattern. A constantly changing snowflake pattern. One that you got only a glimpse of before it melted.

Marina's notebook hung in the back of his mind like a frosted sheet on a washing line. While he doubted her psychic abilities, maybe others didn't. And whether she was psychic or not wouldn't obviate the danger. He guessed he should report her absence to the police, but knew he would hold back. Yet Muxloe's insistent reminder he was no longer on the force played on a loop in his head. He liked responsibility, but at what point should he relinquish it?

Truth was, he was his own man. Beholden to none.

The car ahead of him containing Hammerton was the car that had been tailing him.

This explained how it had been so easy to lose him. It also explained how it was so easy to keep on his tail. He doubted if Hammerton had even noticed his vehicle at Muxloe's. Amateur. What it didn't explain was what Hammerton was doing at Muxloe's in the first place.

As they approached the city lights, dark followed behind them, rushing them towards the centre. A storm was brewing. It was darker than the seasonal norm. Hammerton popped on his lights. Mordent held back before following suit. Other traffic converged as the number of lanes increased. He stepped on the accelerator. Fat drops of rain hit the hood, advanced up the bodywork in a car-wash rush. His vision became blurred, wipers shoved water this way and that, ineffectual twin Moses. Hammerton's red rear lights fuzzed, haloed by mini-refractions, making them one-colour rainbows. They descended into the heart of the city, were swallowed up by the beast.

Mordent had really only needed confirmation that Hammerton was the driver of the vehicle, but he stuck to his rear as the rain fell in sheets.

Lightning punctured the sky, the slithering of golden eels in blackened waters.

Rainwater sprayed up from car wheels, ran in rivulets into storm drains. Mordent felt as if he were driving a speedboat. He decreased his speed as Hammerton did likewise. Blurred faces within passing cars foreshadowed their deaths, mimicked decomposition. Within his vehicle, Mordent experienced a bubble of unreality, a distinct protectiveness of environment that didn't actually exist. Pseudo-safety amidst the downpour. A lulling of security that almost guaranteed he could swing a right and the car next to him would do likewise. As if they would repel each other like opposing magnets. The hum of the rain on the roof a dangerous soothing. The descending dark pulling his eyelids down with him.

He jerked his head upwards, shook it. Hammerton's tail-lights loomed larger. Mordent stamped on his brakes, juddered the car in short successive movements, almost grazed his bumper. Stopped.

The silence inside the car was perforated by the rain and the blaring of a dozen horns.

Mordent watched as Hammerton clocked him in his rear view mirror.

The traffic resumed its movement, snaking a way into the city, the hiss of rubber on wet roads accentuating the imagery.

A space opened up on the right and Hammerton took it. Mordent was blocked out. They edged forwards, a slow car chase, a soft shoe shuffle. Another space appeared and Mordent was behind again. They proceeded in this fashion, like an elongated tile puzzle, gaining and losing moves, until the pattern coalesced and they were outside a brownstone a few hundred yards from the university. Hammerton parked up. Remained in his vehicle. Switched off his lights.

Mordent wasn't gullible enough to miss the steam rising from the exhaust.

Engine running. He was ready to scoot.

Mordent switched off his lights. Left *his* engine running.

The rain was a curtain between them. A wet sheen dividing audience and stage. If each drop was a thought, then Mordent knew they must mirror the number running through Hammerton's brain. Thundering.

Another fork of lightning tore a hole in the sky, like a magnesium burn.

Mordent opened his driver door. Put one shoe onto the road. Into a puddle. He could hear Hammerton's engine turning over. He opened the door wider. Wondered how wide it would have to be before Hammerton took off. He didn't want to leave the vehicle. The street wasn't busy. It was just the two of them. A Mexican standoff with a difference. The difference being Mordent was sure Hammerton wouldn't have a gun.

Another inch and Hammerton's vehicle revved away, leaving white smoke signals. Message understood. Mordent slipped his foot back into the car and onto the accelerator. His tyres squealed as they span in the wet, then gained purchase and lurched forwards. Stalled.

He swore. Started his engine. Watched as Hammerton took a right at the end of the street. Lights still off. Mordent wondered what he was scared of. Even if this cat and mouse went Hammerton's way, it wasn't as though Mordent couldn't trace him. Yet it was the freshness of the information that Hammerton had been seen at Muxloe's that invigorated them both. Adrenalin created flight or fight scenarios. It seemed that Hammerton wasn't one to fight.

He took the same right, glimpsed Hammerton doing a left. He stopped, reversed and turned, took the other side of the square and found himself at the entrance to the college car park. It was still manned at this hour. He flashed his PI badge, and whether the operator couldn't care less or didn't want to extend his head out of his metal container Mordent wasn't sure, but the barrier rose and he found a place to park.

Two minutes passed, then Hammerton opened the barrier automatically with a key card. He drove slowly, lights on. Parked up and sat for a while. The rain ceased. Emerging from his vehicle, he looked around quickly. Looked like a man who didn't expect to see anything. Taking a case from the passenger side he locked up and walked into the building.

Mordent followed at a distance. The car park was uneven. Frequently his feet descended into water, soaking him through to his socks. He shielded himself with parked cars. Students who had waited under the veranda at the front of the building began to exit in the drier weather. Hammerton and Mordent walked against the grain.

Inside, Mordent stood by the doorway as Hammerton took the first flight of steps. He followed. Then the second. At the end of the corridor a fire door slammed shut. They were in the science wing. Bunsen burners stood on desk tops like miniature smoke stacks. Gas taps always reminded him of gas chambers. Rubber hose had similar connotations. Large glass condensers were tubular sculptures.

At the end of the corridor, another corridor held a wall of lockers. Hammerton stood by one of them, key in hand.

His shoulders slumped when he saw Mordent. Resignation.

Mordent squelched towards him.

'Why the hurry?'

'Pardon.'

'You know what I'm talking about. Is there somewhere quiet we can go? You might want to take that briefcase with you.'

Hammerton shrugged. 'It's course work. I'm not sure what you're talking about.'

'Don't make it hard. You thought I'd picked you up from the highway, but I was following you from Kirby Muxloe's.'

'Oh.'

'Yes. Oh.'

'It isn't what you think.'

'What makes you think I'm thinking anything?'

Hammerton shrugged again, the way young people do.

A couple of students passed them in the corridor. This seemed to focus Hammerton's mind, and he led Mordent into one of the labs. The only seats were stools. Mordent pulled one up. Sat on it. Expected to see a bar mirror on the other side of the table.

Hammerton didn't look as cocky as when Mordent had first seen him with Sue Sweeney.

'You know I'm investigating Patrick Davenport's disappearance. You probably know he's been found dead.'

Hammerton nodded.

'Any idea where he was found?'

'None at all.'

'At the back of a truck in a container that belongs to one of Muxloe's business rivals. Someone by the name of Bataille.'

Hammerton stood. Rested his hands palm down on the work surface.

'You see how it looks,' Mordent continued. 'You knew Patrick, you know Muxloe. There's not much doubt that Muxloe planted the body in a tit for tat situation. The only puzzle is where Patrick and/or his body have been for the past three years.'

'I wouldn't know that,' Hammerton stumbled.

'It won't just be me,' Mordent said. 'At some point the police will also put the connection together. I imagine you had a promising career lined up. Jail kind of knocks that into a cocked hat.'

Hammerton's eyes widened. 'Jail?'

'I can only surmise on the information I have.'

Hammerton took a couple of deep breaths. His body was tense. Shaking controlled. Just.

'What do you want to know?'

'How do you mean?'

'You're suggesting a deal in exchange for

information. What do you want to know?'

Mordent raised his eyebrows. 'What do you want to tell me?'

'Look. It isn't what it seems, okay. I don't know anything about Patrick's body.'

'So what were you doing at Muxloe's.'

Hammerton started to pace. 'He's funding a research project here that I'm majoring in. I got an invite to go and see him. I hadn't a clue what it was about. Or how it was related to Patrick.'

'This doesn't quite hold up. Why did you run when you saw I was following you?'

'Because I didn't know why you were following me?'

It was a question, not an answer.

Mordent stood also, grabbed Hammerton by the shoulders, creasing his shirt.

'You can stop giving me the runaround. You've been tailing me for days.'

Hammerton shook, in addition to being shook.

'Coincidence?' he blurted.

Mordent slapped him once, hard, across the side of the face.

Hammerton tried to reach up, but his arms were pinned.

'You can't do that.'

'I can do what I like.'

Mordent grabbed Hammerton's head, pushed it down to the desk opposite a gas jet. Turned it on. Reached inside his pants pocket and pulled out a lighter. Flicked it.

'What the fuck!' Hammerton struggled, but Mordent's weight was over his body and he was pinioned against the desk. 'You can't do this.'

'Then it isn't happening, is it?' Mordent snarled.

The flame trembled.

Mordent's muscles bulged.

A gleam mirrored the flame flicker at the back of his eyes. Hammerton saw it.

He started to sob.

Mordent turned off the gas. Kept Hammerton down while his body continued shaking, as though holding an epileptic steady.

'Easy. Keep it calm. Breathe slowly.'

Hammerton started to cough on the residual gas.

'I can't breathe.'

'If you can speak you can breathe. Shall we start again? Why have you been tailing me?'

'I didn't like your attitude when you asked Sue and me about Patrick.'

'My attitude.'

'You suspected something from the start.'

'You make it sound like there's something to suspect.'

'I don't know what to say.'

'Just keep it coming.'

'I knew something happened between Sue and Patrick before he disappeared. I thought you might find out about it. Draw the wrong conclusions.'

'You thought I thought you'd killed Patrick in a fit of jealousy.'

'Something like that.'

'How close are you and Sue now?'

'On and off; it's strained. You're hurting my back; are we done?'

'You've forgotten Muxloe.'

'It's as I said. I got an invite. Muxloe is funding research here. Ask the principal if you don't believe me.'

'So you tailed me to see if I was getting suspicious about you, and Muxloe wants you for his golden boy.'

'I dunno about that. But you're right about the tailing.'

Mordent released his grip, and Hammerton rose stiffly.

'It's just so damn weird it might be true.'

Hammerton rubbed his arms, massaged his shoulders. 'I could report you for this?'

'Who to? I'm my own boss.'

Hammerton shrugged, with difficulty.

'But you won't.' Mordent replaced the lighter in his pocket. As he did so, Hammerton attempted a punch. Mordent caught the fist in his other hand.

'Lazy.'

He twisted his grip and Hammerton cried out as his wrist followed.

Mordent let go.

'You could still be in the frame for the Davenport boy. Watch your back.'

Hammerton shook his arm. 'Jesus.'

Mordent hefted himself back onto the stool. 'Tell me about Muxloe. You said why you were there, but what did he want?'

'If you know why I was there why don't you ask him yourself?'

'I'll drop him an e-mail. But for now I'm asking you.'

'I was offered a scholarship based on the research I'm doing.'

'And that research would be ...'

'Stem cell research. Extending the life of cells. There's a key gene that keeps embryonic stem cells in a state of youthful immortality. That was found some years ago. We're looking into further possibilities.'

'For immortality?'

'Immortality? I wouldn't go that far.'

'Wouldn't you? There's those who would.' Mordent sighed. 'Listen kid, don't try and take a swipe at me again. I might break your fingers next time.'

Hammerton stepped back. He had regained some confidence. That ineffectual swing had gone some way to restore his manhood. He'd tried. He nodded.

'I should tell the police you were at Muxloe's.'

Hammerton shrugged. 'It's college business.'

'I think there's more than coincidence linking the two of you. And if that's so, I'll find it.'

Hammerton nodded. Quiet acceptance.

Mordent stood again. 'Just think about what I've said. How did you respond to Muxloe?'

'I told him I was interested in taking up his offer. My parents can't fund the whole of my studies. This would be a fantastic opportunity.'

'Just be aware of who you're mixing with.'

'Mr Muxloe is well known for his business and charitable concerns. There are a couple of other students here who received bursaries from him. He practically funds the entire science faculty.'

'Spoken truly and naively. I guess you should run along.'

Hammerton reached for his briefcase, but Mordent's hand was there first.

'I almost forgot about this silly thing.'

Hammerton's hand tugged at the strap. 'This is private.'

'I imagine it is. What I'm wondering is why you brought it here. The only reason I can think of is you didn't want me to find it in your possession.'

'I was dropping it off before college tomorrow.'

'Doesn't ring true to me. What am I going to find?'

Hammerton's grip remained steady. 'Nothing to do with Patrick.'

Mordent wrenched the case free. 'Funnily enough I didn't think so, but now you've got me curious.'

Mordent slid the latch open as easily as depressing a key on a keyboard. He made a show of tipping the case upside-down so that the contents fanned out onto the table.

'Hey, careful with that.'

Mordent handed Hammerton the empty case, flicked through the coursework until he came to a manila envelope. The end was folded inside itself, so he flipped it open. Inside were half a dozen glossy glamour shots. Four were softcore poses. Two were hardcore. Sue Sweeney was the model.

She didn't look like she was enjoying the experience.

Mordent knew what fake looked like.

He looked at Hammerton. 'You didn't take these.' It was a statement of fact.

Hammerton shook his head slowly, thinking.

'You get these from Muxloe?'

'I don't see what that's got to do with you. These are private.'

Mordent considered the Sue Sweeney he knew. A bit retro-hippie, confident but sweet. He considered the circumstances that might have led to these photographs being taken. He considered coercion.

He pointed at one of the images. 'This body part, that Patrick's?'

Hammerton didn't glance down. 'No.'

'And it's not yours, right? Too big.'

'Very funny.' Hammerton went to snatch the photos away, but Mordent was quicker.

'I've no legal right to keep these.' Mordent put them back into the envelope. 'But I will remember them. Tell me something. This deal Muxloe extended today.

Your bursary. Were these photos part of that deal?'

'I want the funding,' Hammerton said, his expression blank.

'And I'm guessing Sue's need for the funding wasn't so great.'

Puzzle pieces interconnected. All the edges fell into place. Mordent knew the frame.

'Muxloe approached three kids. Patrick, Sue and you. Maybe more. My guess is that Patrick said no. Then he disappeared. That could be coincidence – I'd buy that. Then Sue said no. These photos are blackmail for keeping her mouth shut. Or maybe something else. Whatever. They exist. Then you said yes. But you knew about the photos and you might have known about Patrick. So you did a deal. Thing is, Muxloe's usually the dealer, so if you were able to do that deal then the stakes mean a lot to him.'

Hammerton kept silent. Yet his face was awash with relief.

'You don't have to tell me I'm right. Patrick was the smart one, correct? Smarter than both of you put together. Smart enough to be approached three years ago. Whereas you and Sue, you were second and third options. But still smart enough for him to want you at all. Which I guess is pretty smart. Fair where fair's due.'

He handed the photographs back to Hammerton. 'You will be giving these to Sue, right?'

'I was going to destroy them.'

'Let her watch you destroy them. That way she knows they're gone.'

Hammerton nodded. Came onside. Asked: 'There could be more, though, couldn't there? I didn't get any negatives.'

Mordent smiled. It didn't sit right on his face, like a cat on a pointed fence. 'I thought it was me living in the '50s. I doubt there are negatives. You never heard of digital cameras? One wrong step from you and these are all over the internet. Don't mention it to Sue. Keep your nose clean and it will be okay. I've got to contact Muxloe anyway. If he knows I know about these images maybe he'll make sure to hold back.'

Hammerton muttered a *Thanks*.

'I'm not doing it for you. I'm doing it for the girl. Look after her.'

Mordent watched as Hammerton replaced the contents of his briefcase, clicked it closed. He was just a kid who thought he knew better. Rattled and scared and hungry but didn't want to show it. Muxloe would rip him to pieces once he got what he wanted.

Unless Mordent ripped Muxloe to pieces first.

20
A Blueprint For Courageous Action

Before heading to Marina's, Mordent stopped at his office. Early evening was warm. The cloud cover having trapped the heat rising from the Earth's surface. Outside smelt of wet earth, clear rain. It was vibrant. Proof that the Earth was alive and not a spent commodity chained and changed by man. All it would take, Mordent thought, was one international disaster and the world would be reclaimed by the elements. Mother Earth was a woman, and so couldn't be tamed.

Outside his office door, despite the late hour, sat Mrs Mouse. A ghost of the woman who had waited there four days previously. She wore the same cardigan, but it seemed faded. Cream pants with a sharp crease instead of the skirt. She remained unattractive, but she had that right. She had just lost her son.

She stood as Mordent approached. Red rims underscored her heavy eyes. He had been hoping to avoid this.

'I'm sorry, Mr Mordent. I know it's late, but you left the light on in your office and I imagined you might return. I tried to phone, but got no reply.'

Mordent pulled out his cell phone. Saw the missed calls. It wasn't locked and had switched to silent. Maybe he'd sat on it.

'That's no problem.' He unlocked the door. 'Come in.'

Once they were seated she pulled a folded-up piece of tissue from the left sleeve of her cardigan. Blew her nose. Repeated that she was sorry.

'I understand your circumstances,' Mordent said. 'There's no need to apologise.'

'I came as quick as I could,' she said. Her voice soft, mechanical. 'I formally identified Patrick's body today. He looked. Well, he looked different.'

Mordent remembered the corpse he had seen. He couldn't imagine that corpse looking anything like it had done when it was alive. There was no surprise that it looked different.

Yet he had an inkling what Mrs Mouse was going to say.

He pre-empted her.

'You think he looks older? Older than he was when he was alive.'

Her eyes lit up. 'Why, yes.'

'I thought so too. Although I didn't know him. Of course.'

'A mother knows her son, Mr Mordent. I'm sure he died recently, but the medical examiner confirmed it was three years ago. They'll be an inquest of course. They're still not sure of the cause of death, other than a blow ... a blow to the head. But I don't believe he's been dead these past years. I would have felt it. Intuition. I know that sounds silly but I would. I'm sure of it.'

Mordent wasn't sure of anything other than another connection to Robbie Constantin.

'I've made enquiries,' he said slowly, 'although I'm not sure if there's progress or not. I can't reveal what I've found so far because it might be nothing. But can I ask a question about Patrick's studies?'

'Of course.'

'He was majoring in science. Did he mention being approached about a bursary to enable him to continue his studies after graduation?'

Mrs Mouse thought carefully. 'I can't say that he did. Is it relevant?'

'As I say, it might be.'

She wiped her eyes again.

'I'm a single woman, Mr Mordent. My husband passed away ten years ago and I brought Patrick up on my own for those years. A bursary would have been useful to him.'

Mordent nodded. He imagined the accusing finger of the dead Davenport boy wavering in the corner of the room, dissipating.

'I'll report back once I've made further investigations. Of course, now a body has been found this is largely in the hands of the police. But as I said over the phone, I'll see what I can do.'

Mrs Mouse stood. 'I'm very grateful.' She held out her hand and he shook it. A trace of her tears remained on his fingers, but she hadn't noticed. He slipped his hand into his pocket and dried it.

At the door she said, 'Do you think the police would lie to me? I'm sure he died recently. That's why I came.'

Mordent shook his head. 'They may be many things but they're not liars,' he said. And at the back of his mind he thought, *at least not when something can be proven.*

'I'll trust your professional opinion, Mr Mordent, but they are mistaken. Of that I am sure.'

He closed the door behind her as she left.

Clocking his watch he saw it was approaching eight o'clock. He wanted to contact Martens but it was too early for his shift. A blow at the back of the head?

Any manner of death was reasonable. But how had he got off that ferry?

Nevertheless, things were moving.

He turned on the PC and checked his e-mails. There was one from Constantin.

I was wrong about my brother. Thanks for your help.

He'd never seen an e-mail that so obviously hadn't been sent by the person it appeared to have been sent by. Even those that were viral.

He closed down the PC.

On the way to Marina's apartment he stopped off at an independent convenience store. It was packed floor to ceiling with an assortment of goods. Even so, he couldn't find the brand of cat food he was hoping to buy. He chose something mid-range. The Chinese owner with tufts of fluffy white hair that curled like smoke from his head smiled approvingly. Mordent left the store a satisfied customer.

Once again dark hemmed in on his vehicle, as though a black blanket had been thrown over the car and sewn tight on all sides; the streetlights bright stars pinpricking the background, the hum of the engine a lullaby, a soporific. The longer the time between his and Marina's last meeting, the more he wanted to see her again. He recalled the touch of her hands on his skin, her mouth, tongue on his lips. As he replayed their romantic entanglement back in his mind he found himself with an erection. Maybe he shouldn't have dismissed her psychic claims so quickly.

Unsurprisingly, since his encounter with Hammerton, there was no longer any indication he was being followed.

He parked outside her apartment block. Again, he pressed a few buttons simultaneously. Made a mental note to check out a spare key once he gained entry. No-one responded, so he tried again. Eventually an elderly voice came through the intercom. 'Who is that, I'm trying to sleep?'

'It's your son,' Mordent said.

'Barry? What do you want?' The voice wasn't frail, but strong. Violently strong.

'I left my coat in the hallway.'

'Idiot.' The door was buzzed open and Mordent slipped through. *Take it*, he heard. *Then leave me alone.* The door swung shut behind him.

Thankfully the security on the internal doors wasn't as complex as it was out the front. Electronic locks were always harder to pick. At least in his experience. It took but a moment to re-enter Marina's apartment, and there were no signs it had been disturbed. Due to the warm evening, and the thick modern windows, the rooms were baking hot. He checked the thermostat, tapped it, wondered if it were broken. Then turned off the heating he had started earlier that morning and located the notebook on the radiator.

The pages were bent and twisted like a Swami's fingernails. Browned like curly fries. He picked it up delicately. It was brittle to the touch. The top page fell free, floated like a sycamore seed. He held it like parchment retrieved from the National Archives. A piece of the Magna Carta. His will.

The cat was mewling. Sniffed the paper on the floor and looked up at him expectantly. Meowed again. Its teeth were needle sharp.

He placed the notebook on the table. Opened the box of cat food and peeled open one of the sachets. Whitefish. The cat mewled louder.

He did all this deliberately, slowly; was aware that once again he was delaying what needed to be done.

There might be answers in that notebook, there might not. Sometimes he needed to know the answers, sometimes he didn't. If there was an indicator that the notebook would tell him something he wanted to know then he would have checked it immediately. But there wasn't, so he wouldn't, and he didn't.

Instead he watched the cat chew the fish. Wondered to what extent the cat wondered about its existence. Presumed that it didn't. Wondered whether that benefited it or not. Was it consciousness and a sense of self that determined the course of the human race? He liked consciousness. Maybe it was good to be alive, after all.

The question over whether or not Marina was alive halted his musing and he sat at the table. Held the notebook.

He turned each of the approximately fifty pages slowly without reading them, ensuring it was malleable, wouldn't break up. When he got to the end he started again at the beginning. Marina's choice of pen seemed to be blue biro, probably the best option when it came to defrosting and reheating. A fountain pen wouldn't have cut it, pencil scratchings would have been erased.

Nevertheless, some of the pages were Rorschach tests in blue. He recognised a butterfly, splayed legs, a heliograph. He found one that mirrored his head, twice, a conjoined twin. He found half-words, musings, interlinked words that may never have had any meaning other than the early morning jottings of dreams: *the bananas were in the fridge, cantaloupes, when the haberdashery was on fire, sex, Julie told me nothing, euphoria.*

What was it Bruce Wayne had said in the '60s *Batman* TV show: *A dream. What is a dream but a blueprint for courageous action!*

Mordent needed a dream that would lead to that action.

Ten pages into the notebook there was a page where the watermarks extended just around the edges, as though framing the contents. Marina's lettering was typically female: rounded, circles rather than dots on *i*'s, seamless joined-up writing that indicated an equally well-rounded personality. Whatever she might have been, it seemed she had been happy. Yet as for all of us, the dreams were sometimes dark.

Last night I dreamt that I went to the doctor's. It was a backstreet doctor in a disused warehouse. She was Chinese, female. I thought I was pregnant so she threw water over my belly and scanned me with what looked like a sweeping brush.

A shadow came up on the image of the baby and I knew it was possessed! It was rolling a cigarette and then holding a gun. I had to turn away, I couldn't look at it, and then it shot the doctor.

I went next door. The doctor's brother was lying in a sort of bath tub in the dark. The baby shot him in the eye, which produced a blue light.

Underneath, arrows pointed to some of the words. Some arrows were double-headed, suggesting links. Question marks populated the text. Mordent found it fascinating, a way into Marina's head, even if there was nothing there he could use.

There was vulnerability, intrigue, an over-abiding sense of despair. All the familiar elements of dream.

It wasn't what he was looking for.

He turned a few more pages. Saw the first reference to what he assumed might have been Patrick. It tied in with what Marina had told him in the bar.

There's a boy. Water coming out of his mouth. Bubbles. Upwards looking. Wooden slats. Coffin(?). Sky through the slats.

Yet, Mordent knew, Patrick hadn't died at sea. Or at least, hadn't drowned. A blow to the back of the head, Mrs Mouse had said. He looked at his watch. It was after ten. Flicking open his cell phone he found the number of the morgue. Picked up Marina's house phone to dial.

'Martens?'

'Mordent. I was wondering when you would call.'

'What do you know?'

'In layman's terms, blow to the back of the head, which led to bleeding in the brain. Looks like he might have been in the sea at some point. Traces of saltwater, but minimal. The body has also been tampered with ...'

'Not by you, I take it.'

'Oh c'mon. When are you going to let that go?'

'Depends on how many years there are left in me. So how do you mean, tampered?'

'It's hard to describe. I'm not going to fob you off with medical descriptions, but essentially someone has gone to some length to make him look older than he was when he died.'

'And when did he die?'

'Three years ago without question. I would say at the time he disappeared.'

Mordent stroked his chin, felt the bristles. 'Kovacs been down there?'

'Personally. Apparently. Not on my shift.'

'You getting the connection with Davenport and Constantin?'

'They're running similar tests on Constantin now.'

'Anyone else come in similar?'

'Nope.'

'Okay, Martens.' Mordent paused, added thanks. Hung up the phone.

Maybe there were slices of truth in Marina's notebook.

Although despite what Martens had said, Mordent knew as a layman that everyone dies of the same cause: lack of oxygen to the brain.

He turned a couple more pages. Found a one-liner, underlined:

I was trying to strangle myself to show that it could be done.

Further on, another detailed dream:

I'm walking to my car. There's a Chinese restaurant with a blue and white chequered floor. I write a word on it.

My phone vibrates. There's a text of a foot that is a little swollen, and then later another one that is bleeding. Then a message from someone called 'Celon' about setting something up because the wrench has been brought over.

Scene changes: my camera is returned to me and there are hundreds of photos! There are dark ones of my sister sitting in her middle room playing on a games console wearing purple. Some have two babies sitting at the table. Some are of the TV screen; lots of light and maths equations. I'm looking at the TV when I see your face and wake up.

Mordent re-read. *Your face.* Who were these written to?

He turned a couple more pages.

Here, another oblique reference to Patrick. No doubt the one that had led Marina to tip Kovacs off about the body.

There's a truck. Someone struggling. A box. Not struggling physically. Mentally. I see bread, rolls, baguettes. Cake. The word 'police' was circled after this brief vision.

Mordent detected a pattern. Detection being his forte. Short, staccato sentences indicated visions; longer segments indicated dreams. He flicked back to the short,

ANDREW HOOK

staccato sentence where Marina imagined strangling herself, then looked for more that might be nearer the end of the book.

On the final page before they went blank was circled the letter *M*.

Muxloe, or Marina? Or neither.

It was impossible to tell the age of the book, but he presumed that it was new judging by the placing of the visions and what he knew about when they were reported. The blank pages at the end were proof it was her last journal. He remembered the page that had fallen to the floor, picked it up. Unlike the other pages this was dated. Only two weeks earlier.

So there must have been other notebooks.

He made another search of the room. This time looking for what wasn't there rather than what was. It didn't take long to find it. In the living area stood a bookcase. One of the shelves was half-full, with a stone Buddha taking up most of the second half. When he picked the Buddha up there was no circle of dust delineating its base. The unit had been recently cleaned, but there was dust at the edges of the books.

Where the Buddha stood would have been space for a good twenty notebooks of similar size to the one he had found.

He pulled over a kitchen chair, stood on it. On the top of the bookcase, where it couldn't be seen from head height, there was a rectangle of dust at the centre. The Buddha fit perfectly in that space.

So the notebooks had been taken and the statuette moved in the process; either to hide the gap or just for convenience.

Whether Mordent did or not, someone had taken Marina seriously.

He replaced the Buddha in its adopted home.

Replaced the chair. Then he returned to the last page of the notebook.

    M.

    Muxloe or Marina.

    Or Mordent.

21
A Lattice Footprint

Mordent spent a second night at Marina's apartment. Twice he had slept with her, twice he had slept in her bed. At no point had those circumstances converged.

He awoke with the cat beside him. They yawned simultaneously. Stretched. Mordent's fingernails were not comparable to its claws. He scratched the cat around the ears. It nuzzled him. He imagined Marina waking up to the cat. He imagined him waking up to Marina. He wondered what might have happened if he had taken her more seriously. He wondered if she might be here.

He wondered if she might awake. Ever again.

Dark thoughts clouded his mind. Outside the weather was a mimicry. He had left the curtains open. Storm clouds gathered like street hoodies with a brooding menace. Roiling and tumbling, light flashing across the sky like a blade. The darkness was omnipresent. His thoughts rolled with the clouds, churned, coalesced. He imagined Marina standing by the bedroom doorway, pointing an accusing finger.

He didn't want her to be dead.

He got up. The cat slid off the bed, clawed a scraping tune. He needed to report Marina's disappearance. Should have done it earlier. He wasn't playing at being a detective but he was no longer a cop. Withholding information only worked in movies and cheap pulp novels.

He searched for breakfast but consigned the bread to the bin. Blue mould had increased. There were no other options. It smelt sweet, cloying with a hint of death. He coughed its memory from the back of his throat. Spat in the sink. Washed it away.

He wondered again whom Marina had been writing her dreams to. *You.* He remembered the reference to a sister, re-read it. Not a hypothetical sister – a dream sister – but a real one. She was for missing persons to trace. He didn't have the energy. As his lines of enquiry intermingled, tied knots, he became less sure of his abilities. The case was bigger than he was; he was just pissing in the wind. His only client was Mrs Mouse and the money wasn't enough. A body had been found. That should have closed his case, but he'd persisted and unravelled and wasn't going to get paid for it. He had his own bills. A smattering of other clients.

Truth was, it had started to get personal.

And when it got personal, he tended to crumble.

Keeping it cut and dried, clean, smooth, no edges. Watching it progress like a shadowplay, black and white. That was what he was about. Muxloe had it right. He aspired to the noir overtones of his employment. The basics: dames, murder, missing persons who turned out either not missing or dead. Ploughing the obvious. Stamping his image, his expectations. Taking the hard line. Yanking it through.

Injecting Marina into the mix. A dame no more than a two-night stand. It had wrong-footed him. His hand couldn't hold all the cards that were in it. It wasn't often he let personal judgments cloud his vision.

He'd had affection for Simona. Her with the heels and the bubblewrap. Yet he had shot her when he had to. A simple bullet.

He needed to be tied up again.

Just a little something to release the tension.

His thoughts rambled, were confused. That was all.

The storm needed to break.

He fed the cat.

*

Mordent found himself washing up, doing a few domestic chores. It was another way to put off the realisation there was little else that needed to be done.

Mid-morning he telephoned Missing Persons, used his history to report Marina's absence without needing to attend the station. He stressed a possible link to Davenport and Constantin. Mentioned Kovacs.

He didn't mention the notebook, but placed it in his jacket pocket, opposite his holster. He thought of cigarette cases saving lives in pre-nuclear world wars.

Outside Marina's door there was a lattice footprint.

The direction of the toe pointed towards her apartment.

He bent down. Mud that had caught in the crevices of a sole had dislodged in one section, a grid. He traced smaller particles back to the elevator. And from there down to the ground. Someone had entered the building, taken sufficient steps for the imprint to be dislodged like shaking clay out from a mould. The raised profile was like a fingerprint, but many shoes were the same. What mattered most was that it hadn't been there that evening. Someone had approached her door while he had slept.

He opened the door of her apartment again. The secret way. A reminder to find her spare key. There was no trace of mud on the inside.

Whoever it was had stopped at the door. Listened? Knocked?

They wouldn't have known he was there. Why hadn't they entered?

Or had it been him they were tailing.

Nothing made sense.

Marina had a spare set of keys in a tiny cupboard where she hung her coat. Mordent took them.

Then he went back to the landing. Took a cell phone picture of the print. Rode the elevator to the ground floor. Got in his car.

Traffic was light. No trace of a tail. As he turned into the traffic like pastry being folded over he realised there were at least three unanswered questions.

Small, but specific.

How had Patrick got off the ferry?

Who had taken a pot shot at him outside Hubie's?

Why the lattice footprint?

There were others of course. More serious questions. But Mordent found it was in the detail that the larger answers hid. Crack the small print and the rest might follow.

He had gone several blocks before he took a well-worn, little-known turn.

The side road was one-way, and like a rat in a maze he took it through several twists and turns; slowly, the metal edges of rubbish bins close to leaving silver trails on the sides of his vehicle, his wing mirrors protruding precariously at corners. Steam rose from restaurant grilles. Mordent closed his window, wary of the intermingling of smells. It was a road meant for traffic from days gone by. Or alternatively, the surrounding buildings had grown around it, squeezing the road narrower, a pencil.

On the final sharp turn, however, the road opened out into a circular car park. From the air, the layout was crop circle, from the ground it was less attractive.

Instead of golden strands of wheat the area was littered with hypodermics. An adult game of pick-up-sticks mixed with Russian roulette. Graffiti coloured the surrounding buildings, as though he were inside a panoramic 3D photograph, a modern art installation. Brown grass, killed by urine, disconsolately pushed its way through pavement cracks. A scabby hairdo.

Yet, it was all a front.

Behind the half-moon of seemingly broken apartments worked some of the highest class hookers Mordent had ever known.

What the girls who worked hotels like the Hilton and the Marmaris didn't appreciate and would greatly increase their trade was that most guys turned to whores for sleaze. It was the dangerous, out-of-the-box scenarios that added the edge. That was where the money was. And while Mordent didn't have the money, he most definitely needed the sleaze.

Even at this hour the parking area was littered with Jaguars and Mercedes. He parked up. Should have made an appointment but had decided to take the risk. In the back of his mind whirred the preference that she would be unable to see him. Knock that one on the head. His visitations were often tinged with regret, but when the urge came, it was a persistent, insistent thrumming that emanated as though through a boombox within his entire body. Rattled his heart and his lungs. Jiggered his penis. When he needed to clear his head, when he needed to think, that was when he came here. It was a remedy.

Anna was on the second floor. The exterior steps were littered with decaying leaves, the handrail was paint-worn and rusted. A smartly-dressed gent passed him, head down under hat. You didn't recognise anyone here, regardless.

He stopped at 219. Pushed the buzzer. Anna opened the door in a kimono that revealed nothing. He raised an eyebrow. She nodded.

He entered the apartment.

Anna would never be Simona. For a start, the bonds were too loose. The bubblewrap popping too mechanical. She didn't emanate the same animal power, give him the same sense of helplessness. Yet she was the only whore on this block prepared to indulge his peccadillo. Ironically, it was because it *wasn't* extreme that he could get no other takers. Bubblewrap, for many, wasn't inherently sexual. Because of that he was somehow a weirdo.

Pop pop pop.

He watched the silver point of her heels pierce each bubble. The underside of the sole was worn, a grey ghost of its former self. She had changed into a business suit. Pin-stripe, sharp creases. The straps of her shoes dug into the arches of her feet. She walked with a swing in her hips, catwalk model pose. He was naked. His penis protruding from a network of ropes, a criss-cross of shame.

He had paid for thirty minutes. Towards the end of that time she knelt down beside him, the material of her suit straining against the curvature of her body. Wrapping bubblewrap around her hand she then enclosed her fingers around his penis. Masturbated him slowly, each increase in grip causing a further pop, until he came violently, jettisoning tension.

Anna smiled. 'That's what we in the trade call a heavy cummer,' she said.

She said it every time. Said it to all of her clients, no doubt.

He waited for her to untie him. She didn't initially. Sat down on the sofa and smoked a cigarette.

The ropes were so loose he could pull himself free if he needed to. But this wasn't what he was paying for.

'I've got to tell you something, honey. Someone was asking about you. A client of a colleague.'

'A client of a colleague?'

'We double-up sometimes. You know this even if you can't afford it. I think he knew you came here, but didn't know who you visited.'

'You got a name?'

'I can't divulge it, honey.'

'You got a reason?'

'Curiosity?'

'If you're going to tell me a little you might as well tell me the lot.'

She sighed. Took a long pull on the cigarette, blew out a smoke ring. Mordent was impressed. Just before the extremities of that ring dissipated he could have jumped through it.

If he wasn't tied and immobile on the floor.

'Someone's trying to get an angle on you, honey. I'm guessing blackmail. There's a lot of it in this game, but we didn't divulge anything, of course. Bad for business.'

Mordent shifted his weight on the carpet. Without the excitement of sexual promise he was getting cold.

'So, are you going to untie me?'

Anna nodded. Stood. 'Sorry,' she said, 'I almost forgot.'

Mordent dressed. Anna seemed to be watching him dress as intently as he might watch her undress. He was no more than a john to her, but unfailingly he developed a one-sided connection with whores. The difference being that for her it was only a transaction, for him it was always more.

Was he, inside, just a softie. Or was it just need, a sense of wanting to belong? Again he thought of Maria, of Marina. Wondered what they would have thought of the previous thirty minutes. Although if Marina was psychic then she knew anyway. And while Maria wasn't psychic she might as well have been.

As he left, he kissed Anna on her lips. Something tingled inside him. She only ever kissed clients as they left, and he knew it was a pull to bring them back.

He returned to his car. His heart and his wallet feeling lighter. Yet despite the sleaze, the apartments were maintained by the girls themselves. There were no pimps here to cream off the cream. It was a legitimate business concern that benefited everyone. This is what he told himself as he opened his car door.

The exit route from the properties was also one way, along a similar road. Overgrown urban hedging edged branches along his paintwork, scratched secret names. The tops of the buildings above him appeared to converge with distorted perspective, funnelled him out of the area as if he were being repelled down the barrel of a gun. When he hit the street he was travelling too fast, swerved a left to avoid the traffic. Then he was back in the flotsam and jetsam, his time with Anna forgotten, just another day in the life of a PI.

Constantin. Constantin was his next destination. Another dollop of sleaze, but more than the veneer; right through the centre. Bad to the bone. He cut through traffic like de-coring an apple, homed in on Constantin's address. The riddle of the ages.

22
The Accusing Finger

Come mid-afternoon, as the traffic thickened in expectation of rush-hour, there was a glow on the horizon reminiscent of fireworks in fog. Mordent squinted at the reddening sky. Too early for sunset, it was as if the air itself was turning autumnal, a reflection of the leaves that scattered the ground. Yet it was also more than that. As Mordent turned off the main highway and headed towards Constantin's apartment, the breeze became peppered with ash. Black and grey spitfires twisted and turned. The building where he'd rescued Lexi Leigh was ablaze.

Mordent parked his car a good distance away. Behind him he could hear the sirens of fire engines, negotiating traffic. Yet Mordent knew there was little they could do. The remaining occupants stood outside the building, holding what few belongings they'd managed to salvage. Approaching twilight made shadows out of them, accentuated by the flickering flames. Already, they were less than what they had been. These people had had little to begin with. Now even that was being taken away.

Mordent scanned the meagre crowd for Constantin.

He had a feeling he would be found inside his apartment. Maybe with a head wound, maybe strangled. The fire was probably a cover up. Mordent never saw a fire without thinking there was arson about.

It would certainly solve a lot of people's problems. Perhaps, even, his own.

Next thing he knew he was out of his car, pushing through the crowd, bounding up the steps of the building.

The glass doors hung open, sucking in air. He held a handkerchief to his face. The ground floor ceilings were high, smoke billowed upwards, but the immediate air was breathable. He took a few gulps, assessed the situation. The stairwell seemed flame-free. He took the steps two at a time, heat in his lungs prickling their insides, tickling, daring him to cough.

Second floor: the smoke was thicker, lower to the ground. But the fire wasn't here, which was why he was in the building. From outside he had seen the flames in the floor above, knew that when covering a death through fire you avoided starting it in the apartment where the body was. It was a dummy, a double whammy. The fire a deception, its location a second one. Even so, he stumbled to the ground, crawled to where he remembered Constantin's apartment to be. The door was ajar; again, to facilitate the fire. Mordent crawled inside.

Smoke clung to the ceiling like a wraith. An open window created a breeze, whorls of grey spiralled in tiny eddies, a suffocating vortex. Mordent's eyes stung. The air was hot and thick beneath his handkerchief, which in itself wasn't particularly clean. Knowing the layout of the apartment he quickly scanned the living area. A table had been knocked over; there was no-one about. He found his way into the kitchen. Stood and ran a tap. Wet a towel and placed it over his head, then continued on his hands and knees along the hallway and into the bedroom.

The curtains here were drawn. The room was close. Smoke hadn't quite filtered in the same depth down the hallway. Constantin was on the bed. Mordent knelt beside him, reached for his wrist, felt for a pulse. None was clear. His face was in the pillow, head down. When he turned him over it was clear there was suffocation. No doubt an autopsy would prove there was no smoke in the lungs, but there had to be a body for there to be an autopsy. And to be sure of that, Mordent had to get him out of the building.

Constantin was of only average build, but Mordent wasn't fit. And to carry him meant standing. He took three swift gulps of air at floor level, rolled Constantin off the bed and onto his back and tried to rise. It wasn't happening. Constantin slipped onto the floor, a dead weight.

Mordent held the man's flaccid arms, tried to hook them around his neck, but there was no purchase. He sat the body up, grabbed Constantin under his armpits. Pulled backwards. Pain spread along the base of Mordent's back. He slumped to the floor. Wasn't going to get Constantin out that way. Tendrils of smoke fingered their way through the door, darkened the room. There was something not right with it, something sweet. The only way was out. Mordent stood, pulled wide the filthy curtains and opened the window.

Cool air assaulted his face, make him cough. He sucked in mouthfuls, realised how clogged he had become. From here he could see the lights of the fire engines, recently parked, strobing the area with a blue intensity. As he raised Constantin up, propping him against the windowsill, the blue gave the dead body's face a pallid glow. Its eyes refracted the light; an imitation of life.

But there was no life there. And when Mordent

hefted the body over the windowsill and it plummeted to the ground, the screams that came from below were totally unnecessary.

*

A crime scene is a crime scene.

Once the flames had dispersed the area was striated with yellow and black tape. A redundant chalk outline delineated where Constantin's body had fallen. The body itself was on a gurney, covered with a sheet and waiting by an ambulance with its engine ticking over.

Mordent had watched the body land. It had bucked the ground, as though the earth had risen up to meet it, attempted to cushion the fall. Constantin's right arm had extended in that movement, the fingers splayed outwards, almost pointing. As if in accusation.

Mordent had gulped more air and returned to the floor. Crawled his way out of the apartment and stumbled down the stairs. Now he sat near the ambulance, a grey blanket over his shoulders. A few remaining residents milled about. He imagined they had nowhere else to go. Possibly, once the fire engines had dispersed, they would flip themselves under the warning tape and head back to their apartments. Likely most of them were squatters, anyway.

'You did a stupid thing,' one of the firemen said. 'Who goes into a burning building to rescue a dead body?'

Mordent's voice crackled like burnt paper. 'Evidence.' His throat was raw.

'Could have gotten yourself killed.'

Mordent knew it. Couldn't answer. Wasn't sure if it had been worth the risk. But if it could be proven

Constantin was killed before the fire was started then the police had something to work with. He had no allegiance to Constantin, but the man might have a mother somewhere. Mordent once had a mother somewhere, too.

There was a campfire stench to his clothing. Again, the smell of something sweet. He knew he should be able to place it. Couldn't. His head was frazzled. As the fire trucks left they were replaced by police vehicles. He returned the blanket, had a few words with one of the officers he recognised and voiced his suspicions about Constantin.

'Ignore the broken back.'

He tried to laugh, but it caught in his throat and he coughed violently. Thick sputum jettisoned into the darkness. He cleared his throat, coughed and spat again. It hurt.

'You need to get home, buddy. Get some rest.'

Mordent shrugged.

'Seriously. We can take your statement another day. It's not that we don't know who you are.'

The accompanying smile was friendly, reassuring, but Mordent was spent.

He raised a hand. Sat inside his car. Closed his eyes.

Clouds of smoke rolled behind his eyelids, forced them open.

When he coughed, a key appeared in his hand.

He looked for the bus stop but it had disappeared. Constantin stood there, waving, his arm around his brother. His dead brother.

When Mordent looked down there was a duck at his feet. The white plumage impossibly bright.

He blinked and it changed to a peacock, multi-eyed. Blinked again and it was a robin. Again, a raven.

The bird flew. He watched it soar over Constantin's head, circle in the air then disappear out of sight. Not into the distance, but out of sight.

His fingertips were warm. He looked down. Saw smoke emerging from under his fingernails, pulling grit from them as they did so, leaving them clean.

He put a finger into his mouth. Blew on it. Smoke came out of his ears. He was laughing.

Laughing, then coughing. Dirty grey smoke buffeted out of his body, billowed out of his mouth, his nose, his anus. Then he was choking. Choking on the fresh air that surrounded him.

It was clean. Ice stretched into the distance. Sparkling. At first he thought he saw a skater, but it became a polar bear. It was hard to tell if it was getting closer or further away. Or making a circle of eight.

He banged on the window of the car.

He banged on the window of the car.

He banged on the window of the car.

He banged on the window of the car.

He coughed again, violently.

Someone was banging on the window of his car.

He fumbled for the handle. Unlocked it. Fell out sideways, his legs twisting under the pedals. Someone held him.

*

Mason, the cop he had spoken to previously, explained about the marijuana that had been under the bed.

'You took a trip.'

Mordent's head felt it was encased in bubblewrap.

He wanted to sleep but he was being walked around, in a circle like a circus horse. His legs came back to him slowly. Feeling returned to his fingers. His feet, which dragged on the broken tarmac, began to pick up.

'You should go to the hospital, buddy. Get yourself checked out.'

Mordent mumbled something he wasn't sure he understood.

'You were in a bad way there.' Mason gesticulated to the car. 'Banging your head against the window.'

Mordent reached up a hand, could just feel the raised surface of a bruise under desensitised fingertips.

'My daughter told me you lose sixty brain cells every time you bang your head. She's eleven. We wrestle. She slaps my head each time she says it.' Mason smiled. It appeared wonky, then Mordent's sight refocused and it shifted back into place.

'Keep on swimming, just keep swimming.'

Mason was getting annoying.

'Hey!' Mordent grunted, forced himself away from Mason's grip and sat on the floor. It rose with him, like a magic carpet. Hovered two inches above ground. Then settled.

He sat bolt upright. Took deep breaths.

Mason crouched beside him.

'You know,' he said, 'they still talk about it on the force. What you did with Kovacs. That slap.'

Mordent nodded.

'We'd all like to do that, sometimes.'

Mordent spoke. His tongue thick in his mouth. 'That was a long time ago. He's not bad, just different.'

Mason nodded.

'As I say, they still talk about it. You know what I'm saying?'

Mordent knew. It meant his past successes overcame his recent failures. But a man was only as good as his last action.

'You sure you don't want to hitch a ride in the ambulance, buddy.'

Mordent nodded. Stubborn.

'Sit it out here a bit.'

He sat.

*

When it got too cold he returned to his car.

The engine started first time.

There was no reason for it not to.

His thinking was still strained. As though his mind was a pair of tights tied over the end of a drainpipe. His father filtered rainwater that way, ensured debris didn't get into the water butt. But instead of the clear water being the focus, his mind was blocked by the fabric of the tights.

Nevertheless, he drove.

Constantin's death played on his mind. He had expected it. Had assumed Kovacs might have allocated some protection. Constantin had been the living link to Bataille. Proving he had been murdered wasn't as good as having him alive.

Traffic horns blared when he changed lanes. His reflexes a star jump behind everyone else's. He pressed on. Wanted to get home. To get sleep. But he wasn't surprised when he pulled up outside Marina's. Her home was more home than his, nowadays.

He remained outside her apartment. The warmth of his car a buffer against the clear night sky. Gradually, his senses were returning, like college kids' after a fraternity party. But even with clarity his thoughts were jumbled. Constantin's accusing finger almost poked his eye out.

There were those he let down because he had promised to help but couldn't.

There were those he let down for whom he felt responsible but shouldn't.

Then there were those he let down.

He shrugged. Left the car. Ascended the stairs to Marina's apartment. The lattice footprint had gone.

As soon as he entered he knew something had changed.

He stood with his back to the door. Flicked on the main light. From here he could see the door to the bedroom but not inside. From here he could see half of the kitchen.

What was it?

It was more than the cat.

There was something else.

He unholstered his gun.

His back to the wall, he traversed the outlines of the apartment. All was quiet.

The doorway to the bedroom was a night-time yawn, all black and open. It reminded him of a girlfriend, he no longer remembered her name, who always wanted to make love in the dark. Once, when he'd switched on the light out of curiosity, he'd seen the delineated mark of a scar he'd already traversed with his tongue. She'd screamed at him, called him names; eventually thrown him out. But for him, it had made no difference. The scar had been entirely incidental and always would have been.

Always.

Always was a very long time.

There was no-one alive in the apartment.

He turned on the light.

She lay like a flamenco dancer. One arm arced over her head, the curve bridging her hair that fanned cilia-like on the pillow, the other a mirror-opposite across her belly, as though she were cradling the lost child that would never grow inside her womb.

The remains of the cat were strewn alongside her.

An outstretched paw. An accusing claw.

23
Dissecting The N

Mordent sat on the bed. His head in his hands.

Chased a disappeared pulse.

Uncharacteristically he leant over her body. Kissed her forehead. Remembered her dreams.

There was so much about her he didn't know. Maybe hadn't wanted to know. But nevertheless never would know.

She had wanted to tell him something.

Another unknown.

He tried not to look at the cat.

Maybe because it was the cat he felt most upset about.

He rose from the bed, took a look around the rest of the apartment. No signs of a disturbance, nothing missing.

This was a warning. For him.

He picked up the phone. Dialled police. Reported a murder.

If Muxloe and Bataille were interested in immortality they had a funny way of showing it.

He watched from the window. The night sky sparkled clear, the stars a reflection of the neon signs on the street; headlights, traffic lights. He thought of all the stars that couldn't be seen due to light pollution. Camouflage for the nature generation. Sequins on a dark blue cushion, pinprick flesh through stretched black leggings, bubbles rising in a bottle of bourbon, cats' eyes unblinking in night-time photography. The stars we couldn't see.

The stars we couldn't see but those we should be able to see. If it wasn't for man's presence on the Earth.

Analogies abounded but he wasn't having any of them. He could be maudlin all he wanted, but it brought none of them back.

Even if he disappeared into the night, sometime it would be daylight.

You couldn't escape into noir nor could you escape from noir.

And if you embraced it, then you had to take the rough with the smooth.

He shook his head. This was the closest he came to emotion. The realisation that all his efforts were redundant.

After fifteen minutes of looking out into the night he heard a knock on the door. Turning back to the apartment his eyes still saw the dark, a negative version of looking at the sun and then finding a retinal imprint. Shadows surged across the room, blackness permeated the surroundings, sank into objects like ink, discoloured everything.

He stopped feeling sorry for himself. If this was how they wanted to play it, then this would be the way *he* played it.

Kovacs headed the cortege. He put a hand on Mordent's shoulder. Told him to sit down and placed an officer with him. The team followed like a shoal of fish, filling the empty space, pouring life into the apartment. Quiet life. Conversation was minimal except for Kovacs' barked orders.

Mordent was numb but it was no longer from the marijuana.

It seemed like an age before Kovacs sat beside him.

'Two deaths in one night. This is exceptional, even for you.'

'Nail it Kovacs.'

'Just doing my job Mordent.'

'Your career is littered with dead bodies.'

'Not just mine.'

Kovacs looked around at the white-suited forensic team in the bedroom. 'Rather my job than theirs.'

'I haven't touched anything.'

Kovacs sighed. 'I'm sure your fingerprints will be all over this apartment. Sweet on her, were you?'

Mordent shrugged. 'We had something. But it didn't last.'

'You reported her missing this morning. From this number.'

'I did.'

'When did she go missing? I'm guessing you made your own enquiries.'

'A few days ago. I put that in the report.'

Kovacs nodded. 'Yes, you did.'

'I think Muxloe or Bataille are mixed up in this.'

'Tell me what they aren't mixed up in.'

Mordent picked up a salt shaker from the table. Turned it in his hands.

'I need to be doing something.'

'Sounds to me like you've done plenty this evening, Mordent. Rescued a dead body from a burning building, taken a trip, discovered this ...'

Mordent slammed the shaker onto the table. Damp salt encrusted around the dispenser shook out. Kovacs reached for it, picked some up in his fingers and threw it over his left shoulder.

'Frustrating, isn't it.'

Mordent growled, 'I didn't know you were superstitious.'

'There's more to me than you think, Mordent. Multi-faceted. That's me. Not one dimensional.'

'Like me?'

'I didn't say that.'

Mordent sighed. 'It's all just routine to you, isn't it?'

'It's all just routine to you, Mordent. Just sometimes you get too close to the fire.'

Kovacs smiled. Added: 'Literally.'

Mordent grunted. 'You established a cause of death for Constantin yet?'

Kovacs shook his head. 'Early days.'

Mordent nodded towards the bedroom. 'And in there?'

'You saw for yourself. Bluish marks around the neck. Looks like strangulation to me.'

For some reason Mordent thought of BuzzCut. And Robbie Constantin.

'Tell me something, Kovacs. What do you think of immortality?'

Kovacs laughed. A rare sight. 'What is this? Harking back to my theory of Zeno? That's a long time in the past. I was green.'

Mordent ran a hand through his hair. 'Just tell me what you think now.'

'Well, there's a difference, isn't there. Between immortality and invulnerability. Then you've got the problem of ageing. Let's face it, it's not scientifically possible.'

'I know.'

'So, where are you going with this? You caught some of what Constantin caught?'

'I dunno. What did he catch?'

Kovacs stood. 'I haven't got time for a round the houses conversation. It's late. I suggest you go home and get a good night's sleep. But we'll need a statement. There might be implications.'

'I didn't kill her.'

'And are we charging you? No. Go to sleep and get to it. Everything's always brighter in the morning.'

Mordent left. He knew most mornings weren't bright. They were dull.

*

He didn't sleep.

Or if he did, he didn't dream.

Faces and names ran through his head. His bed felt alien. It was all wrong. It had been wrong from the start, from the moment Mrs Mouse had entered his office. From the moment Marina had picked him up in the bar. Was it Virginia Woolf who had said life was made up of perfect moments? The opposite was the truth.

He needed facts. Not intangibles. And what he was holding was a list of intangibles.

Being a PI was different from being a cop. He didn't have back up. He needed resources, rather than scraps of information. The frustration was building; like standing in a post office queue. Something needed to be done.

When his phone rang, the last person he expected to hear was Maria.

Her voice was soft, a memory of better days.

'Hello.'

He recognised her instantly. Sat up in bed. The cover rolling away from his torso like surf.

'Maria?'

'Yes.'

Silence weighed between them. He couldn't speak.

'I know it's been a long time. Can I see you?'

'Yes.' The word was out of his mouth before he knew it.

He could almost feel her smiling down the phone. A certain smile.

'Whenabouts? Today?'

He nodded. Realised what he was doing, and said *yes* again.

They arranged to meet at his office. She knew that he was busy.

Hanging up the phone made him realise how much he loved her.

Yet the feelings of love were confusing.

He couldn't gruff it out.

Was there a twisted logic that had drawn him to Marina through the simple dislocation of an *N*? He wasn't prepared to discount it.

Suddenly the morning was clearer. Maria was due at eleven. He imagined lunch. There was that Chinese that delivered. Singapore chow mein and a pancake roll seemed pretty appetising, almost breakfast food. He whistled: a slow, long tune that he hadn't heard before. His shirt seemed extra starched, snow white. Even his gun felt comfortable against his ribs. Outside the skies were clear, a pale blue that illuminated the condensation on his windowpane.

Sometimes, even when it was all wrong, it was all right.

What had Marina been, after all, than a few shots in the sack? The projected relationship had been only his imagination, moving images on a cinema screen. But with Maria, he had already been to the flicks.

Traffic was light on the way to his office. He wound down the window, his elbow nudging outside, air on his face, fingers gracing the steering wheel. The entire expanse of the world opened up in front of him, a cornucopia of choice. Days like this were rare. Those when you could eschew the detritus – when even the shit didn't matter. It wasn't all Maria however; he knew it was Marina too.

Nothing brought down a man as much as the desire of a needy woman.

Marina's death was his freedom.

Those hard facts were often the worst to acknowledge.

He still had her key in his pocket.

*

He kicked the morning over in his office. Watched an episode of *The Simpsons* online. Shuffled a few files. Googled immortality but knew he wouldn't find the answers he was looking for.

Mid-morning he combed his hair, watching his faint reflection in the windowpane.

Memories came two ways. Disparate, dreamlike, unreal. Or wholesale. He could no longer remember how he and Maria had separated. Distance shoehorned between them. Physical. Mental. One moment she was there, the next gone.

The next moment she was there.

A gentle rap on the door. Recognisable perfume. A warm embrace.

'How are you?' he asked.

'I'm good, good.' She smoothed down the cotton material of her skirt before she sat. Smiled at him. 'How are you?'

He shrugged. 'Surrounded by confusion and dead bodies.'

'Ever the dramatist!'

He didn't know what to make of her. The eighteen months they had been apart didn't show. Her soft black hair curled at her lobes. Lipstick red. Cheeks pale. Eyelids lined and fluttering. She was always down to earth, but she was coming up again. A second wind. Maybe that was why she was here.

'I'm serious,' he said. 'Four murders, same case. Although I don't know if there is a case. What do you think about immortality?'

'It wouldn't suit you,' she said. Laughed.

He found himself smiling. 'Shall I order in Chinese?'

'Same old, same old.' But there was affection, not disparagement. 'If you want. I'll have sweet and sour chicken.'

Mordent made the call. Once he had done so the moments passed slowly, as though the conversation was stymied until the food arrived. He broke the silence.

'This case,' he said. And he told her all about it.

Their food was delivered. He tipped the chow mein out of the aluminium container as though he were building a sandcastle. Some of it was gritty. His pancake roll sweated steam as he cracked the surface, the bean sprouts hot and moist, crunchy in his mouth. Maria ate slowly, savouring instead of shovelling. Yet as Mordent ate he found he couldn't remember his last meal.

'Seems to me,' she said, 'that you need a woman's intuition.'

'Tell me about it.'

'Why don't you leave it to the police?'

Mordent chewed his lip.

'The only money you're getting out of this is from the Davenport mother, right?'

Mordent nodded.

'And it's not enough, is it?'

Mordent kept silent. He wondered if this was why they had split up. Maria was more direct than any other woman he knew.

'There's a code,' he said finally. 'Call it honour, call it what you will, but you don't leave something unfinished.'

'How about us? Are we unfinished?'

'You know we are.'

Maria picked a piece of chicken from her teeth. 'What if I came back?'

'What's stopping you?'

'You were a bachelor for far too long. That was the problem.'

'I was never sure there was a problem.'

'And you're scared of strong women.'

'These are facts?'

'That should be a statement, not a question.'

Mordent finished his meal. Felt bloated. 'Are you going to help me with this case or not?'

Maria laughed. The sound of it caught him unawares. As though he had just woken up beside her.

'Is that all you want me for?'

'No.'

He stood. Moved around to her side of the desk. Bent his head and kissed her sweet and sour mouth.

The last woman he had kissed was dead. He didn't tell her this.

They lingered. The kiss was hard and soft simultaneously.

As he tried to pull away she pulled him back.

'I've missed you,' she said, once they separated.

'I've missed you.'

'So,' she said. 'Immortality.'

'Yes,' he said. 'Immortality.'

24

The Immortalists

When Maria left they kissed again.

It wasn't as good. But it was good enough.

He told her to remain in her apartment. That she shouldn't move in with him until everything was sorted. Until the heat had blown over.

Maria had worked out how Patrick had left the ferry. It was a hunch he was prepared to gamble on. She had also had ideas on how tit for tat had escalated. He needed her insight; although when she had said she was the cat to his Hong Kong Phooey he had laughed it off. She had blamed it on the Chinese food.

So. Tit for tat. All he had to do was decide who to see first. Bataille or Muxloe.

Bataille was closer.

His lips were still humming when he started his engine. They resonated through the vehicle, along the chassis, the windows, the doors, the pedals. They started his engine without him turning the key. The first couple of miles he ran petrol free.

The road undulated like a flexed muscle underneath his vehicle. If the night was a black panther then the day was a different beast. The city was a tiger come to life. All colour and camouflage. Suddenly he could sense the urgency and determination of the populace. On the surface of it, they were grey faces, making the daily plod into work. He could always see the scum under the veneer, the dirt under the fingernails, the mould at the bottom of the windowsill. Yet today he could also see the drive, the purpose, the need for work as a benefactor of food and shelter. The persistent strive for survival. Today, it was admirable. Not to be despised.

Regardless of whether the city sucked it out of you.

And the homeless, the bums, they too were provided for by charitable organisations, social security. Sure, they were on the edge, addicts and wastrels the lot of them, but a safety net was there should they choose to clamber into it. And like the sinewy beast that moved with stealth and purpose, so the city carried everyone with it, to the good of the city, to the heart of its people.

And Mordent was part of the tiger, riding shotgun to weed out prey. To keep the city streets clean. To rehabilitate those who wanted out of the scheme of things. Not to remove them completely – unless their sense of self-destruction gave him no other choice – but to imprison them within the belly until such time as their time was done.

If the city streets ran with blood it was cleansing, leeched.

He parked up outside Big Cake, where BuzzCut had taken him to see Bataille. The interior office had indicated it was Bataille's main base. A good place to start, if nowhere else.

As he entered the store, one of the girls serving caught his eye. He walked over to the counter, selected a vanilla slice, took it from her.

'Thanks. Say, is Bataille here today?'

The girl gave him a look. Her long eyelashes were accentuated. He suspected they were false.

Mordent touched the side of his nose. 'He knows me.'

The girl looked from side to side. All the other operatives were busy. Maybe she wanted a manager, some reassurance. Then, taking the initiative and looking pleased about it, she walked around the side of the counter and led Mordent to the security-coded door. She punched in the numbers.

'Follow me.'

He watched her ass as she ascended the stairs. Her starched white uniform delineating a skimpy pantyline. He deliberated whether to comment, but Muxloe was right, too much noir-speak came out of his mouth for this world. Just patting it would be a sexual offence.

They traversed the long corridor in silence. He could smell her perfume mixed with fresh bread, cream. The bread provided the base note, the vanilla essence the top note. Tufts of blonde hair curled where her mesh hat touched her neck. He wanted to kiss her there, to have her melt in his arms. The feeling was transitory, but it was as real as day. By the time they reached the end of the corridor he was panting.

'Wait here,' she said. Her voice a sexy saline drip.

She knocked and slipped inside. Mordent pressed his ear to the door. Couldn't discern a conversation. After a moment the door opened and she slipped out. He could see Weasel-Face over her shoulder. For his benefit as much as his own, Mordent did pat the girl's ass as she returned down the corridor. She gave him a look of astonishment that wasn't quite tinged with a smile.

Then he entered Bataille's office.

He was seated behind his desk as before. An average room for an average-looking man. This time his secretary wasn't in sight. It was probably for the best.

Weasel-Face stood behind Mordent, blocking the exit, as he approached the desk.

'Ah, Mr Mordent. An unexpected pleasure.'

'Less of a pleasure for me, Bataille. More of a necessity.'

Bataille gestured for him to sit down. 'I see you wish to dispense with the pleasantries. Very well, why are you here?'

'I want some answers to some questions.'

'And I would give you these because ...?'

'Because you don't want any trouble. And I can make trouble. A lot of trouble. If I want to.'

Bataille sat up. His eyes were hard. 'I assure you, Mr Mordent, I answer to no-one. And I can also make a lot of trouble. A lot of trouble for you.'

'The thing is,' Mordent continued, 'I don't have anything to lose. But you do. I'm not police, you know this, and it won't be long before the police know what I know and won't be far behind me. But it's not you I want. It's Muxloe. You give me Muxloe and I can mess things up enough that you won't have to get involved. I know Muxloe was behind the killing of Marina Gonzales and I want to nail him for it.'

Bataille returned to a more comfortable position, but he didn't look comfortable. He made a triangle with his fingers, opposing digits touching. 'Am I supposed to know who Marina Gonzales is?'

'You tell me. I'm not suggesting you implicate yourself in anything you don't have a part of. I'm here to talk about Constantin and the Davenport boy.'

'Isn't this a conversation we've already had?'

'Last time you had a conversation with me. This time I'm having the conversation with you.'

'And the last I heard, Constantin was dead.'

'You have anything to do with that?'

Bataille raised his eyebrows. 'Constantin was my man.'

'So was his brother, Robbie. According to Constantin, you killed him.'

Bataille raised his hands. 'Do I look like a strangler?'

'You don't. But I didn't say he was strangled either.'

Bataille shrugged. 'I read the police reports.'

'I'm sure you do. And you know what I'm saying. Constantin was a witness to his brother's death.'

'On your reckoning, Mr Mordent, he was a witness who held his breath for over four years. Doesn't seem opportune that I should dispose of him now, does it?'

'His brother's body had only recently been found. Rubs salt into old wounds, doesn't it.'

'Possibly. What are you trying to hang on me?'

'Constantin told me that you – or someone in your employ – strangled Robbie. Constantin's dead. I'm not. That's my angle.'

'And you come here to trade information, to bribe me in order to get Muxloe. Is that it?'

'I know you dumped Robbie's body in Muxloe's container, and you know you got the Davenport boy in return. Logic suggests Davenport was killed by Muxloe's goons – although a few years ago. How come you're both storing dead bodies? Doesn't make sense to me.'

'But this third body, the Gonzales woman. Was she killed years ago?'

'She was killed last night. A psychic trusted by the police. She indicated to them the whereabouts of Davenport. Puts you in the frame, don't you think?'

Bataille's eyes were cool again. 'If I were put in the frame for every dead body in this city I'd already be dead myself. You seem to think my businesses underhand, but you've got one of my cakes in that bag. Doesn't that make you complicit in any theoretical illegal activity?'

Mordent had forgotten about the cake. He pulled it out of the bag. Some of the icing had stuck to the sides. He bit into the pastry and cream oozed sideways in both directions. He licked around it. Bit again. Licked again. Finished the cake and sucked on his fingers.

'I have no complaints about the cake.'

Bataille nodded, vaguely amused. Yet a frown ploughed across his forehead.

'You say I'm in the frame, but you believe it was Muxloe. Why?'

'Because Muxloe has more balls to pull this off than you. You're a two-bit crook with your finger in more than a few literal and theoretical pies, but Muxloe is the one who wields the greater influence. Just look at his funding of the college science programme for example. All the money he's pouring into immortality research, while all you can do is hire a buzz-cut goon fresh out of security at a laboratory.'

The air in the room seemed to increase a few degrees. Mordent could hear Weasel-Face shuffling around behind him. Just waiting for an opportunity, for a sign. Mordent held Bataille's gaze.

'We hang this murder on Muxloe, that's going to put a serious dent in his reputation. The college isn't going to like it.'

'You couldn't place him there.'

'No. But one of his goons was there the previous day. His fingerprints will be all over the joint. I know because I caught him. But what's to say he wasn't there later? There's only me who knows what time he left the building, what day he left the building.'

Bataille sighed. 'This has been very amusing, but I don't see how I'm supposed to assist in the implication of Muxloe.'

'Straightforward to me. You also implicate him in the death of Constantin. Double whammy.'

Bataille raised his average eyebrows on his average face.

'I was there when Muxloe's men picked up Constantin, remember? For all I know that's the last he was seen alive. All you have to do is admit that Robbie Constantin was murdered on your turf. That's the deal.'

Bataille laughed. 'You're confusing me.'

Mordent smiled. 'You unravel it.'

Bataille was ahead of him. 'You want a fall guy.'

'BuzzCut, Derby Boy, whatever you call him.'

'He wasn't in my employ at that time.'

'But he could have been.'

'I don't see how.'

'Look, no fall guy and you're implicated in the deaths of Constantin and possibly Gonzales. It's not you I want. Muxloe is going to fall for those and I don't really care who is responsible. We can swing it for Muxloe, but Derby Boy has to go. Capiche?'

Bataille stood. 'I really don't see why I should go along with any of this.'

'Because I'm the only person who knows you killed Constantin's brother.'

Bataille roared, 'But you're asking me to admit to Robbie's murder.'

'Figure it out.' Mordent stood. 'When the police come, admit Robbie was killed on your premises but say you only just found out about it. Blame it on Derby Boy, or Constantin himself, I don't really care. You take that blow and I'll make sure Muxloe falls for the other murders. Whichever one of you did them. Think of the business opportunities it would free up.'

He turned and walked to the door. Weasel-Face stood his ground, until evidently Bataille motioned behind him and he moved aside. Mordent didn't look back.

He continued down the corridor. Expected the door to open behind him. Wondered if the corridor was soundproofed. But he made the stairs without event, and latterly the warmth of the cake shop. He looked around for the girl, but she was gone.

He hoped he had confused Bataille as much as he had confused himself. Bataille was right. It didn't make sense. He didn't want it to. If it made sense then Bataille would know what he was working with and ease himself out. The best way to make a rat strike was to corner it. A confused rat struck randomly, then ran. He wanted Bataille to run and he wanted to see where he ran. Maybe that way, he would get some answers.

It might also rattle the cage of BuzzCut too.

That was part of the advice Maria had given. Bang their heads together. Knock the biscuit on the table and watch the weevils run out.

He sat in his car for a few minutes. There was no obvious movement inside the shop, other than the usual press of customers and staff alike. So he hit the gas and headed out of the city. There were two players in this game, and he had an appointment with the second that certainly wasn't going to be by e-mail.

*

He was there within the hour. Traffic was sparse as if it knew something he didn't. The wind had picked up, leaves skydived with parachutes tangled, twigs scattered without purpose on the highway. Driving over them sounding like fingers breaking.

At the wrought iron gates Girl-Voice cooed his way through the intercom.

'It's Mordent. I need to see Muxloe now.'

'I think you'll find Mr Muxloe is indisposed, perhaps ...'

'Listen. It's the organ grinder I'm after, not his monkey. Run the name Gonzales by him. He'll want to see me.'

After a short pause the gates began their mechanical opening and Mordent tore through, inches from damaging his wing mirrors.

It was all show.

When he parked, small stones flipped an arc like Chinese gymnasts. Girl-Voice was waiting at the entrance, nonchalant and demure. He led him down a different corridor, past the room where Mordent had seen Hammerton, an alternate twist and turn, a buck of the trend. More doors were open, more opulence. A girl who seemed stoned lay semi-clothed on a table, rolling like a lioness. A languid man in another room drew on a cigarette in a holder. It was as though Muxloe had amassed a cast of freaks and throwbacks. If Mordent lived in the '50s, then Muxloe was in the '20s.

At the end of a T-junction they turned right. Another short corridor, another set of double-doors. It was all wood-panelled and polished. It stank of money and something else. A modicum of indecency.

Muxloe was standing when he entered. He seemed taller that way. Girl-Voice closed the doors behind them softly. Mordent imagined him lingering, an ear to the door, a hand over the gun that was no doubt pocketed and cocked.

'This is getting boring.'

Muxloe's voice was drawn. There was a trace of impatience, but also unease. Mordent knew he had been expected. Mordent knew Muxloe wasn't sure why.

'Nietzsche said that to ward off boredom at any cost is vulgar,' said Mordent.

Muxloe snorted. 'I don't expect you to be quoting Nietzsche.'

'Always expect the unexpected. Oscar Wilde.'

'You're wasting my time. Why are you here?'

Mordent walked up to the desk. Leant over it and opened the right-hand drawer. Took a sweet.

The wrapper crackled like a dry leaf in his hand. He pulled at the edges and the sweet was uncovered. He popped it into his mouth. Lemon.

He tried to keep a straight face with the sour taste.

'I think you know why I'm here.'

Muxloe threw up his hands. 'Again the noir-speak, trying to draw the truth out of me when you don't really know it yourself. Isn't that what detective fiction is all about – the cop or PI as a cipher for the story? Not actually discovering anything, just uncovering? Well this isn't fiction, Mordent, and I'm not a caricature willing to play those games.'

Mordent sucked slowly. 'There are four bodies,' he said, 'that I'm interested in.'

Muxloe's brow furrowed. 'Four?'

'Constantin and his brother. That's two. The Davenport boy that you dumped on Bataille. That's three. And the other one. The other one is Marina Gonzales. You know her?'

'I know that you were sniffing around after her whereabouts the other day. Believed some goon employed by me was involved. For which I sent you away with a flea in your ear.'

'That's not quite how I remember it.'

'I'm not interested in how you remember it, Mordent. I'm interested in fact.'

'Go ahead. Fact me.'

'I'm a man of integrity, Mordent, despite what you think. And a man of order. Fact one: the body of Robbie Constantin was dumped on us and was duly reported to the police. You're not pinning that on me. Fact two: this Davenport boy was not found on our property. Maybe Bataille dumped it to look like revenge. Who knows the mind of that twisted fool? Fact three: Constantin died in a fire, as I understand. Fire kills, Mordent. Another fact. Fact four: I still don't know who the Gonzales woman is. That's all there is to it.'

'The Gonzales name got me in at the gate.'

'I got you in to get rid of you. Seemed easier that way.'

Mordent cracked the sweet between his teeth. Inside was a sour goo. Released fumes penetrated his throat. He coughed.

Muxloe smiled. 'Cough sweets, Mordent. They replaced my cigars a while back.'

Mordent swirled saliva around the inside of his mouth, tempered the taste, regained some composure, aware that his face had reddened and a vein stood out on his neck.

He swallowed.

'Here are the facts as I see them, Muxloe. Fact one: Bataille killed Robbie Constantin, of that there is no doubt. Fact two: you arranged for the death of the Davenport boy because he wasn't willing to play your immortality game. Fact three: Bataille killed Constantin because he was a witness to his brother's death. Despite the years that had passed, he felt he could no longer trust him. Fact four: Bataille killed Gonzales. You want to know who she was? A psychic who had ascertained information valuable to the police. I get the feeling both you and Bataille were after that information, but he got there first because he's smarter than you. Whatever: I'm not interested in that. I'm interested in nailing Bataille. You assist me with that, and I'll ensure nothing will stick on you.'

'Sounds to me you've got it all figured out.'

Mordent shrugged. 'That's how it falls into place.'

'You've got nothing to link me to the Davenport boy.'

'Maybe nothing hard. But I've got Hammerton and I've got Sue Sweeney. I've seen the photos.'

Muxloe nodded. Took a sweet out and unwrapped it. Was thoughtful.

'I knew I shouldn't have trusted the Hammerton kid.'

'Leave him alone. I found him, he didn't find me. Besides, you deserve each other. He's got the same morals, deep down.'

'You have me at a disadvantage over the photographs. But you still can't link me to the Davenport death. I would respectfully suggest that's a matter for the police.'

'This is the deal. I can pin Robbie's death on Bataille and his cronies. Constantin gave me enough info for that to stick. Whether it was you or Bataille who arranged Constantin's death is immaterial: Bataille had more of a motive than you. The sticking point is Gonzales. I'm sure I could identify the goon who was at her apartment, and I'm sure he could identify you. I keep quiet about that and the rest is easy. You just have to own up to the death of the Davenport boy.'

Muxloe almost laughed. The sweet rattled in his mouth as his tongue made an attempt to stop it. 'And why on earth should I do that?'

Mordent leant on the desk. 'Sue Sweeney. I have the photos.'

'And ...'

'I'm sure you can be identified. Rape isn't a charge you want hanging round your neck, is it Muxloe? Certainly not the rape of a student into whose faculty you've been pouring money over the past few years.'

Muxloe snorted. 'I hardly think framing me for a murder makes it any less a charge than rape. I'll take my chances, Mordent. You've got nothing on me.'

'Think it over.' Mordent turned to go. Turned back: 'Think over what I know and how it can be used. Think over the advantage you'd have with Bataille out of the way. We're all after our own slice of immortality, aren't we?'

'Again with the teaser, again with the nuance. You don't know anything.'

'I know how Davenport got off that ferry,' Mordent said, his voice level.

'Sure you do,' Muxloe retorted. But there he wavered and Mordent knew it.

'I'll see myself out.'

Mordent opened the double doors. Girl-Voice was but a hop, skip and jump away down the corridor. He might well have done that. By the time Mordent reached him he had only then regained his breath.

'Guys with ears your size tend to end up wearing concrete overcoats,' Mordent said.

Girl-Voice reflexively reached a hand to the side of his head. Lowered it. 'This way.'

'I can find my own way,' Mordent grunted.

'My apologies, but that wouldn't be permitted,' Girl-Voice insisted. 'You must be escorted off the premises.'

'Maybe Muxloe's afraid of what door I might put

my head through,' Mordent said. 'Of what I might or might not see.'

'This way,' Girl-Voice reiterated. He strode ahead, Mordent followed behind.

They walked in silence, retraced their steps. The languid guy was no longer smoking a cigarette, the stoned girl had disappeared. It was as though their decadent traces had been erased, a little too late for Mordent not to have seen them.

They stopped at the entrance. Mordent turned to look back at the corridor. It stretched away like the interior of a long beast. Girl-Voice was itching to go. Mordent held him longer.

'You trust your employer?'

'Naturally.'

'Wouldn't think he'd frame you for anything? Murder, perhaps?'

'Of course not.'

Mordent nodded. 'Of course not.' He moved over to his car. 'Be seeing you.'

He didn't have to be psychic to know what Girl-Voice was thinking.

He drove back down the drive, looked out for squirrels but could see none. Soon they would be hibernating. He had caught Muxloe and Bataille on the verge of that same hibernation. Keeping their heads low until the heat blew over. No doubt Kovacs would be heading his own investigation but would be tied with red tape and doing things correctly. From experience, Mordent knew the right way didn't always reveal the right answers. Those who knew the system would know their way around it. He didn't have a system. Unlike Tinkerbelle who had faith, trust and pixie dust, he had subterfuge, fear and insinuation. One of those usually pulled the carpet hard enough for someone to take a dive.

Maria's notion of how Davenport had left the ferry was simple. He hadn't.

At least, not until later. Chloroform. Strong arm. Hiding place. These were all possibilities. He wondered if the police had examined the CCTV footage on the days after the date of his disappearance.

It still didn't explain why the body had surfaced three years later.

Puzzle. Edges. Sky. Trees.

All that was needed now were the people and their positions.

Then he could bring down the immortals.

But before that, he needed a drink.

25
Conspiracy Theories

Morgan's Bar was caught between afternoon and evening drinkers when he arrived. The comings and goings resembled revolving doors. He eased himself onto his usual seat, his outstretched hand curling round an imaginary drink even before he put in his order. Morgan was wiping a glass with an off-white cloth. He nodded to Mordent and poured out his usual. Then leant an elbow on the bar, touched his nose.

'What do you think of conspiracy theories?'

It was rare when conversation developed, yet occasionally Morgan found a subject that demanded he share it.

'Kennedy assassination, 9/11, Princess Diana, Roswell. Which one you talking about, Morgan?'

'The Moon landing.'

'We talking shadows?'

Morgan's face fell slightly. He didn't get out much. Mordent realised he was hoping his information might be new. He elaborated roughly as a result: 'I mean, isn't there something about there being no shadows on the Moon? I dunno much about it.'

Morgan leant closer. Mordent could smell stale alcohol on his breath.

'The conspiracy is that we never went to the Moon. There was a space race going on. Us versus the

Russkies. They'd already – theoretically – put a man in space. We had to get to the Moon first. We're the goddamned U S of A for God's sake. So the pictures were faked, directed by Stanley Kubrick based on a story by Arthur C Clarke. That's what they're saying. We never went there. It was easier to fake than it was to go.'

'I've heard some of this. How come it got to you now?'

Morgan shrugged. 'Programme on Channel 21 after I closed down last night. Been checking the internet on it in the back room all day.'

Mordent slugged his drink, ordered another. 'Go on.'

'You're right about the shadows. They reckon they had arc lights. Also the flag was waving, but there was no atmosphere. It was a cover up, from start to finish. We had to beat the Russkies. You get that? Plus Vietnam. The space programme stopped at the same time we withdrew. It was a tactical diversion. All that money the government raised for the landings could have been diverted to pay people off. Buzz Aldrin punched someone in the face. You know that? It was all very emotive.'

Mordent nodded. 'I've only heard some of this,' he said. 'But what would it matter?'

'Eh?'

'What would it matter if we went or not? Isn't it only important that we thought we went?'

'I don't follow.'

'I'll use another example. If we give money to charity but the money doesn't get to where it's supposed to be going, does that matter to the person who has given the money? They get the feel-good factor regardless. Just a thought.'

Morgan stroked his chin. 'In theory, that's right. But if we're all being lied to ...'

'But we *are* all being lied to. We're being lied to all of the time. What difference does another lie make?'

Morgan grumbled something under his breath that Mordent didn't catch. He supposed conspiracy theories were fine so long as they remained theories. They input a bit of intrigue into the day. But in comparison with the greater lies we face on a daily basis, and in the wider context that nothing was important at all in the scheme of things, their value was undermined.

Mordent believed that. That nothing was important at all. When all could be snuffed out by lack of oxygen to the brain then all the life, the love, the genuinely good and great things didn't matter a hoot. It was the false lie of a God's existence that facilitated the importance of the other lies. Yet if all we had was nothing – Woody Allen's *black, empty nothingness* for a future – then what did it matter if we went to the Moon?

As Morgan wandered off to serve another customer, Mordent understood two things. If we were immortal, then everything would matter. And if we thought immortality was possible, then everyone would be happy.

That was all that anyone ever needed to know.

He pulled out his cell phone, the glow from the screen casting a blue aura over his face. Accessing Maria's number, he sent her a text: *everything set. x*

He nursed his drink, regarded his face in the bar mirror, waited for her reply. When it came it was short and sweet: *good! Take care. x*

He closed his phone, re-pocketed it, left it at that. It felt comfortable being back with Maria. He just wasn't sure yet how comfortable he wanted it to be.

Mordent ordered another drink. Although it was quiet, Morgan didn't revisit his theme of faked Moon landings. He sat at a stool, at the opposite end of the bar, looking towards the door as the sun went down behind it, casting an orange sunburst around the edges like in some cheesy science fiction movie. Mordent wasn't into theories or speculation. Some would even question if the Moon's existence was hard fact. All he knew was the taste in his glass, the touch of a woman, and the satisfaction in closing a case.

Maybe, if he struck it lucky, all three simultaneously.

He downed the remainder of his glass, the liquid scorching the back of his throat. Night burned at the back of his eyes, forcing sleep. He needed to rest. The events of the past week were catching up. Something tugged within him: the knowledge that he would never sleep in Marina's bed again. It had become more comfortable than she had.

Mordent stood. A bead of sweat ran from the base of his neck down the back of his shirt, becoming absorbed where the shirt tucked in at his waistband. He was also hungry. A handful of ready meals were sitting in his freezer, but hardly beckoned. He decided to eat at the all-nighter called *Bukowski's* that he sometimes visited, a couple of blocks away. He could use one of their famous ham on ryes.

As he left the bar Morgan glanced up, didn't say anything. Not that he ever did.

It wasn't just the lack of food that made his stomach feel empty. There was a sonorous emptiness, an echoing, that made his muscles clench as he walked. Each step felt slow. The drink had muddled him more than he imagined. Yet there was something else. Something that nagged at him. He couldn't place it.

The residue of sunlight outlined the skyscrapers in gold and silver. Glass-fronted façades created prisms that refracted like searchlights across the city. Mordent stepped into a beam. Stepped out of it. Five seconds of fame. As the sun descended, buildings showed their true colours, the drabness of brown, the permanence of dirt. His mood fell with the sun, emotions shadowed by unknowns. The colours dripped out of his world.

Other shadows joined his. Yet it wasn't the speed of twilight. There was pain in his shoulder blades, his legs kicked out from under him. A blow to the jaw left him with nothing except the sensation of being bundled into the back of a car. Face pressed against leather, an elbow in his chest. Another punch and his life went black.

26
The Buzz Of The Cut

When Mordent awoke, the empty ache in his stomach was supplanted by the ache from the punches. A swelling over his right eye hampered his sight. The room was tiny, a basement, perhaps. A light bulb hung from the ceiling, the walls were bare brick. Somewhere, someone was cooking. There was pain in his back as though something was digging into his spine. There was. It was his wrists. Tied and pressed against the back of the chair. His feet were tied too.

Under other circumstances, with Simona or Anna, this situation would have been pleasurable. Here it was different.

The bulb didn't illuminate much of the room. As Mordent's eyes refocused, it looked more like a garage than a basement. An assortment of car tools hung on the walls. What seemed like the floor disappearing into darkness in front of him was just that – the pit to examine the underside of a vehicle. And then the shadows that moved at the back of the room resolved themselves into figures. One was Weasel-Face, the second BuzzCut.

When Mordent tried to speak he found his mouth was numb.

'Not so smart now, huh?'

BuzzCut's voice resonated within the garage. He stepped further into the light. The bulb hung just above the top of his six foot frame, the filament matching the blondness of his hair, as though the 'idea bubble' in a comic strip sketch.

Although in this case the bulb was the wrong way around.

'You've been bugging me,' BuzzCut continued, 'ever since I was sent round about Constantin. You've got the habit of keeping your nose in business that doesn't belong to you.'

'You're mixing your metaphors,' Mordent tried to say; but the numbness in his mouth hampered it. He realised it was a gag. All he could mutter was *mmmmmmmm*.

BuzzCut moved closer. Placed his palm against Mordent's cheek, where it rested hot and sweaty. Then pulled it away sharp. Mordent flinched at the blow that never came. BuzzCut laughed.

'As I said, not so smart now,' he reiterated.

Weasel-Face came to stand beside him. 'Told you his bark was worse than his bite,' he said. 'All hot air and nothing behind it.'

BuzzCut nodded. 'See,' he said, 'back where I come from we have ways of dealing with people who double-cross us. He looked around for a tool, picked up a wrench from the wall and slung it heavy in one hand. 'Just imagine the pain you'd get in a knee cap.'

Mordent could imagine only too well. He struggled to spit out the gag, tried to push it with his tongue. But it wouldn't budge.

'Devlin here,' BuzzCut gesticulated towards Weasel-Face, 'reckons you tried to set me up with Bataille. Needed a fall-guy. I don't like people making plans behind my back. Know-what-I-mean?'

He dropped the wrench onto the concrete floor. It made an awful clanging sound. Mordent avoided looking at it.

Weasel-Face drew alongside. Handed BuzzCut a saw. Smiled.

'You see,' BuzzCut continued, 'sometimes you just gotta look out for number one. Devlin here, he knows what's good for him. He knows what's good for me and for Bataille too. This way, Bataille doesn't get his hands dirty. We all get what we want. You understand.'

Mordent only understood that his logic was shot through. Bataille wouldn't know what was going down here. He wouldn't be told. If he did want to make BuzzCut the fall guy then whatever happened to Mordent would make no difference. But it had all been a blag, anyway; something to stir him up. He could tell BuzzCut that if he could dislodge the gag from his mouth.

BuzzCut bent the saw into a horseshoe shape. Held the bent end up to the side of Mordent's face. Let go.

The effect held more impact than BuzzCut had thought. The metal flipped forcibly against Mordent's flesh, left a toothed mark along his cheek, drawing blood in two places. It sounded like it stung and it did. Mordent's head shifted twenty degrees to the right. His jaw clenched down on the gag, compressed to the extent that it spat out of his mouth.

Mordent wanted to speak, but found himself gasping for breath. The residue of the gag was a toxic lipstick burn at the edges of his mouth. Now it was out, the taste became stronger, a semi-olfactory memory.

Weasel-Face went to reach for the gag, but BuzzCut put a hand on his shoulder. 'What's the good of that when you want to hear him scream?'

He placed the saw on Mordent's leg, its teeth against his pants. Leant on it.

Mordent bit the side of his mouth. The material took the brunt of the blade; there was just a pinprick along his nerves, which was bearable. Yet he grimaced, made it look worse than it was. That was the secret to torture. Cop out soon. Managing to hold the pain inside simply led to more pain. That he could do without.

'Bataille doesn't know what you're doing,' Mordent managed to whisper, his voice dry.

'So what if he doesn't? This is personal. You and me.'

'But it isn't, is it? There's a wider picture. You burn your bridges with Bataille and you burn your shot at immortality.'

BuzzCut laughed. It was an ugly laugh. One that you wouldn't want to be seen in public with.

'Bataille might believe that shit, but I sure don't. Try something else.' He leant on the saw again.

Mordent gasped.

'But that's why you came to the city. To sell Bataille information. To get up the ladder. Bataille and me had a deal, ask Weasel-Face over there. If I go missing, Bataille will take the rap. I know stuff. This is a knee-jerk reaction. Maybe Devlin didn't tell you the whole story.'

BuzzCut laughed again, offspring of the earlier sound. Babies you would bludgeon at birth.

'I said it before, you're not so smart. Not as smart as you think you are. Same with Constantin. Think you know what's going down, but don't. Make excuses? Plea bargains? Try to put off the inevitable? Well, it ain't happening. This is the end of the line.'

Mordent glanced over at Weasel-Face. Although

he hadn't been speaking, he still had gone quiet. He was thoughtful. There was a tinge of doubt. Mordent knew it wasn't the accusation that something was being held back, more that he was wondering how far BuzzCut was prepared to go.

This was new to him. He didn't want to get his hands dirty.

Even so, a weasel-face was a weasel-face. Mordent doubted he would intervene.

'Spare me some last minute answers. Who killed Marina Gonzales?'

There was a lightness of pressure on the saw.

A flick of puzzlement across BuzzCut's face.

'Don't tell me you don't know who she was?'

Mordent could tell BuzzCut wanted to say something to someone. Only there was no-one in the room he wanted to say it to.

'Found dead yesterday. Cause of death currently unknown. Her cat took the hit too.'

BuzzCut dropped the saw to the floor. It made a noise like the first few bars of a bluegrass number.

Given the reaction, Mordent held fire on saying he'd slept with her.

BuzzCut looked to Weasel-Face.

'I don't know nothing. He mentioned this broad's name when he was with Bataille, but it didn't mean nothing to me.'

BuzzCut nodded. Ran a hand over his chin. Stroked that day's stubble.

Weasel-Face glanced at Mordent. It was clear that he didn't know what to do. Or say.

'Give me a minute.'

BuzzCut re-entered the shadows. From the creak of wood Mordent guessed a staircase led upwards. As if in confirmation, a halo of light lit BuzzCut's hair as a door opened. When it closed, a semi-circle imprint glowed over Weasel-Face. Mordent turned his gaze to him.

'Looks like he's rattled.'

'I don't need no talk,' Weasel-Face said.

He looked in limbo. Didn't want to be with Mordent. Didn't want to go upstairs. Uncomfortable with Mordent being tied, now they were alone.

'As I say, looks like he's rattled. When people are rattled they tend to get nervous. When they get nervous they get twitchy. When they're twitchy, they're unreliable; you know what I mean? At the moment, you're party to kidnapping and torture. I don't know your background, but I'm guessing you've been in and out of jail a few times. You know what it's like there and you don't want to go back. If he kills me, you're party to murder. And that's a long rap. You let me go, and I'll be pressing no charges. Think it over.'

Weasel-Face shifted his feet. Looked everywhere but at Mordent.

Somewhere, either a clock ticked or water dripped.

'There's only one way out of here,' he said, finally. 'The same way he went.'

Mordent nodded.

'And if I let you go, I'm in trouble with him. It won't cut. Will it?'

'No, it won't.'

'I mean, it's not like you could have got out of those alone,' he gesticulated at the ropes.

'That's right.'

Weasel-Face rubbed a callused hand over his chin.

Mordent shifted in his chair, as much as he could. 'This isn't cartoon violence. This is the real thing. You got a wife, kids? You got a conscience?'

Weasel-Face shook his head. Mordent wondered to which question.

'What do you think he's doing now?'

There was no response.

'He seemed pretty upset about the Gonzales woman. Maybe he had a thing with her.'

'I never heard of her.'

'Maybe he kept it quiet. I mean, you're not buddies are you? You've got no particular allegiance to each other. You might have told him about my deal with Bataille, but that was just to feather your own nest. Maybe you look up to him. He's got the talent, the looks, he's a rising star. You ride in his wake and you get closer to the top. Better that than just opening and closing the door in Bataille's office. Just another heavy that he doesn't need to get close to. But why worry about Derby Boy? Why not make it big with Bataille? He wouldn't want me wasted. You help me, you help yourself.'

'I dunno.'

'I repeat: you help me, you help yourself. What does Derby Boy owe you? Nothing.'

Weasel-Face shrugged. 'I don't wanna end up in that chair.'

'Go on up and speak to him.'

They exchanged glances.

'Go on. I can't get out of here.' Mordent made a show of struggling. 'Just go and make him see sense.'

Weasel-Face turned towards the stairs. Turned back. Turned around again.

Then, as though a decision was made for him, he headed up the stairs.

The room fell quiet. Mordent tried to flex his wrists, but there was no give to be had. His legs were numb. The taste of the gag hadn't dissipated with talking. He couldn't feel if his gun was still in his jacket pocket, suspected it wasn't. The room was too dark to determine its whereabouts. The mark of the saw on his cheek stung like a paper cut. There was nothing for it other than to sit tight. Literally.

The clock or the dripping water seemed to be working to a different time scale. Seconds passed imperceptibly.

Those joints that weren't numb were stiffening.

The ache in his eye wasn't lessening.

His sight wasn't improving.

He listened for rats. Couldn't hear any.

Listened for voices. There weren't any.

He wondered what BuzzCut was up to. There was no doubt of his involvement with Marina. It made him ill just to think about it.

Had they slept in the same bed? Maybe the *You* in Marina's diary had been BuzzCut. It didn't make a lot of sense, but then sometimes puzzle pieces for different pictures cropped up in the same box. There could be no other link than coincidence.

Whatever. That link might have saved his life.

More listening.

More waiting.

It crossed his mind they might simply have left him. It was unclear in the gloom whether the garage was frequently used. If he were underground, then would anyone hear him shout? Yet they couldn't be underground, the stairs couldn't be the only exit. The mechanics' pit that yawned in front of him was testament to that. Behind him, he figured, were double doors.

Mordent shifted his body weight to the right hand side, then the left. The chair creaked, without any perceptible rise. He tried again, repeated the movement, repeated it again, kept it on repeat. With each rock, the chair groaned louder, with each rock a leg seemed to move further from the floor. It was hard to tell exactly. Sometimes, through the effort, his movements were exhausted, the momentum was lost. It was like licking a pussy. The tongue would tire just as the girl was ready to cum. Then you had to start all over again.

He kept trying.

Kept rocking.

Just kept swimming.

Eventually it wasn't the rocking that did it, but the left leg cracked away from the base of the chair, splintered into his own leg, although he could no longer feel it. The chair tipped to one side, went over. He held his breath as he hit the concrete floor, as if that might negate pain. It didn't. His left arm took his weight. Maybe a fracture, maybe not. He lay still, waited for movement from upstairs, waited for his legs to regain their strength. The rope curled away from his feet now the chair leg was broken, but his lower body remained numb.

Gradually, tiny pinpricks started to run through his legs as the blood supply was re-established. Or maybe a porcupine was humping him. He couldn't tell from that angle.

The clock ticked.

Or the water dripped.

Feeling took hold of his legs. He moved them gingerly. Over the course of four minutes he manoeuvred himself onto his knees. BuzzCut had made a cardinal error with regards to the rope: had used the same length for both hands and feet. Once one was unravelled, the other followed. He tugged repeatedly, gaining a mild burn, until eventually it came loose and free.

He leant on all fours, waiting for his strength to return. His arms were so weak he fell forward, grazed his chin on the floor. Again he lay still. Waited for a noise from upstairs. But still there was none. It took another ten minutes before he could stand. Another five before he relocated his gun.

It had been left carelessly on the side, chamber intact.

Picking it up, he found he couldn't remember the last time he'd actually used it. Yet it was as necessary as the beat in his heart.

As he moved in the semi-darkness, so the shadows moved with him. Like being in fog he could see only his immediate area, altered subtly with each step. The glow from the light bulb was minimal – a low wattage, unsuitable for the garage and detailed work. He imagined the place must be disused. Behind the chair, as he thought, were heavy double doors. They seemed to be locked from the outside.

There was nothing for it but the wooden staircase. BuzzCut and Weasel-Face.

On his way to the steps he picked up the wrench.

There was a banister that was shaky, but his legs were now firm.

He eased open the door at the top of the steps. Wondered why he held the wrench rather than his gun, a momentary lapse of reason. He found himself in a small kitchen. Two plates, some knives and forks and an upturned cup were long dried beside the sink. The linoleum floor was peeling, curled at the edges like bread left out overnight. Scum delineated the area between the bottom of the cabinets and the floor.

He took in these details professionally. Could see no signs of his kidnappers.

In the next room, the living area held grease marks on a tattered sofa. A torch stood face down on a coffee table. A generic watercolour of a riverbank scene was wonky on the wall. Beside it, a singing fish. One that waggled its mouth and tail when a button was pressed: sang *Mammy*, or some other inappropriate nonsense. Two sets of heavy workboots stood legless beside a door.

He passed into the other rooms. A grubby toilet with cracked yellow limescale engrained in the rim, a sink with a toothbrush bristling wildly. Further on, a bedroom, sheets unmade, curtains closed. If he didn't know any better he might have been in Constantin's apartment. It was equally grubby, rundown, uncared for. Indistinguishable from any number of apartments in an equally grubby, rundown, and uncared for city.

His good mood established earlier that day had long disappeared. The same way as BuzzCut and Weasel-Face. He suspected the former had some enquiries to make over Marina, the latter had not been prepared to turn him loose. He thanked the vulnerability of the chair leg, then let himself out of the apartment, tried to determine his whereabouts.

The night was wet as well as dark. Rain fell slowly in thin sheets, glazing the ground with shiny reflections. Mordent knew his location. He looked up at a faded white sign painted on the wall, clocked the name of the garage. It was long disused. Hubie's office was two blocks away. Just as the rain accumulated individual drops to make one puddle, so information drip-fed into his puzzle. A date with Marina, a gunshot in an alleyway, a vacant garage frequented by one BuzzCut known as Derby Boy. A cat and mouse game of jealousy under a veneer of immortality.

He sighed. Sometimes it was that simple.

Yet regardless of the epiphany, he couldn't get a taxi. Being mugged was more likely in this district. He moved stiffly up the street, his limbs aching now they were getting used to activity. He felt like he'd been shoved in a box and kicked downstairs. Placing his fingers against the saw mark on his cheek he traced the zigzag. Another story to tell the grandchildren he imagined he would never have.

He set off for Hubie's office. Rain soaked into his clothing, yet it was warm and he felt encased by the weather as though impermeable to other influences. The jacket of water felt like a PVC protector. It caressed his wounds, relaxed him as much as a warm bath. Inside Hubie's building, however, the absence of outdoors negated the rain's effects. As he ascended the stairs he became simply cold and wet, his suit dragging down each step, his socks making paddling pools out of his shoes.

He knocked on Hubie's door. It was already ten in the evening. The soft glow of a light from the bedroom illuminated the glass section of the door. He was in bed then. Probably not asleep.

He knocked again.

Again.

Behind the door a shadow loomed. The key turned.

Hubie opened the door in his dressing gown, the tassels twirling.

'Oh, it's you.'

'Who were you expecting? Lady Godiva?'

Hubie shrugged. 'Something like that. I've got an appointment.'

'At this time of night? And in your dressing gown?'

Hubie opened the door wider, let Mordent through. 'Don't you start being judgmental. I know your track record.'

'It's the long winter nights.'

'And it's not even winter.' Hubie opened a cabinet beside his desk, pulled out two glasses and a bottle of J D. Poured some shots. 'I take it this isn't a social visit.'

'I was in the area. Needed somewhere to dry out. Somewhere neutral to think.'

'No information?'

'Not as such. Well, maybe. About two blocks from here there's a disused garage. You know of it?'

Hubie nodded. Took a sip of his drink. 'I don't know who owns it, if that's what you're asking. Haven't seen anyone use it, either.'

'That BuzzCut guy. The Derby Boy I mentioned before. You seen him hanging about?'

'Nope.'

Mordent rubbed the back of his neck. It ached.

'You want to get those cuts seen to,' Hubie said. 'Look, I've a spare suit in the bedroom if you want. But don't be too long about it. As I say, I've got a visitor.'

'It's just a little rain.'

'It's more than the rain, Mordent. You taken a look in the mirror recently? Your clothes are scuffed, ripped in places. Looks like you've been rolling on the floor with an Eastern European hooker.'

'And if I had, you'd be asking me for her number.'

'Whatever.'

Mordent took his drink down in one. It cleared his head. In Hubie's bedroom he stripped down to his underwear, hung his jacket and pants on a coathanger over the window frame. Hubie was right, the elbows and left hand side of the suit were badly damaged. The fabric furred where the rope had dug into it. The side where he had fallen was covered in wet dust, a negative image of the other side, which remained black. He felt vulnerable in his underwear and gun. Hubie remained in his office, seated on the corner of his desk.

'Seems like you're unlucky recently, Mordent. First you get shot at, then you get roughed up.'

'If I didn't know any better, Hubie, I'd be blaming that on you.'

Hubie's laugh was hollow.

'Seems like you might need a shot of immortality yourself. The way that you're going.'

'Neither of us believes in that.'

'I certainly wouldn't bet on it.' Hubie's voice picked up, imbued with the excitement of a frequent better. 'Hey Mordent, if you think about it, it's an impossible bet. *Carpe Datum*. Even if you were immortal – how would you prove it?'

Mordent shrugged. Rooted around in Hubie's wardrobe for something serviceable. 'By not dying?'

'But when? Even if you lived two hundred, three hundred years. Four hundred, even. You would never know if you were immortal. There would always be death hanging over you. Even if we forget about the physical ageing problem, or the possibility of accidental death. Immortality is something that can never be proven. A betting agency would never pay out on it.'

'I guess that's true.'

'Of course it's true. It's also true that should Bataille ever believe he's found a cure for death – or however you want to call it – then he could never be 100% sure. Imagine how that might bug him.'

'That's something I'm working on.'

Mordent re-entered the office, a silk kimono over his burly frame. 'Look, I can't find your suit.'

Hubie stifled a laugh. 'Very fetching.'

'Can it. Take a look for me, will you.'

'Sure.'

Hubie made a move towards the bedroom, but was stopped by another knock on the door. He opened it. A tall, curvy, black girl stood in the doorway. Knee high black boots, a short denim skirt and a halter-top were barely concealed under a long fur coat. Where her skin was visible, it gleamed the colour of an eel in night-time waters. Her red lipstick entered the room before she did. Her afro matched her 1970s appearance.

'You said nothin' about two of yous, honey,' she drawled. 'That'll be extra.'

27
Just A Man In A Tight-Fitting Suit

Mordent, freshly-suited, waited for his taxi just inside the entrance of Hubie's apartment block. The suit clung in all the wrong places. He remembered the English comedian, Alexi Sayle. Found a comparison. Outside, the rain continued to fall, a curtain of reflected light, as though he were standing in a cave at the back of a waterfall. His body still ached, the side of his face razor-cut as though through shaving. He wanted Maria to kiss that side of his face. He wanted to kiss her all over.

Upstairs he had declined the services of the prostitute. Despite her attractiveness, bedding down with Hubie wasn't on the cards. He did take the number of her agency, however. *Retro Hookers*. They came in all shapes and sizes. All decades. You never knew when a girl like that might be required.

Inside his mind, cogs were turning. Puzzle pieces slipping into place. Like most conclusions to investigations, the solution was simple. Just like quiz show questions when you knew the answers. All he needed to work out was who might take the rap for it.

He needed to see Kovacs, but it was too late for that. He needed sleep.

He wanted to lie next to Maria and not imagine she was Marina.

Names of women flitted in and out of his mind. So many interchangeable, so few permanent.

His gun was packed hard against his body, the tight suit delineating its shape as though embossed on the material.

He fingered his cell phone. Probably too late to send Maria a text, too late to turn up unannounced. Besides, he didn't want to lead anyone to her. Unlikely as it might be that he was being followed.

Just where had BuzzCut gone?

Just where was his taxi?

Lights pooled two circles at the end of the street, as though in answer to one of his questions.

It pulled up outside the apartment block. A yellow submarine.

Mordent opened the rear door, got in. Barked out Morgan's Bar as his destination. The driver wasn't the talkative type. Maybe it was down to where he was heading, maybe it was the inappropriateness of the suit. Whatever, he was glad of the quiet. He lay back, rested his head against the backrest. Watched the journey through the rear window of the cab, streetlights staccatoing the sky above, strobing the tops of buildings, the rain glinting like silver pin-pricks, the warmth of the vehicle cocooning the night.

Morgan's closed late, so it was open when they arrived. He paid the driver and entered the bar. Individuals were pocketed in corners of the room like pool balls. He recognised most of them, but knew none of them. His usual seat was taken, so he took another. Ordered a beer for a change. He needed liquid, felt dehydrated. Morgan served him with a look of disapproval at the change of his regular drink, and not without a little humour at his attire. Nevertheless, he said nothing. Neither about his appearance nor about the faked Moon landings. Despite the late hour, it was busy. Mordent always wondered why Morgan never had help behind the bar. Yet no-one was ever in a rush. Time was different here. It felt so on each occasion. A glamorous barmaid, however welcome in other joints, would destroy the atmosphere. Worse, she would talk.

The beer felt good as it coursed its way through his body. The deep yellow colour brightening inside out. The taste slightly tart on his tongue. At Hubie's, Mordent had cleaned the blood from his face. The saw-tooth had created a flesh wound that didn't look like a scar. He wasn't sure whether to be pleased or disappointed. Each time he raised the glass to his mouth, however, he was reminded of the tightness of the suit. It felt as though the onset of arthritis lingering at the periphery of his health had been heightened. At least once home he could take the suit off.

Before that journey he had another to make. Finding his car, he remembered his hunger. He drove to the all-nighter and ordered a baguette stuffed with ham, olives and cheese. Knocked it back with two cups of black coffee. He wondered what he would have been doing if his previous journey hadn't been interrupted. Probably asleep, unhurt, not in an ill-fitting suit. As sometimes happened, he pondered the philosophy of bad timing.

Right place, wrong time. Wrong place, right time. Truth was, there was no right or wrong time. There were just instances of moments of existence. Individual realities that sometimes connected, sometimes didn't. Your world was perfect, discounting other people. Yet you had to engage with other people in order to live.

Whether he ate the baguette now, earlier or later made no substantial difference to him. But it had for BuzzCut, for the deli-owner, for Hubie, for Weasel-Face, for the black whore, for the taxi driver. Timing was everything, but none of the clocks ever worked. Bad timing. There was no such thing.

He wiped crumbs from his mouth. Drained the remainder of the coffee. Headed back to his car.

And as usual, he changed his mind. Bad timing had caught Martens with his hand in a corpse. Good timing had meant Mordent saw it.

He always had that favour to call in.

The drive to the morgue was uneventful. Traffic remained light. The rain cleaned the streets of debris, of bums, of partygoers. His wheels created mini-waves, occasional tsunamis. The wipers shouldering rivers left and right. He turned up the jazz in the car, immersed himself in an equal wave of sound. Instruments crashed around him, punctuated his thoughts. Drums the heartbeat of the city.

Martens wasn't in the morgue when he arrived. He bypassed the security system through boredom, took a look through some of the cabinets, turned the sheet back from a cadaver on the gurney. Thankfully, no-one he recognised. He wondered what the autopsy would turn up on Marina. Whatever it might be, it certainly would have zero to do with ageing after death. She hadn't been dead long enough for that to have happened.

When he heard footsteps he stood behind the door hinge. Watched as Martens entered the room, a sealed-sandwich in one hand, a can of *7-Up* in the other. Martens didn't see him. He walked towards the gurney, placed the sandwich next to the body, and his finger under the ring pull of the can.

'You're breaking health and safety regulations,' Mordent barked.

Martens let out a high-pitched squeal in a girlish

tone. The can dropped from his grip, hit the ground. Half-opened, the can span like a Catherine Wheel, spraying drink over the floor. Martens glanced over at Mordent, swore, picked up the can and pushed his thumb against the hole. It accentuated the pressure. The carbonated water jetted towards his face. Martens ducked and it dampened the sheet covering the cadaver. Still clutching the can, he ran nimbly over to the sink, dropped it there. It hissed a few moments more before it stopped.

Martens' face was red. 'You're a fucking idiot Mordent.'

Mordent beamed.

'Several health and safety regulations, in fact.'

Martens pulled a couple of paper towels from the dispenser, wiped his face. 'What are you doing creeping around anyway? Could have given me a call.'

'I was in the area, thought I'd drop by.'

Martens opened a floor-length cupboard, pulled a mop from a bucket, began cleaning the area by the gurney. 'Where have you been? Some kind of fancy dress party? That suit doesn't fit.'

'It's a long story. One you won't be getting.' Mordent paused. 'Had any ageing bodies down here recently?'

'Nope. And not likely to either. We dug a little deeper. They'd undergone some kind of cell degeneration treatment. So they'd not had a life preservative. Moreso the opposite.'

'They'd been deliberately aged?'

'That's right. Different techniques.'

'So why would that happen?'

Martens shrugged, squeezed out the mop. 'I don't get paid enough to even think about it.'

Mordent kept his idea to himself.

He watched as Martens replaced the mop in the cupboard, pulled the sheet off the cadaver and replaced it with a fresh one.

'What happened to her?'

'Road traffic collision. Just trying to work out whether it was deliberate. Or not.'

'She's pretty.'

'For a corpse.'

'Just the way you like them. I prefer mine stone cold sober, you prefer yours just stone cold.'

Martens returned to the sink. Deliberated drinking from the half-empty can, then decided to pour it away. 'You owe me one, now.'

'I don't owe you anything.'

'I got some more information.' A sly smile crept across Martens' face. 'I'm sure you'd be interested.'

'Go on.'

'Heard you were sweet on the Gonzales girl. Did you want to see her?'

Mordent thought it over. For half a second. He didn't.

'Not now.'

'Been told you were in the frame for that one. Fingerprints all over the place. Might take some explaining. Only they know it wasn't you. Pills suggest suicide.'

Mordent couldn't remember an empty pillbox near the bed. He could remember the cat.

'They're not serious?'

'Maybe.'

'But her cat ...?'

'No cat came through here Mordent.'

'Then it's a cover up. What were inside her?'

'Barbiturates. Enough to kill a regiment of rhinos. No sign of forced entry. Either end.' Martens grinned.

Mordent shook his head. 'It wasn't suicide.'

'Maybe she did the cat, then herself. Stranger things have happened.'

'Not that strange,' muttered Mordent. 'There were bruises around her neck.'

Martens shrugged. 'I've got things to be doing,' he said.

Mordent nodded. 'So have I.'

He turned to leave, suddenly overcome with tiredness. Martens called out to his back.

'You wearing that suit for a bet?'

Mordent raised a finger. Left.

28
The Calm Before The Storm

Mordent's head hit the pillow, sank through it straight into dreamland.

He was at a party with Maria's relatives. Hadn't seen them for some time. In his peripheral vision were glimpses of Marina. She flitted in and out like a butterfly with St Vitus' Dance. It wasn't clear if she were really there or just a figment of his imagination. He hugged his mother-in-law. There was real love there. But this was at the end of the evening. Crumbs from sandwiches lay on plates alongside cocktail sticks. One of their dogs had been allowed back into the living room, was asleep in the corner. Something was skewed, but he couldn't place it.

He went into the kitchen. His father-in-law was washing some glasses. Tight white wiry curls sprung from his head. His face was red, as though he had been exercising. Again, there was a hug. He had a feeling he hadn't seen them for a very long time.

It was quiet. The noises he associated with a party weren't present. He looked around. He could see people talking, but they were making no sound. It was like watching television with the volume turned down. Maria entered his line of view, glanced at him, glanced through him.

When he turned back to his father-in-law he had

gone. Marina was at his elbow. *They can't see you*, she said. *You're dead.*

He awoke in a sweat, his head pounding. The thin sheet covering his body was wet. He sat up. It was still night. His curtains were solid rather than transparent with daylight. For a sudden moment he had a fear there was nothing beyond the window, and he stood and tore them open. Stars percolated his vision, the expanse of the sky a backdrop to the muted colours of the city. He eased the window ajar, traffic noise a low hum like the sound of a refrigerator. He gasped. Realised he'd been holding his breath. The LED lights on his retro alarm clock read 4.17 am.

He ran his hand over his head, collected moisture. Wandered into the bathroom and splashed water on his face. His eyes were red in the mirror. He closed them. Felt himself drifting away even as he was standing. Back in the bedroom he folded himself under the covers, curled up as best he could, imagined himself in his old bed at home, as a child. Before the discovery of a dead body in the garden and the first accusing finger. Before the world turned and weevils fell out of it, like a giant ship's biscuit.

If he dreamt the second time around, then he didn't remember.

Morning came with a bright kick. He awoke with his eyes closed, an orange glow permeating his lids, accentuating veins. Reaching over to his cell phone he accessed a message from Maria: *Morning sweetheart. Maybe this will be the first day of the start of the rest of our lives. x*

His text back: *Maybe ;) x*

He looked at his reply after he'd sent it. Wondered if he was right.

He had to see her. He wanted to see her. And then

he would see Kovacs, and then there would be the showdown between Bataille and Muxloe. If they didn't get to him first.

He got dressed. Hubie's suit discarded on the floor beside the bed like a deflated costume. He still felt stiff. The side of his face ached, but the wound was already healing. He wondered how many mornings of stiffness were to come, as arthritis replaced the aftermath of beatings. He wondered how many beatings might come. How long he could stay in the game. And how long he wanted to stay in the game.

Yet he loved it. Deep down. It ran through his bones. Defined him. To remove it would be to remove his skeleton. Without it he would be no more than a suit on a floor, or a bum in a bar – slowly drinking without a reason to do so.

He wondered if there would be a loud *clunk* when everything finally fell into place.

Heading out of the apartment, he made his way towards his office. A quick check of his e-mails revealed nothing of any importance. He was living a hand-to-mouth existence. Even if, as he suspected, this case would be concluded that day, there was no guarantee Mrs Mouse would make payment. He wasn't sure there would be anything to tell her.

A girl in the corridor winked at him when he passed. Or it might have been his imagination, a shadow of the kiss curl on her forehead.

His eyes lingered on her rear as she opened the door to the agency. Considered, for a moment, swapping their sign with his.

Back on the street the sky was a bright blue. The day luminescent. Telephone lines bisected the view, cut it into segments like cheese wire. Leaves had found their way into the city, billowed in a slight breeze around the heels of pedestrians, danced stem to stem around dog shit and debris. The day wasn't cold, but it wasn't warm enough to have cleared all the rainfall. His tyres splashed dirty water onto the sidewalk, monochrome Pollocks. Where leaves were in the puddles he surfed.

Maria's apartment was on the Upper East Side. He'd sent her a text from his office, told her to wait. As he parked he looked up at her building. It was almost identical to his own, but cleaner, better cared for. She buzzed him in and he rode the central elevator with iron doors to her floor, six storeys up. It wasn't quite penthouse, but the view was spectacular.

She opened the door smiling. He took her in his arms, lifted her feet slightly off the ground. That smile had been missed far too long. When they kissed, everything they had shared came rushing back, truncating the time they had been apart into one continuous romance. A perfect, unassailable moment. Yet it was just a moment, and as they separated, real life re-exerted familiar influences. All the concerns and petty-mindedness associated with love. They weren't there now, but would be, over time.

He just hoped that he could live with that.

'How's it going?' She led him into the kitchen, steam rose from a kettle, water freshly boiled.

He pointed to the side of his face. The fact she hadn't noticed was of some comfort.

'Poor you. What happened?'

He told her.

But not everything. When they had spoken in his office he hadn't mentioned the extent of his relationship with Marina. That choice detail was also omitted now.

'I need to lay a trap,' he said. 'I've got both Bataille and Muxloe thinking but I need to get them together. I need it to kick off.'

'Invite them on a picnic.' Maria smiled.

He laughed. 'Maybe.'

They drank coffee. His was dark and bitter. Not quite how he liked it, but the way he had tolerated it during their marriage. One of the tiny compromises that had enabled them to live as a couple.

'So,' she said. 'Looks like we're continuing to get back together.'

He nodded. 'Looks like it.'

'Just one thing,' she said, her eyes sparkling with a base note of intent. 'Don't give me any shit, okay? I want to open myself back up to you, but I'm vulnerable and hurt. I *was* vulnerable and hurt. I feel strong enough now to open my heart, but it's more fragile than it was before. You need to know this, before we go any further.'

'I know I'm not the best person to live with.'

Maria smiled. 'That I can deal with.'

'Then ...'

'Then it's everything else. And if you need to ask what it is, then there's already a problem.'

Mordent sighed but didn't show it.

A slippery slope of implication.

The female route of preference.

He kissed her, hard. 'Let's just get to bed.'

There was a taste of coffee on her tongue.

*

Kovacs was less easy to please.

Mordent found himself in his office, with the usual cajoling and camaraderie along the way. It wasn't true, regardless of what Muxloe had intimated, that he had left the force because he could no longer hack it. The fact was that the force had changed and he hadn't. Strict down-the-line cops like Kovacs had made it more of a business, less of a job. The thrill was in the chase, not the accountability, the paperwork that followed. It wasn't to be written up like a book, it was to be lived like a story. And until that final moment when he had been immersed in the river, that story had been his life.

Hooper sidled up to him as he pulled a white plastic cup from the dispenser, grabbed himself a free dash of liquid.

'Hey Mordent, good to see you.'

'Likewise.'

'Kovacs is out.'

'So I see. His office locked?'

Hooper laughed. 'Of course.'

'Keep a look out for me?'

Hooper glanced from side to side. The department was busy. There must have been over twenty cops there. Some leaning into computer screens as though they were getting facials, others chatting, others filling out multitudinous forms, two arm-wrestling, another mid-way between emptying a locker and eating a cheese sandwich. The rest just a blur of humanity.

'Eh?'

Hooper hadn't got the joke. If there was anyone in the office Mordent would have asked to keep an eye out, it wouldn't have been myopic Hooper.

'Just kidding,' Mordent said. 'I can wait.'

He sat on one side of a desk, paperwork creasing under his rear. Then he remembered Hooper was the guy who had been a point of contact for Marina. He decided to ask him a few questions.

'Hooper. We chatted about Marina Gonzales, remember. A few days ago.'

'Course I remember.'

'You know what's happened?'

'I know that she's dead.'

'You know I made the call.'

'Sure I know.' Hooper blinked twice, in quick succession. If he'd had the sense to have worn glasses he would have pushed them up the bridge of his nose.

'Hear anything else?'

Hooper shrugged. 'Just that you were in the frame for a while. You were everywhere in that apartment, from the bed to the kitchen to the fridge to the shower. Shedding DNA all over the place as though you were living with her.'

Mordent held back on the information that he had never been in the apartment when she had. It smacked of stalking.

'So when was I out of the frame?'

'Pretty quickly. She killed herself. So many pills she rattled when we moved her. She'd taken them herself. No signs her mouth had been held open, no traces in any of the glasses.'

'No pill box, that I could see.'

'A lack of evidence isn't evidence.'

Mordent wasn't sure he could follow that.

Behind Hooper's head, he could see Kovacs approaching.

Conversation trailed. Mordent gestured to Hooper, eased himself off the desk. Wandered over to Kovacs' office and waited.

What had been in Marina's notebook that had made someone so desperate to get it? To kill her for it?

Maybe it had nothing to do with anything after all. Paranoia on Marina's part. Sometimes, even once the puzzle was completed there were pieces left over. They looked like they should fit. But they didn't.

If his life story was a puzzle, what would be the picture on the box?

Yet there was no time to answer that question. Kovacs headed in his direction, head down charging like a bull, fiddling with a cell phone. When he reached Mordent he looked up, faux surprise on his face. Mordent saw lines there indicative of age.

'Just like a bad penny.'

'Or the bottom of a pair of pants.'

'Tradition against anarchy, as always, Mordent. What can I do you for?'

'Time for a quick chat.'

Kovacs nodded. Pulled out a key from his pocket and unlocked his office door. 'In there.'

They entered. The room was a greenhouse. The windows closed, the heating on. A cactus on the filing cabinet was wilting.

After Kovacs had closed the door and headed to his desk, Mordent leant against it.

'Just what is it with Marina Gonzales?'

Kovacs sat down. 'I was expecting this.'

'She didn't kill herself.'

'How well did you know her, Mordent? Not well enough, I'm guessing.'

'I knew her cat.'

Kovacs ignored him. 'She had a history of attempted suicides running back to when she was fourteen and thought she was hearing voices. The only difference this time is that she didn't get her stomach pumped.'

'And I suppose the cat had a history of self-mutilation?'

'A cat doesn't have the same legal rights as a person.'

'Meaning?'

'Meaning case closed. We chose not to investigate.' Kovacs leant back in his chair. 'You should be grateful. You were in the frame.'

'I think she's been framed.'

'Think what you like. Case closed.'

Mordent could feel his fists clenching. He didn't look at them. When the words came, each had equal emphasis. 'We saw the strangulation marks. Whose thumb are you under, Kovacs?'

Kovacs didn't do him the courtesy of looking up.

'Case closed.'

'I'm serious. I'm about to blow the lid off this thing and I need to know who you're gonna get burnt standing next to.'

Kovacs looked up, this time.

'Ever the dramatist, Mordent. This isn't the '50s. Police work is different from those pulp novels you used to read. I needn't even be having this conversation with you. You're not in with us and you're not in with the DA. You go running around, you'll burn yourself, no-one else. If you want to take that risk, I'm going to let you.'

Not for the first time since Mordent had slapped Kovacs' face he felt compelled to do so again.

Didn't.

He also resisted picking up the cactus and throwing it against the wall.

Instead, he turned to go.

'One more thing,' Kovacs said. 'That guy you were asking about. Derby Boy? Real name is Clarence Meech. We picked him out of the river this morning. Single gunshot wound to the head. Dead.'

Mordent nodded. Left.

Clarence. What a laugh.

Meech. The *M* in Marina's notebook.

29
Moon Race

He left his car in the police compound, walked several blocks to Prospect Park, found a bench and sat on it.

He'd forgotten to ask Kovacs about Constantin. But then he knew his death had been no accident. Loose ends were being tied, but it wasn't him doing the tying. That would have to change with Bataille and Muxloe. If he could tie their shoelaces together then they would stumble and pratfall. He'd pay to see that.

Pigeons congregated at his feet. He didn't have any bread for them, but they didn't know that. Maybe that was why Marina had been killed. Either Bataille or Muxloe had thought she had something, and whether she did or didn't was immaterial. If she'd previously sat at the park bench with bread then who was to say she wouldn't again. He would probably never know what she had wanted to tell him in that phone call. And even if the police eventually decided against that ridiculous suicide verdict, then BuzzCut would be the likely fall guy. Seemed like Bataille might have followed through with his recommendation. Only with a dead man rather than a live one.

He moved his feet forward amidst a rush of feathers. Rats with wings: that was a common description of pigeons. Mordent didn't mind rats, and he didn't mind pigeons. It was rats with guns that he hated the most. Rats who were content to consume whoever was in their path to attain some semblance of glory. Rats like Bataille and Muxloe, who managed their covert operations within the boundaries of the law, yet who ran underground concerns that contaminated the city. That everyone knew about, but no-one had the balls to shut down.

Truth was, their businesses were the lynchpins that held much of the city together. They contained it, held it, were part of the foundations. Pull that apart and too much would crumble. Those in high places thought the city needed the bad and the good to survive. Mordent knew it was more about maintaining their own positions rather than for the good of all. If he could pull out the right block, he would do so. No matter who fell.

Everything was set up for a confrontation. If they weren't rattled, then at the very least they were inconvenienced. People who inconvenienced them ended up dead. If Mordent was going to poke a stick in the hornet's nest then he needed protection. That wasn't going to come from Kovacs, so he'd have to arrange it by himself.

Protection didn't always mean heavies and goons. It meant working out an escape route, making sure of a location. With that in mind, Mordent looked around the park. Joggers kept a pace on the paths, females with hard midriffs exposed by tiny crop tops, their rears compacted into shorts that were little more than panties; males packing salami, chest muscles rippling, strutting rather than jogging. Pseudo-athletes the lot of them. They were welcome to their military sex and hard attitudes, but that was a distraction and not what he was looking for.

Further up was a children's play area. From woodchip ground rose colourful metal structures: slides, climbing frames, swings. It was a new construct, everything was clean, untarnished, free of graffiti. New mothers chatted while the children played, the air around them fresh with overtones of laughter.

Elsewhere, couples sat on the grass, lone elderly men fed the birds, a couple of solitary students read books. The day had brightened sufficiently for the pale sunlight to relieve the ground from the rainfall. It was almost balmy. Here, Mordent thought, would be the best location for a showdown. Out in the open where he could see both parties and there were plenty of witnesses. It might be an unnecessary precaution, but on the other hand it might be essential. He wasn't prepared to take the risk.

He glanced at his watch. It was early afternoon – past twelve, so a high noon scenario was no option. Pulling out his phone he accessed directory enquiries, called up the number of the bakery and dialled. He bypassed the cake order and said he wanted Bataille. After a short wait he was put through to a girl he assumed was his secretary: the blonde with the legs and the lipstick. Her voice was rich and sensuous. He drifted with it, for a while, then snapped back when she tried to stall him.

'Can it, doll. Just get Bataille for me.'

'I beg your pardon?'

'You heard, sugar.'

There was silence. At first Mordent wondered if he'd been disconnected, then Bataille's voice entered his ear, a tone higher than in person. And with a nasal twang that the telephone conveyed more succinctly than he was sure Bataille would have wanted to hear.

'Mordent.'

'That's me.'

'What do you want? You got your fall guy.'

'I got a dead guy. No more, no less.'

'You didn't specify, Mordent. Next time you'll have to learn to be more specific.'

'Your grammar ain't great Bataille. Where were you brung up?'

'Listen, Mordent. I've no time for small talk. You promised me Muxloe if I gave you Derby Boy. What's happening with that?'

'You think that's something I'm gonna tell you over the phone? Immortality is a hot topic.'

'You've got information?'

'I've got information.'

'Come on over. You know where I am.'

'Listen Bataille, you want this info, you come and get it. I'll be on a bench in Prospect Park at 3pm. Don't be late.'

Mordent hung up.

He ran a hand through his hair. He'd been joined on the bench by a lady with a brown paper bag. She looked to be in her eighties, white hair, cream cardigan over a white blouse. Her limbs were thin but she wasn't shivering. The pigeons came to her like old friends.

He dialled directory enquiries again. They gave him a number for Muxloe's mansion. He hadn't thought it would be that easy.

It was less easy getting to speak to the man himself. After passing through two secretaries – neither of whom, he suspected, were as sweet as legs and lipstick – he arrived at Girl-Voice.

'I'm afraid Mr Muxloe is busy, Mr Mordent. I believe he gave you instructions to contact him by e-mail.'

Mordent told him what to do with the e-mail.

Then he told him a lie.

The shaky tone that ran around the edge of Girl-Voice's voice indicated that he bought the lie. Or at least, enough of it to handle the call the way Mordent wanted it handled.

After a few more moments he was through to Muxloe. He could swear he heard a sweet wrapper unfolding in the background, unless there was static on the line.

'What is it?'

No formalities then.

'You wanted me to stitch up Bataille. That deal still on?'

'I don't think I used those words, Mordent.'

'Nevertheless, the intention was there. You owned up to the Davenport murder yet?'

There was laughter. Cold and quiet. 'You couldn't expect me to buy into that deal. And it's certainly nothing I'm going to discuss on the phone.'

'You've pre-empted my intention, Muxloe. I've got some information through Bataille that I think will be of use to you. At 3pm I'll be on a bench at Prospect Park. You're gonna be there or the Sweeney photos go to the police, plus the knowledge I have of the Davenport boy.'

'You haven't got anything, Mordent.'

But Muxloe's last sentence went to dead air.

Mordent closed his phone. Then he closed his eyes. The cooing of the pigeons was a constant. It was impossible to distinguish one from another; it was a wave of noise that hummed and soothed. When he opened his eyes the old woman had gone. As had the pigeons. In fact, forty minutes had passed.

He stood. Stretched his legs. There was another hour at least until showdown. Ideally, Bataille and Muxloe would approach from opposite directions, wouldn't see each other until too late. He didn't want either pulling out before he'd spoken to them. Didn't want any goons with them either, although whether that would happen wasn't up to him. Still, the kids and the joggers and the mums and the bird-feeders would be his insurance policy. Plus the gun that rested snug at his side.

Those were the sureties.

Everything else was bluff.

He took a stroll through the park. The ordinariness of the surroundings was at odds with the complexities of the case. It struck him how many individuals never had to come into contact with criminals or the law. That the way of life that for him was ingrained would be totally alien to those people. Something to watch on television, either as a drama or a reality show, but never infringing on their existence. Like toy dolls on a production line they moved ceaselessly and silently throughout their lives, never quite touching. Whereas for him life was a battle, a constant rub against the detritus of society, sorting out lives gone awry, morality blurred.

He knew which side of the fence he would always choose.

Even if he was sometimes so tired.

Leaves circled to become mulch on the ground. The circle of life was so evident at this time of year. He thought again of Davenport, of the likelihood he had been smuggled off the ferry, or perhaps tipped overboard and later picked up by Muxloe's men. He knew why it had taken so long for the body to surface. And again he thought of Robbie Constantin and inter-gang wars. Normally they were for more obvious reasons: drugs, liquor cartels, money laundering. But he supposed immortality was as good as reason as any.

And he thought of Marina. His swift sweet romance. And of how he had dumped her as soon as she was dead and Maria had re-entered his life. If he were Martens maybe the romance would have continued, but even so his complete negation of what they had slightly astonished him. Yet life was for the living, even in this stumbling city, where brightly-dressed children played on swings and fluorescent lycra joggers blurred peripheral vision. The underbelly, the scum around the reality bath, could be scrubbed away. Even when it inevitably returned, it was changed.

Constants. Those he could deal with. The gun in his holster, the décor of Morgan's Bar, the kiss of a woman and the certainty of death. Those who railed against those would come to no good. Bataille and Muxloe thought they were living at the edge, but they were going down the plughole. He doubted he would nail them, but he would put them back in place.

He checked his watch. Five minutes until they arrived. He wandered back to the bench, heavy with information. This was it, the culmination of the past few days, the readdressing of the pointing fingers of the dead.

The bench was six foot long. Enough for three people. He sat in the middle. Waited.

The park was flanked by two highways. One led from the direction of Bataille's bakery, the other would be the through route from Muxloe's country house. Was it too much to hope that they would arrive simultaneously from opposite directions? Would advance facing each other as if in a duel?

As it happened, that wasn't the case.

He watched as Bataille and Muxloe walked together. Both had hands deep in their coat pockets, their collars pulled up against the increasing cold. At a slight distance to their rear, Weasel-Face and Girl-Voice followed, less familiar with each other. Weasel-Face twitchy, his eyes darting from side to side, no more sure of himself than he had been in the garage. Girl-Voice nonchalant, just taking a walk in the park. Yet Mordent knew not to drop his guard. Girl-Voice wouldn't be where he was if he was as innocent as he looked. So he kept his hand inside his jacket pocket, his index finger lingering on the trigger of his gun.

Bataille and Muxloe were chatting, as though old friends meeting up after a gap of several years. Yet the conversation was strained. Mordent detected lines at the edges of their mouths, as if they were biting back what they really wanted to say.

Easy camaraderie didn't come easy to either of them.

Muxloe spoke first, his voice soft, controlled.

'Seems we're here on a wild goose chase, Mordent. You're playing the joker but it's just a mirror, held up to your face.'

'Sit down. Keep the goons at a distance.'

'Always the noir undertones,' Muxloe continued. 'You're like a Japanese soldier still fighting in the jungle long after the war has ended. We got rid of our trilbies and Thompson submachine guns long ago.'

Mordent glanced at Bataille, who was smirking.

'You're worn out,' Bataille said. 'Your time is past. We've had an interesting chat getting to this bench. You've got nothing on either of us, it's all speculation. You can't set both of us up.'

'And yet still you came,' replied Mordent. 'I repeat: sit down.'

Muxloe rubbed the top of the seat with his hand before he sat. Bataille looked like he was about to do the same, but changed his mind. Neither of them wanting to emulate the other.

Weasel-Face and Girl-Voice hung back. Leant

against a tree. Weasel-Face pulled out a cigarette, glanced at Bataille, who nodded. He lit it, shook out the match, which left a smoke curl heading up through bare branches.

'Back in the '60s,' Mordent began, 'there was the space race. Both the Russians and the Americans wanted to be first on the Moon. As you know, the Americans got there first. It's a theory, however, that the landing was faked.'

Muxloe snorted. 'So what if it was? What has this to do with us?'

'It was a matter of pride, some would say of national importance, that we got there first. The Cold War had been running some twenty years, a mixture of political conflict, military tension, games of one-upmanship. The Cuban Missile Crisis hadn't long passed. I've heard that it would have cost us less to fake the landing than it would to go there. Also, the space race was a diversion from our activities in Vietnam. You don't have to believe the conspiracy theorists to see how the odds were stacked against the Moon, and yet we still managed to get someone there.'

By the tree, Girl-Voice was poking at something between his molars with a toothpick. Weasel-Face had lit another cigarette. Bataille's hands were still deep within his pockets. Mordent could sense vibration along the bench. Muxloe was cold, was rubbing his hands together.

'The thing is,' Mordent continued, 'you two aren't far from being the Americans and the Russians. Each of you tapped into this immortality scam, and neither of you wanted the other to be first, or to fall behind the other. That's all well and good, until you start taking down the people around you. That's when I get involved.'

Muxloe stood. 'I really don't need to hear any more.'

Mordent tugged at his coat, pulled him back down. 'Remember those photos,' he growled.

Girl-Voice stepped away from the tree. Muxloe waved him back.

'The way I see it,' Mordent continued, 'you're both pushing your noses against a glass window. Looking at immortality on the other side, but really it's a reflection of the life behind you. You're big time losers. Both of you. Yet you can't be seen to be losers. So what happens? Bataille: you kill Robbie Constantin because he rips you off, and then get his body delivered to Muxloe suitably aged. A cheap trick, but that's just right for someone like you. Four years later and it's found, and it looks like you're ahead in the immortality stakes, his brother running around like a headless chicken claiming the fact as though its fact, and doing all the publicity for you.

'It doesn't matter that it's shot through with holes. What matters is that Constantin believes it. That kind of belief is catching.

'Meanwhile, Muxloe's killed a student who refused to play ball. A warning to other students who might decide to follow suit, and a surety he's not going to spill the beans on your operation. You've still got the body though, kept it on ice to cover your tracks. So when Robbie Constantin's body turns up you get all competitive, try to play Bataille at his game. Doctor the body and make it look like you've been working successfully with cadavers. Truth is, neither of you are any closer to the secret of immortality, and the whole idea is just as ridiculous as believing I'm stuck in the '50s.

'Play it how you want. Deceive each other. Stick

your flag on the Moon. Make shadows. Truth is, you're both idiots. You're both bums as much as those who sleep on the streets in this stinking city. Both deserving of all that is coming to you.'

Mordent stood. 'Don't tell me I can't prove any of this. I don't have to. I'm Constantin's mouthpiece avenging his brother's death, and Davenport's ghost bringing down Muxloe. If I find out who killed Marina Gonzales then one of you'll take the rap for that too. And there's no good trying to buy me off or kill me. There's an envelope with all this information on Chief Kovacs' desk as we speak. He knows we're here. The park is surrounded.'

Bataille stood, pulled on his arm. 'This is nonsense.'

'Is it? You become obsessed with something long enough, you lose your sense of reality. Muxloe reckons with me its noir fiction, all wet streets and hoods. But though I have a predilection for those books, those times, my reality is grounded. You guys think you're king of the heap, invincible, yet your goons would swap sides in a moment if they thought you were losing it. You're only as good as your last scam, and this immortality drive is shot through with holes. And that's fact, even if you know it already and are just using it against each other. Fact.

'You're going to die and it'll have nothing to do with me. Its hard fact: neither will win.'

He turned his back on them, winked disconcertingly at Weasel-Face and Girl-Voice, then left the park with Bataille and Muxloe rooted around the bench. Ironically, he heard sirens in the distance.

They weren't coming for them, of course. There was no envelope on Kovacs' desk. They were right. He couldn't prove any of it. Didn't have to.

Sometimes all you needed was to get the criminal scum to face some home truths. Show them for the fools they were. You'd hold a mirror up to those who thought they'd got it good, and that was just about as much satisfaction as you could get. It wouldn't win any wars, but would certainly dent some pride, particularly when it was a double whammy.

He sat on another bench, just outside the park. Watched as Bataille and Muxloe stood staring at each other, wandered around, kicked up leaves. The sun went down, casting an orange glow over the scene, almost sepia tinted as the day finally edged over the horizon, speckling the remaining leaves with gold, tessellating the sunlight. At that point, Weasel-Face scratched his nose, turned to leave. Then left. Girl-Voice hovered, caught with indecision. Followed. The two businessmen remained in their Emperor's New Clothes – static, silent, motionless.

Mordent left them. Headed for Morgan's Bar, wondered how long it would be before they tumbled and went their separate ways.

He could still hear sirens more than two blocks from the park.

30
Solace

The two drinks he had in Morgan's Bar weren't exactly celebratory. The mild euphoria he had felt when exposing Bataille and Muxloe slowly dissipated, just as the seemingly hot fluid burned the back of his throat. Everything wasn't always as it seemed. The bourbon had a kick but wasn't temperature hot. He had had *his* kicks, but the case had run cold. Maybe Kovacs would eventually be able to pin something on both of them. He would certainly report Constantin's allegations. As for the Davenport boy, he was dead. But Sue Sweeney was very much alive. Any suspicions he had of Muxloe's involvement needed to be buried. She'd had her morals and kept them, didn't need them to be raked over.

So what had felt like a minor victory just became another notch on a bedpost. At least exposing them both together had dented their egos.

At midpoint during the evening, he pulled out his cell phone. Read the text he'd received earlier. The vibration on the bench. Just for a moment, through the calming fog of booze, he misread both the text and the name.

back! Worried? :) Marina x

He blinked, looked again:

You back? Worried! :) Maria x

Everything wasn't always as it seemed.

He returned a text: *all sorted, be over later. x*

Then he called Morgan and lined up another shot. He raised it to his lips, then, watching his face in the mirror over the bar, raised the glass higher. Toasted Marina and the times they had and would never have. When he slugged the alcohol back he could barely taste it.

For a moment then, he considered his own death. Whether it would be under a hail of vengeful bullets, caught in the middle of a revamped St Valentine's Day Massacre between Bataille and Muxloe, or whether he would be wracked with a different, lingering kind of pain: through cancer unaided by arthritis, or a slow, agonising heart attack where the remaining seconds of his life would tick by in slow-mo, each to be savoured bitter-sweetly because they would be his last.

He couldn't decide whether he wanted it sudden or prolonged, whether he needed to have an indication that he was dying or be snuffed out without warning. Regardless of the manner of his death, the thought was abhorrent. He remembered Muxloe's words, *Everyone believes they're immortal until they die, Mordent. Then they don't believe anything anymore.* He also remembered Kovacs, back in the day when they had been tailing a punk called Laszlo, quoting from Godard's *À Bout de Souffle*: *I want to become immortal, and then die.* Maybe Kovacs would understand if he span him the immortality angle, although Mordent doubted it. For most, immortality came with the flush of youth. As you aged, it became a red herring, a golden goose. Something you couldn't tempt yourself with because considering it forced consideration of the opposite: a life of death.

He picked up his phone again. Regarded the *x* he had placed at the end of his text to Maria. Natural, reflexive, genuine? He decided the latter. It was time to start again.

Thumbing through his address book he dialled Mrs Mouse.

'Mr Mordent?' There was more than the query of his name in the question.

'I'm off the case. I believe I know what happened to your son but I can't prove it. I doubt the police will be able to either. I can't keep taking your money knowing it's a dead end. I'll send over an invoice for my outstanding fee, then we should call it quits.'

'Will you tell me? Your suspicions, I mean?'

'I'll put them in the letter. Oh, and one thing. Bury the past, Mrs Davenport. Bury it good. You can't live with ghosts.'

'I'm beginning to understand that, Mr Mordent. It should be easier, now Patrick's body has been found.'

Mordent agreed, then backtracked out of an invitation to the funeral. After he hung up, he wondered how much he could get away with charging her. It didn't make him feel good.

He stood, walked to the window, looked out at the night. It had been raining again, a persistent downpour, washing grime off the buildings and onto the street, which was wet black like in an old pulp novel. He felt comforted.

Leaving the bar he drove to a convenience store, bought some mints and some flowers. The pull towards Maria was both terrifying and permanent because he knew without a doubt that this time it would last.

ABOUT THE AUTHOR

Andrew Hook is an established writer with over 160 separate short story sales and several books in print. He has been a British Fantasy Award finalist, an award-winning editor, and a radio presenter. In addition to his crime novels his most recent books are *Frequencies of Existence*, a collection of SF stories, published by NewCon Press, and *O For Obscurity, Or, The Story Of N*, a biography of the Mysterious N Senada, written in collaboration with the avant-garde San Francisco art collective known as The Residents.

Andrew is a member of the Crime Writers Association. There are four other books featuring his ex-cop turned PI, Mordent, available from Head Shot Press. Be sure to check them out.